MW01633759

From the Dust

ALSO BY DAVID SWINSON

A Detailed Man

The Second Girl

Crime Song

Trigger

City on the Edge

Sweet Thing

From the Dust

A Novel

David Swinson

MULHOLLAND BOOKS

Little, Brown and Company

New York Boston London

The characters and events in this book are fictitious. Any similarity to real persons, living or dead, is coincidental and not intended by the author.

Mulholland Books / Little, Brown and Company
Hachette Book Group
1290 Avenue of the Americas, New York, NY 10104
mulhollandbooks.com

First Edition: March 2026

Mulholland Books is an imprint of Little, Brown and Company, a division of Hachette Book Group, Inc. The Mulholland Books name and logo are trademarks of Hachette Book Group, Inc.

ISBN 9780316528658
Library of Congress Control Number: 2025945575

Printing 1, 2026

LSC-C

Printed in the United States of America

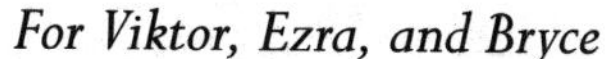

For Viktor, Ezra, and Bryce

Will there come a time when I no longer ask why the world is like a mean street, because I shall take the squalor as normal? Does grief finally subside into boredom tinged by faint nausea?

—C. S. Lewis, *A Grief Observed*

From the Dust

1
The Birdhouse

It began here. A small town in upstate New York, bisected by the Erie Canal, where the days were short and the nights long because sleep was hard to find. Acres of rich farmland surrounded the edge of town. The corn was always tall, and the smell of fresh manure lingered in the air. Not a foul odor, something more warm and earthy. Felt like the beginning of growth. My father would also help enrich a tiny portion of the soil. He wanted a green burial. His body would naturally decompose to feed the small Eastern Red Cedar I planted behind his headstone.

The interim pastor of our dad's church, Simon Guerre, conducted the burial ceremony. Pastor Simon had inherited the congregation after the previous pastor took ill, and he would remain in place until a new one was hired. Only a handful of people attended the funeral—neighbors and friends my dad got to know over the years, including William Finn, the chief of police for the eight officers, one sergeant, and lone investigator of that small town. He was chief for life and about my age, maybe a couple of years older. He had known my dad for a while and had always been there for him and my younger brother, Tommy, when needed. No relatives showed up. Most of them were either too old, too dead, or too alienated by my father after the great divorce.

Tommy couldn't make it either. He tried, but his agoraphobia got in the way. It was difficult for him, so I gave him credit for trying. It was my father's death that brought me here, but my brother's condition and need for company that made me stay. Not like it was a new start—I wasn't running away from anything. It was just something I felt I had to do, especially since I could no longer keep my head in the game with the investigations I had to work. That was my only regret: leaving and not working my last two cases through. I left them open, probably soon to be cold.

After I retired from DC's Metropolitan Police Department, I packed my life and what I didn't need for day-to-day living and had it stored just outside the District of Columbia, in Virginia. It was a six-hour drive from here. A lot of years of life packed away in that storage unit. I moved into the guest room on the second floor of my dad's home and surrounded myself with those life mementos that brought me comfort: the photograph I took of my wife, Elena, on our wedding day; another taken during the last vacation we had together; and, on the nightstand next to the side of the bed where I slept, the urn that contained Elena's ashes.

Death used to be my life, my career, and then it became something personal after Elena's death, much like my older sister's accidental death that occurred when we were kids. You looked at it differently when it involved a loved one. I was thankful that Elena, my sister Dani, and my father's death had not been homicides. There was an odd sense of comfort in that.

My dad's home had been built in 1850: a barn-red, two-story farmhouse, with an unattached barn that he converted into a two-car garage and workshop. The property comprised just over one and a half acres of land—not much, but edged by trees. A refuge. He knew it was where he would die. When it was his time, he just went. Never woke up. Isn't that how we'd all like to go?

In his original living will, he advised that he wanted to be cremated but not until after the seventh day. He wanted his body kept in the morgue until that time. He believed that the mind stayed active long after death. For how long he obviously didn't know, but all his research suggested that the brain was still going through something after everything else in the body had stopped. So, one week to be safe. *Why the hell would you want to stay trapped in your head,* I had asked him, *with your body in a cold morgue?* (Not that he'd feel the cold, but still.) *What if this brain-activity business were true and you found yourself stuck in one helluva nightmare? What was the point? You're not going to come back, so why not go for the ashes as soon as possible?*

Obviously, he told me, no one could ever know until that time came, but he didn't want to take a chance on anything having to do with matters of the soul. He later decided, for reasons I'll never know, that he didn't want to be cremated; he wanted a green burial instead. I don't know. He was a tough son of a bitch, and even tougher to figure out.

Tommy sat on an old rickety rocking chair. It creaked with every rock forward. He was drinking an orange soda out of the bottle. We were on the back deck. Bill Finn was with us. He was on his way to the station but had stopped by to drop off a nice cut of venison tenderloin from a buck he had butchered over the weekend. Bill was a devoted hunter, and the venison was his way of welcoming me to the community. I was sitting on a rattan sectional, sipping coffee. Bill was on a matching rattan chair. The deck overlooked the half-acre of green pasture surrounded by trees. A cozy view. A view I wasn't much used to having.

It was early afternoon, with a comfortably warm breeze. Spring was one of my favorite seasons. Summer was an enemy, mostly because I hated the humidity. It could get humid here too, but nothing like DC. Humidity in a large city was different than anywhere else. Far less tolerable—for me, anyway.

Tommy shot us a half-smile and said, "I haven't grilled in a while," like his mind had finally caught up to the conversation we'd had earlier about the meat.

"Well, now you got yourself a reason to," Bill responded.

"Yeah, Dad said more than once how you were a grill master."

Tommy looked at me, almost like he was about to smile, but then changed his mind. Looked like he might cry instead.

"Looks like you have some mowing to do," Bill jumped in and said, as if he sensed the same thing.

"I can't remember the last time I mowed," I said.

"We have a zero-turn," Tommy advised, and I imagined his large but fit body frame, and his shiny bald head, on the mower zigzagging along the pasture.

"Those are fun. Slip a cold one in the cup holder and off you go," Bill said. He finished the remaining coffee in his cup and straightened up in his chair. "I should go."

"I'll walk you out."

"See you another time, Tom. Don't wait too long on those tenderloins."

"I won't, Chief. Probably tomorrow."

I walked him around the house to his marked Expedition.

Before he opened the door I said, "By the way, my brother said you had a homicide a couple of weeks ago."

"Yeah. We only had two other homicides in three years. One was domestic and the other one a shooting at our local bar, the Birdhouse. That place is a damn thorn in my side. Both murders were easy closures. This one I'm not so sure about. The body was dumped at the bank of the canal off 31. Appeared to have been dragged from the road. Looks like it might be drug related."

"Birdhouse? Haven't heard of that spot."

"Don't go there. I've tried to get the place shut down, but no luck. Lot of the town's trouble comes through there, especially drugs."

"You have a big drug problem here?"

"What town doesn't?"

"True," I agreed with a nod.

"Our investigator retired a while ago and we just promoted an officer to his position. He's solid, but he's still a rookie investigator."

"A good homicide will break him in. Didn't you work a few at NYPD back in the day?"

"That I did, brother. But that was years ago."

"Like riding a bike, though."

"But I'm dangerous on a bike. I always fall and hurt myself."

He opened the car door, stepped in.

I said, "All right then, be safe."

"Always."

Bill Finn gave me an upward nod, closed the door, started the car, and pulled away. I watched as he slowly made his way down the long driveway toward the road. Our driveway was obstructed by a line of large trees, but I could see his car between the tree trunks, moving slowly and turning left onto the road.

My mind pivoted to the homicide because that was in my nature. I wondered why the body had been dragged to the bank, not dumped in the water. I should have asked. In the water, it would have been harder to find. Or maybe just as easy to find, depending on how deep the canal was, how fast the current ran, and whether the killer had thought to weigh down the body. I shrugged it off after a couple of seconds and made my way back to the deck. I didn't have to worry about such matters anymore.

2

The Pastor

I've always been a light sleeper, and so the noise outside woke me. I picked up my iPhone to check the time.

0137 hours. I had it set to show military time.

I got out of bed to look out the window. I had a view of part of the garage and most of the driveway in front. I saw Tommy standing in front of the garage waiting for the door to slide open. He was fully dressed. He entered after it opened. A moment later I heard the car door slam. Our dad had his car parked in there. The car started. The headlights beamed light out of the garage.

What the hell?

It was only a few seconds later when Tommy drove our dad's older model Ford Explorer out and slowly made his way down the driveway toward the road. From this vantage point I couldn't see the end of the driveway, or the road. The trees were tall, their big limbs thick with leaves. The car disappeared. I couldn't even see the headlights. I stood there for a while, until exhaustion overwhelmed me. I didn't know what to think. *Was his agoraphobia all made up? I mean, what the fuck.* I returned to bed.

Sleep did not come easily. It hadn't since I retired.

Tommy was still sleeping when I woke up. I had two cups of coffee, then decided to hit the Wegmans in Canandaigua. It was the place to go for groceries around here. It was about 15 minutes from the house. I used to go to the one in upper Northwest, DC. Tommy told me that Wegmans had originally started as a fruit-and-vegetable cart in Rochester, which was about 40 minutes from town.

"The founders were brothers, like us." Tommy smiled like a kid.

Going to the grocery store had always been something I enjoyed doing. Elena didn't like to. If I had not been there, she would have probably had everything delivered.

I still found myself instinctively grabbing at snacks she loved, like Triscuits, Colby-Jack cheese, or jumbo blueberries. Tommy wanted to grill asparagus with the venison, so I went to the vegetable section after almost taking the blueberries.

I grabbed a bundle.

"Graham Sanderson," a familiar voice said behind me.

I turned to see Pastor Simon. He was holding a plastic shopping basket that contained three apples in a clear bag.

"Nice to run into you here, Graham."

"How are you, Pastor?"

He held up the basket, smiled, and said, "Just got started here, and saw you. How are you and your brother doing?"

"Doing well, thank you."

"Are you getting settled in?"

"Yes, I am."

"Again, I'm so sorry for your loss. Please let me know if there's anything I can do."

"I appreciate that, and I will."

"I know your father was a regular at church before I got there, and your brother attends online, but what about you? Do you join your brother for the sermon online?"

"Afraid not, Pastor. It's not for me anymore."

"Anymore?"

"It's just not for me."

"I understand. It shouldn't be about guilt anyway, so I apologize if I made you uncomfortable."

"You didn't," I smiled.

"Well, good to see you. Say hi to your brother for me—and let me know if you ever need to talk. I specialize in grief counseling. I'll leave it at that."

"Thank you, Pastor. Good to see you, too. I'll keep it in mind."

"Off to the bread section now. You take care."

"You too. Have a good one."

The image of Tommy driving the car down the driveway popped into my head.

"Oh, by the way, Pastor—"

He stopped and turned back toward me.

"I was just wondering... I mean, I know my brother was seeing the previous pastor for online counseling, so I was just curious if he's doing that with you now."

"Is there something you're concerned about?" he asked as though he sensed it.

"I just know my father's passing has been hard on him."

"We do have online sessions once a week. You should talk to Tommy about that. And remember, I'm here for you too."

"Appreciate that."

"You take care, Graham."

Pastor Simon gave a friendly smile and walked away. He seemed pleasant enough, and I felt a little bad that I'd been short with him about attending his church. Elena got me into going regularly, but after she passed away, I got angry at the God she said she had faith in. Dad didn't go to church until later in life, and he had never forced his beliefs on us. Our mother, on the other hand, was Jewish, and she *did* press her beliefs on us. I guess they never took root, because I knew that Tommy had streamed the church service online for years.

I liked driving around here. Long winding roads, farms surrounding small towns, and most of those with a Main Street. Some homes seemed sad, though. Falling apart. Others were grand old structures that have probably been standing for more than a hundred years.

Tommy insisted on taking care of the groceries when I got back. Everything had its proper place, and I wasn't about to disturb that. When he was done, he returned to his comfortably cluttered room. He kept the door shut. Dad told me he felt safe in his room, so I never questioned Tommy about it. For some reason I didn't even ask him about taking the car out last night. I must have been afraid of the answer. Damn, I gave up my life to be here with him, and now I had doubts. Had he been lying to our dad all this time too? All the childhood trauma and the psychiatrists and therapy that followed. I knew all that was true, but the agoraphobia? I would have to talk to him soon.

The extra time I had on my hands was new to me, and something I had to get used to. Work had been my life—more so after Elena's death. I kept myself busy working cases, even assisting other detectives with theirs, until I burned myself out. I had to find other things to occupy myself with here. Sitting around and having nothing to do allowed too much time with my thoughts.

I heard a loud thump. Sounded like it came from upstairs. Then I heard Tommy yell, "Damn!"

I walked upstairs, thinking something must have fallen. His door was closed, so I knocked.

"Yeah," he said like he was irritated.

I opened the door and stepped in. He was standing in front of a wall to the left of his desk. There was a fist-sized hole in the drywall. I noticed drywall dust on his fist.

"Why'd you put your fist through the wall?"

"Don't worry," he said calmly and without regret. "I know how to fix that."

I stood there hoping he'd answer my question, but he just turned and sat back down at his desk.

"What's going on, Tommy?"

"No worries, G. Damn customer just pissed the hell out of me. I'll patch it up later."

"You need to talk?"

"Naw, I need to get back to work." He smiled oddly.

I had never seen him do something like that before. He turned back to his computer screen as though I wasn't there. Before I could respond, he glanced over his shoulder toward the window overlooking the front of the house and said, "Someone's here."

Seconds later, the doorbell rang.

"You mind getting that? I have to work."

"No problem."

I closed his door and walked downstairs.

It was Bill Finn, dressed in his police uniform. I mentally shook off what had happened.

"Hey, Bill. Two times in two days. I feel honored."

"Hope I'm not interrupting anything."

"Not at all. Come on in."

"I only have a minute. I would have called, but I figured this was something I'd rather do in person."

"Sounds serious."

"It is. I could really use your help."

3

The Chief's Nephew

When Bill Finn told me there'd been another murder, I said I'd feel more comfortable talking at his office, where there'd be no interruptions.

"I can meet you there in about an hour," I said.

"Appreciate that."

Truth was, I didn't want Tommy and his uncanny hearing picking up on our conversation. I was still confused after witnessing his early-morning excursion and his sudden outburst of anger, then learning that a murder that had occurred around the same time I saw him driving out. Damn the way I thought! It was ridiculous. This fucking cop brain of mine. It should've retired after I retired. He's my damn brother, after all.

The police station was on the first floor of the town's municipal building. No one was at the reception window, but there was a buzzer to the right of the entrance. I pressed it. A short time later, Bill approached from another room. He saw me through the window and waved, walked to the door, and let me in.

"Good to see you, Graham."

"How are you doing, Chief?"

"Good, good. Thanks for coming down."

"Looks empty in here."

"Investigator Gottert and the three day-shift officers are on the street."

He showed me around the station. It was small. In the central area was a large cubicle with three computers, where the officers could sit and do paperwork. There was also a community area with a large table and chairs (plus a refrigerator, sink, and dishwasher), a locked evidence room, a prisoner holding room, an office for the sergeant and the office clerk (who was out sick), and a vacant office.

Walking back through the main area and toward Bill's office, I noticed a roster on the wall listing the officers and their shifts.

"No women in this tiny department of yours?"

"Not anymore. The one female officer we had left us for the ATF. We currently have four vacancies, but no one wants to be a cop anymore."

"Yeah, DC is hiring too. Even offering some nice incentives and still having a hard time."

"Tough everywhere."

Bill's office had 1970s-style wood paneling, with a built-in bookshelf that took up the wall behind his desk. Police-related textbooks were on the top shelf. New York Giants bobbleheads, awards, medals, and framed family photos occupied the two lower shelves. The other walls were decorated with his plaques; other framed awards, certificates, and accomplishments; and a framed print of the Archangel Michael running a spear through the mouth of a dragon-like creature. The L-shaped desk he sat behind was tidy. The computer monitor and keyboard were on the shorter side of the desk. His handheld radio was next to the phone. One call was dispatched for shoplifting at the local drugstore. Nothing like DC, where I would have heard one call right after another.

"Would you like coffee or anything?"

"I'm good. Thanks."

"Again, I appreciate your time."

"Happy to help, but I'm thinking you'd get more assistance from state troopers or the sheriff's office?"

"I don't want their help with this. I want to keep it in-house, maintain control of the investigation."

"I confess I'm not that familiar with the kind of politics you might have to deal with here. In DC I had to work with the feds, and jurisdictions in Maryland and Virginia on occasion. It could be frustrating, but we were always in control."

"I'd like to keep this investigation close. Not because there's anything to hide." Bill Finn looked away for a moment, like he needed to pause. When he looked back, he said, "The second victim was my nephew, Del."

"Damn. I'm so sorry, Bill. What the hell happened?"

"We were very close. He had his problems, but he was a good kid, and I tried to be there for him. His body was found by a farmer. Appeared as though he'd been dragged from the road, about twenty feet, to the edge of the farmer's cornfield. Here's the thing—he had four cylindrical puncture wounds to the chest area that at first appeared to be gunshot wounds. The medical examiner later found them to be stab wounds made by a tri-edged cylindrical instrument, like a dagger, maybe seven or more inches long. Same cause of death as the first body found at the edge of the canal, and damn-near identical wounds. They probably bled out fast, but somewhere other than where they were found."

"Any characteristic hilt marks on the skin?"

"I asked about that, and no. The stab wounds were deep, but maybe not thrust hard enough to leave something like that on the skin."

"An ice pick is narrow, but it doesn't have three edges. Doesn't sound like a normal knife."

"Gottert is looking into that."

"You still thinking it was drug related?"

"Thought so with the first one. The victim had a criminal record that would suggest that, and bloodwork revealed the presence of cocaine and fentanyl. *Drug deal gone bad or something,* is what I thought. Del . . . my nephew . . . he didn't do drugs, didn't have a criminal record except for a couple of DUIs. Toxicology revealed only alcohol. He is—was—an alcoholic. It cost him a good job, but there was nothing at his home that would even suggest he was involved with drugs."

"Did Del know the other victim?"

"Investigator Gottert is looking into that possibility. Cell-phone records, social media—all that."

"And they both lived in town?"

"Yes. I thought at first it was a robbery gone bad, but both of them had their wallets. My nephew still had his watch on his wrist, and the first victim even had some cash still on him."

"So, not likely a robbery. Stabbing them both four times—that's something else."

"I thought that too."

"Two homicides with similar MOs, in a town this small. There has to be something in common with the two."

"I agree. Haven't found anything yet."

"Looks like you have everything covered."

"Yes and no. I need someone like you. A fresh set of eyes. Walk Gottert through it. Someone with your homicide experience would be valuable."

"I don't want to be that *retired guy* stepping in like he thinks he knows everything. That might not sit well with your investigator or your other officers. That's just not me. Besides, between you and me, shortly after my wife died I dived headfirst into work so hard I burned myself out. Couldn't get my head in the game anymore. And then when my dad died, I knew I was done."

"I can understand that—and I can't imagine what you went through. But all I'm asking is that you come in, stay as long or as short as you want. No pressure. The other officers will welcome your knowledge and wealth of experience. Don't worry about that."

"They'll also do whatever you tell them to do."

"My guys are squared away, Graham. It's not like it was in the city."

I really wasn't sure about all that, and I knew he could see it in me.

"Give it a shot, Graham. Might be good for you."

"Alright. I'll do what I can. I *was* getting a bit bored just hanging around the house."

"That's all I'm asking—do what you can."

"When can I take a look at the case jackets?"

He opened a drawer on the left side of the desk, pulled out two folders.

"Just so happens I have copies right here." He smiled.

He reached across the desk and handed them to me. I accepted.

"I'll review them tonight, if that's alright."

"Appreciate it."

"What are you working tomorrow?"

"I should get in about 7 a.m. until whenever. You know how it is."

"I remember those days. I'll shoot you a text in the morning. I'll stop in."

"Alright."

We shook hands and he escorted me out of the station.

* * *

Tommy was in his room when I got home. I thought about calling up the stairs to let him know I was there, then figured he'd heard me come in. I got myself a beer and went out to the deck to sit and review the cases. Felt good—like I'd been handed a present.

Leaving the body at the edge of the cornfield was like leaving the first body on the bank of the Erie Canal. Just a few more feet and it would have been concealed—and probably not discovered until the farmer harvested the corn. I believed the similarity was intentional: The murderer (or murderers) had wanted both bodies to be discovered quickly. Paul Savell and Bill's nephew, Del Thomas. Their case jackets were thorough and by the book, but not much there yet. I looked over the incident report and the running résumé a second time, and was just finishing up when Tommy came down to make dinner.

"What were you reading?"

I didn't want to tell him about the second murder, so I said, "Bill asked if I'd be interested in volunteering, help out the new investigator."

"With that murder?"

"Just help out the new investigator. No big deal."

"Like a mentor, then?"

"Yeah, I guess. You going to grill up those tenderloins?"

"Yeah, but I can freeze them if you want something else."

"No, venison sounds good. Haven't had that in a while."

"Alrighty then."

I almost chuckled when he said that. Brought back memories. I needed that. He used to drive our dad crazy by repeating that line as a kid. *If you say that one more time I'll stop this car and give you a spanking,* Dad once told him on a road trip. Tommy replied "Alrighty then" without a thought, like he couldn't help it. Dad pulled over and chased him around the car. Tommy was laughing like it was a game—until Dad caught him, that is, and the spanking turned that around. For a while, anyway.

"How was your day?" I asked now.

"Good. I mowed."

I looked out over the deck.

"Don't know why I didn't notice it. Great job."

"I like mowing."

Tommy once told me the property was an extension of the house, so he didn't have a problem getting out and working around the land. It had taken him a while before he could do that, he confided, but eventually he worked up to it. Dad always made sure that Tommy understood it was a safe environment. He had hoped that Tommy would one day work his way all the way out. And maybe he had—but why wouldn't he tell me so? Why was he hiding that from me? I couldn't bring myself to think about it further.

He rubbed the back of his buzz-cut head with the palm of his hand.

"Growing longer back there," I said. "Like a mullet."

"That'll be the day." He suddenly became sullen. "Dad used to have to cut back there because I could never get it even."

I felt bad, so I said, "I'll help you out, Tommy. Might cut you a bit in the process."

He chuckled.

"I would appreciate that. Not nicking my scalp up, though." He looked at me with serious raised brows. "And by the way, I've always wondered how the hell you ended up with a full head of hair and I have to shave down because I'm almost bald? Dad had a full head of hair all his life."

"Luck of the draw. I don't know, it's on the mother's side. Her dad was bald as shit, but he wasn't big like you. Where'd that come from?"

"You saying I'm fat?"

"No, dude—you're like the linebacker you were in high school."

And there was that sad face again. Shouldn't have brought those memories up.

"You're looking fit and healthy, my brother."

He smiled.

Tommy went back to his room after dinner. It was his comfort zone, and something Dad said was nothing to worry about. All that emotional abuse our mother put him through when he was a child. Fortunately or maybe unfortunately, I hadn't been there to look after him. It got worse when he injured his spine playing football at a high school in Arlington. Tommy was lucky he hadn't been paralyzed from the neck down. He had surgery and the orthopedic surgeon advised him that his career as a football player was over. That destroyed him. He lost his college scholarship. Made his life even worse with our mother. He hid the abuse from me and our Dad until he was an adult. By then it was too late. Our dad would have fought to take him if he had known.

I went through the case jackets again, got tired early. I picked up the jackets to take upstairs with me, but not to read; I was going to place them on the dresser—keep them from prying eyes. On the way there, I overheard the muffled sound of my brother talking through his closed door. I was surprised he didn't hear me approaching and stop talking to whoever it was and open his door. I felt nosy, so I listened quietly. Sounded like he was on his iPhone.

"I *am* trying," I heard him say, almost sadly. Then, after a brief pause: "No, I can't accept that. I won't accept that."

He worked remotely for a large insurance company, but this sounded more like a personal call. I shouldn't have been eavesdropping. It was probably his friend.

"I don't know what to say to that." He continued sounding more angry. "Fuck that. I don't care anymore."

He stopped talking. It sounded like he got up and was moving toward the door. I started walking toward my bedroom. When Tommy opened his door, I stopped and turned to look back at him.

"Hey," I said with a smile.

"You going to bed?"

I said, "Yeah, I'm beat."

He was holding his iPhone.

"I thought I heard you talking when I walked by. You on the phone with Henry?"

He hesitated, like he was surprised I'd heard him.

"No. That's done with."

"Oh, sorry. I didn't know."

"That's all right."

"So . . . one of your other friends, or a new friend in your life?"

"Nope. Good night then." He closed his door abruptly.

"Good night," I said more to myself.

4

The Rookie Investigator

I rolled to my side to look at the urn on the nightstand and said, "Good night." Turned off the light, rolled onto my back again, and studied the fictive patterns cast on the ceiling by the light seeping through the window curtains. Some of them made into faces. Glared back at me. Fortunately, no one I knew. My racing mind eventually ran out of fuel and I found sleep, but only for a couple of hours. Repeated the process three more times until daylight found its way through the curtains. I was still having a tough time processing the whole retirement thing—leaving those open cases behind to add to some other detective's already heavy workload. I've never liked leaving anything unfinished, but that's what I had done.

I wanted to loaf around in bed, maybe close my eyes and try to find more sleep, but I wasn't programmed that way. It was going to take some work to get there. So I sat up, let my feet feel the wood floor, and pushed myself out of bed.

After a long shower I went to the kitchen to make coffee. I sat outside when it was done. The clouds were coming in dark. The wind was picking up, too. An awning covered the deck, but that wouldn't help much if the wind turned the rain sideways. About half an hour later, Tommy stepped out to join me. He had an orange soda.

"Looks like rain," he said.

He sat in his rocking chair.

"I'm going to head over to the police station a little later," I told him.

He didn't respond. He did that often. Didn't mean anything. His mind was probably caught up somewhere else. He started rocking. The chair creaking. He was a big guy, so I worried it would eventually break on him. He'd survive, but that'd be a sight to see. His giant six-foot-four frame crashing down to the decking. I'm five eleven and nowhere near as built as he is. Some funky genes in our family.

"You should invite your friends over sometime soon. I'd like to meet them." I couldn't let last night go.

"Huh?"

"Your friend, or friends. I'd like to meet them."

"I don't have friends anymore. Just Dad."

He said that like Dad was still alive.

"Then who were you talking to the other day?"

"I wasn't talking to anyone. You probably heard me streaming something on the laptop, or maybe a customer for work."

"Sure sounded like you were talking to someone you were friends with. Sounded like an argument."

"Naw, maybe to myself. I do that sometimes, you know."

I didn't want to push it. He was in his forties and allowed his own secrets. I certainly had mine. After all, I talked to my dead wife.

Raindrops were gently smacking against the tin roof. It was a comforting sound until it became a hard rain. It passed over quickly, though. Turned to an eerie lull, but only briefly. Then the slow pitter-patter of light rain resumed.

I texted Bill Finn and asked him if around 10 a.m. would be good to stop by. He responded after a couple of minutes with a "yes."

I loafed around a bit longer and got myself ready. I grabbed the case jackets and headed to the station.

A young uniformed officer appeared at the window after I pushed the buzzer. His name tag read R. AGUILAR. He looked squared away.

"Can I help you?"

"I'm Graham Sanderson, for the chief."

"Hold on, please."

He walked to the door that led to Bill's office, came back a few seconds later, and let me in.

"He'll be out in a minute."

"Thanks."

"You can have a seat over there if you want," he said, pointing to one of the three cubicle chairs.

"I'm fine."

He nodded and walked away, disappearing into the other side of the large room. A couple of minutes later Bill stepped out of his office.

"I was on the phone," he smiled.

We walked toward each other. Shook hands.

"You want some coffee?"

"I'm good, thanks. I went through these."

I handed him the case jackets.

"Based on the autopsy reports, they do appear to be connected," I said.

"Yes. I have a town-hall meeting this evening. One murder was enough to stir up the folks here; now we have two. Hard as hell to keep something like this from spreading in a small town. A lot of concerned folks. Come meet my investigator, Mike Gottert."

"Alright."

I followed him across the room to Gottert's office. The door was closed. He opened it without knocking. Gottert was sitting in his cubicle chair, typing on a computer keyboard. He looked up. He was wearing tan khakis and a light green polo shirt with the department's badge embroidered on the breast. His badge was affixed to his belt on the left side, ahead of the leather pouch that held two magazines. His holstered Glock 40 was on the right side. He had a goatee, trimmed short.

"Chief," he said.

"Mike, this is Graham Sanderson."

Gottert slid the chair back, stood up, and extended his hand.

"I've heard a lot about you," he said.

"Likewise."

"I've got to go to my weekly meeting with the mayor," said Bill. "I'll leave you two at it."

"Alright, sir." Gottert said.

"See you around, Chief."

He shot me an upward nod and left.

"Have a seat."

I sat in the chair on the side of his cubicle. A couple of boxes filled with papers were on the top shelf. Another, larger box was on the floor. It was filled with framed photos, a few books, and some other personal items he hadn't gotten around to emptying yet.

"Chief said you worked homicide in Washington, DC."

"Yep."

"That must have been something."

"The city was about to regain its *Murder Capital* title again just before I left."

"So you got out in the nick of time."

"I did."

"I imagine it's a lot of drug-related shit."

"A lot of that, yes. Is that what you're thinking with these two homicides?"

"I don't have enough to go on yet, but it usually is. Chief said you'd reviewed them?"

"I did, and you're right. There's not much to go on. But most drug-related homicides are committed with a firearm. A dispute over turf, or a bad transaction. These could be, I guess. Maybe this killer liked it up close and personal."

"But didn't seem out of control. Each one four times, like he knew what he was doing."

"Like he's done it before. What also stood out to me was why they were dumped where they were. Why make it easy to find the bodies?"

"I never thought about that—where they were dumped. It's almost like a statement, right? I mean that and the stab wounds."

"More than likely, it was."

"So maybe it was a drug deal gone bad and he was sending a message."

I wanted to say, *Maybe on some television crime show, but usually not in real life*. Instead I kept it to myself and said, "Could be."

"I was going to recanvass the area where the second body was found, knock on a couple of doors. You wanna tag along?"

"Sure."

"Great. One of the homes faced the road in the area where the body was found. Looked like it had a door cam."

"You going to have me sign a waiver to ride around with you?" I asked with a smile.

"The chief vouches for you," Gottert said facetiously. "So, no."

"Good. Makes me feel like the real police again."

I don't know why I said that, because I certainly didn't mean it. The last thing I wanted to feel like was a working detective again. *The real fucking police.* The only reason I was here was because I've always had a hard time saying no. But then, there was also my brother.

5

A Suspect

We pulled up the driveway to a ranch home that faced the road. Across from it stretched a large cornfield owned by the farmer who had discovered the body. If we were to take a left out of the driveway, it would be less than a quarter of a mile to the spot where the body was found. Homes in this area were distanced from each other by land. My father's home was about two miles away.

There was a surveillance camera above the door. It looked like it could capture a portion of the road. Gottert rang the doorbell. It was loud, as if the chimes were meant for a larger home or the occupants were hard of hearing. Gottert removed his leather identification wallet from his rear pants pocket.

A wiry old man opened the door.

"What can I do for you?"

Gottert showed his identification.

"Good morning, I'm Investigator Mike Gottert with the Charontown Police Department, and this is Graham Sanderson."

"You related to Carl Sanderson?"

"Yes, he was my father."

"Used to get together with him at the bar at least once a week before he took ill. A good man. I was at his funeral. Sorry for your loss."

"Thank you."

"Your dad said you were a policeman in Washington, DC. You with the police department here now?"

"No sir, I'm just assisting however I can."

"Good for you. This about that murder down the road?"

"Yes sir, it is," Gottert said.

"What are you doing here, then?"

"We're talking to all the neighbors and checking if you might've seen anything suspicious in the area. We're also curious whether your surveillance camera captures the road."

"Haven't seen anything out of the ordinary, and my camera doesn't record. It's just there for me to see who's there."

"Do you live alone?"

"Yes. My wife passed away over a year ago."

"I'm sorry for your loss, sir."

"My condolences," I said.

"Thank you. I don't know what else I can help you with."

"Well, I appreciate your time," Gottert said. "We'll be on our way, then."

The old man shut the door without a word.

"That was a bust," he told me.

"Usually is."

We knocked on a couple of other doors of homes along the road, as well as some on the intersecting street. One of those homes had a trail camera wrapped around a tree in the front yard. It was there to capture wildlife photos. The woman who answered the door allowed Gottert to borrow the camera's flash drive and search through it on the laptop in his vehicle.

"I've never had to search one of those before," I told Gottert.

"Yeah, I imagine they're not really a big-city thing."

Gottert checked the video to see the area it covered. It did reveal a good portion of the road. The farmer had told Gottert that he'd discovered the body at 7 a.m., and that he had also been at that location around 6 the evening before, so we had an accurate time frame to search. It looked like the camera's motion detector was able to capture and record several images. We were hoping to get any vehicles that passed by. The suspect could have driven from the other direction, but you still had to exhaust all possibilities. It wasn't a busy road, so Gottert was able to retrieve the images of only two vehicles. No visible tags. One was an older-model gray Chevy sedan and the other a newer-model red Ford pickup truck.

"The chief's nephew had a red truck. It was parked in front of his town house when we were there."

"Did you search the vehicle?"

"Didn't think to."

The decedent's vehicle wasn't searched? Rookie mistake. It should have been done on the same day the body was discovered, because you never know. I was surprised Bill hadn't caught that, but I kept it to myself.

"Should probably do that—and have your crime-scene tech dust it for prints and possible trace evidence."

"That'd be Sergeant Jimmy O'Born. Got time to check it out with me?"

I guess it had slipped by the sergeant too.

"All the time in the world."

The truck was still parked there. Sergeant Jimmy O'Born—a thick-haired, well-fed man—met us with an extra set of keys he got from Bill.

He examined the vehicle and found what appeared to be dried blood in the bed of the truck.

"If there was more blood, the rain probably washed it away," O'Born said. "I know Del was a hunter, so it could be deer blood. I'll get it towed to the garage for safekeeping and where I can be more thorough."

"What about the truck's navigation system?" I asked.

"I can get a forensic search on that too," O'Born said. "And do I need to get prints from you guys to rule you out?"

"We didn't touch anything," Gottert advised.

"Well, the chief said he's been in the truck but never drove it, so I'll have to get his."

O'Born took photos of the truck bed and the rest of the vehicle, inside and out. The tow truck arrived before he was done.

"I'm hungry. How about you?" Gottert asked.

"I could eat."

"There's a nice diner just outside of town."

"Sounds good."

About twenty minutes later we were sitting in a booth. A pretty waitress with a pleasant smile and a nose ring brought us menus and coffee. She seemed to know Gottert. They were still serving breakfast. Scrambled eggs, country potatoes, and bacon looked good to me. Gottert ordered a BLT.

"So, must be a big difference for you living here."

"It's quiet. I like that. You live in town?"

"Yes, I grew up here. Met my wife at the University of Rochester. Got married after we graduated."

"You get your degree in Criminal Justice?"

"Of course," he smiled. "How does your wife like it here?"

That caught me by surprise.

"My wife passed away three years ago. Cancer."

"Oh man, I'm sorry. I saw your wedding ring, so I assumed . . ."

"No worries. It's such a part of me I don't even realize it's there most of the time."

"I'm sorry. I can't imagine. Chief said you worked some really high-profile homicides."

"I did. Hard not to catch a few of those in the nation's capital."

"Any serial murders?"

"That was always something unspoken with our command. They never wanted to admit we had anything like that, but yeah, I did."

"Sounds political. Like a dirty word, right?"

"Yeah, but I don't think you have to worry about that unless there's a third murder." I knocked on the table.

"That's not real wood."

"Shit—let's hope for the best, then."

"I'm not superstitious, but if we do get a third, I'll know who to blame."

"I've been the fall guy before. I'll take it."

When we finished lunch, I went with Gottert to knock on some doors around Del Thomas's town house. We got lucky with the second home. It was across the street, and they had a door cam. The woman let us in. Her husband was at work. She advised us that the motion setting on their camera was set to *Sensitive* so it could be triggered by cars that passed. They did this because trash was being tossed on their lawn from a car that drove by. She opened the file on a laptop for the camera's surveillance. Gottert searched the time frame before the body was discovered. At 3:39 a.m., Del Thomas's red pickup was seen parking. Possible suspect wearing dark clothing and a black baseball cap got out of the driver's side. Because it was so dark, the door cam had captured only a shadowy profile. Unidentifiable, but the baseball cap had some sort of logo on it. The individual walked out of view.

I was relieved in a way because his physical description was nothing like Tommy's.

"That would be your suspect," I said.

6
Sweet Tooth

Gottert called a deputy at the Sheriff's Office to see if they could enhance the suspect's image. Based on my experience, it was doubtful that he'd be able to get a good facial image, but the logo on the baseball cap was a possibility.

We went to Bill's office and updated him.

"But why would the suspect drive the truck back?" Bill asked. "Why not just ditch it?"

"I've been wondering about that too," said Gottert. "I'm thinking your nephew had to know the suspect."

"Yeah," I agreed. "They must've been out together in the truck. Maybe the suspect drove it back to Del's town house because his car was parked there."

"What the hell did he get himself into?"

"Chief, I have a deputy at the Sheriff's Office working the images. He said he might have something for us in a couple of days. Also, don't you have a friend at the State Trooper's crime lab in Albany who has cell-phone advanced-services software? Hopefully, it might reveal any shared relationships our victims might have. It's a helluva lot more accurate than whatever I can do."

"I do. Sam Beck. He's good at what he does. I'll give him a call."

"The analytical software they have nowadays is damn good," I said. "I remember the day when we had to do that ourselves. It was a real pain in the ass."

"You *are* an old-timer," Gottert told me.

"So is your chief, Mike," Bill advised.

"Yes, sir. I mean, with all due respect." He smiled.

Dinner time came around fast. Good thing about being a volunteer was the department didn't own my life. I felt bad about leaving Gottert, but I was getting hungry and needed to try to get a good night's sleep. Plus Bill did say I could come and go on my own time. So, no guilt.

When I got to my car I gave Tommy a call. Asked him if he wanted a burger from the pub on Main Street. "I can stop there on the way home."

"Nah, I had a late lunch. Not that hungry."

"I'll eat there, then. See ya in a while, buddy."

"Alrighty then."

I hadn't been to the pub enough times for them to know me. It was a local hangout, especially busy at the end of a workday. Nothing in this town stayed open late, though, even on weekends. Only a couple of barstools were unoccupied when I arrived. I took one toward the end, between an older man with a long white beard and an attractive woman who looked to be in her forties. She looked familiar, but I couldn't quite place her. She was talking to another woman seated to her right.

Four large flat-screen televisions were affixed to the wall above the shelves of liquor bottles. There were two bartenders. Both female.

"Anyone sitting here?" I asked the bearded man.

"Nope. All yours."

The woman didn't break from her conversation, so I scooched in. The bartenders were busy, but after a couple of minutes the younger one approached.

"What can I get ya?"

"Guinness, and a menu."

She pulled the tap for the beer, then grabbed a menu and set them both before me.

"Thanks," I said.

"You gonna keep the tab open?"

"Yeah."

She smiled and walked away. Gotta love small-town life. She didn't even ask for a credit card. I sipped the beer, wiped the froth from my upper lip with a paper napkin. I had emptied the glass and eaten my meal (along with a second Guinness) before the friend of the familiar-looking woman beside me got up to leave.

"See you soon," the friend said as she headed for the door.

"Bye," the woman said.

She extended her hand over the bar to get the bartender's attention.

"I'll have one more, Sally."

"Okay, hon."

I could see her in my peripheral. Still could not place her. You'd think I'd remember someone like her. I felt guilty merely for thinking that, as if Elena was still here and I was checking out another woman. Elena was, in a way. She always would be. I went back to my beer. Looked like the bartender had made her a Manhattan. Set it in front of her.

"Thanks, Sal."

The old man was still nursing whatever it was he was drinking. It had started on the rocks but was now mostly watered down.

"You're Carl Sanderson's son?" asked the woman next to me.

I turned to her.

"I am. Have we met?"

"No, but I'm so sorry for your loss."

I'd been hearing a lot of that lately, but I responded only with a smile and a nod.

"I was at your father's funeral. You left before I could offer my condolences. I'm Ada."

Damn, Dad was *known*! But I guess that wasn't so unusual in a small town like this. Quite a few people had attended his funeral.

Ada extended her hand to shake. I offered mine in return. I looked down and noticed she wasn't wearing a wedding ring. Now why had I made a mental note of that?

"Graham. Nice to meet you."

I remembered Ada now. She'd been wearing a black V-neck dress, and she seemed to know most of the people at the funeral.

"How did you know my father?"

"I own the one and only bakery in town. Your father came in once a week every week, ever since I opened it ten years ago. He loved my bourbon biscuits and custard creams."

I was pretty sure those purchases had been for Tommy, because I had never known my dad to indulge in sweets.

"Sounds delicious. He did like his bourbon."

"How is your brother doing? I've never met him, but your dad talked about him often. I didn't see him at the funeral."

"He had a terrible time with the thought of putting our father in the ground." It didn't sound like she knew about his condition, so I left it at that.

"I hope he's doing better."

"Thanks—he is."

"Your dad once told me you're a detective in Washington, DC?"

"I was. I recently retired."

"Well, thank you for your service." She had a nice smile. Lifted her glass toward me. I lifted mine and we clinked.

"Thank you."

She looked toward my ring finger after our glasses met. I always notice even the smallest details; that's what made me a good detective. Had Ada glanced at my hand for the same reason I checked out hers, though?

"How long will you and your wife be staying in town?"

"My wife was taken by cancer about three years ago. I haven't brought myself to take the ring off."

"I'm so sorry. I can't imagine the kind of losses you've had to suffer."

"Thanks. I'm good," I lied. "I'll be here indefinitely, though. At least, that's the way it's looking. I moved here to stay with my brother. You originally from here?"

"Born and raised."

"Married?"

"Divorced. One teenage daughter."

"We never had kids," I said.

We both sipped our drinks.

"And how are you adjusting to small-town life?" she asked playfully.

"Slowly. I'm getting used to not falling asleep to the comforting sound of sirens in the distance."

She chuckled, then stopped all of a sudden and said, "You heard about the two murders?"

"Yes."

"That doesn't happen here. The worst crimes we get are things like theft from cars, and that's usually because the cars are left unlocked. Two murders—that's just frightening."

"It is."

"What kind of crimes did you investigate?"

"Homicides," I said with a half-smile.

"Wow, the things you must have seen. I noticed the police chief at the funeral."

"Yes, my dad knew him. He's a good guy."

"We have such a small department here. I don't know if they're capable of handling two murders."

"They're capable," is all I said, then took a swallow of beer. "They're shorthanded. I'm volunteering my time, though. Helping out where I can."

"Helping with the murder investigations?"

"Wherever they need me."

"Did you and your brother grow up in DC?"

"Yep. It was always home base between countries. My father worked for the government."

"Foreign Service, right?"

That was something he'd been trained to say. Certainly not the CIA, which was who he really worked for.

"Seems like he shared a lot with you."

"Oh, he was a talker."

"Are we talking about the same man? I've always known him to be the quintessential quiet man."

"Maybe it was the bourbon biscuits."

Or maybe he was just being a flirt.

I liked Ada. I felt comfortable with her in a way that I hadn't since Elena. It felt a little like cheating, though.

She finished her drink first and said, "I should be going. It was nice to finally meet you."

"Nice to meet you too. Maybe I'll stop by your bakery sometime."

"It's the Sweet Tooth. I have good coffee, too. Right down the street."

"Alrighty then," I said.

7
The Telltale Logo

The Archangel was a much younger version of my dad. He wielded a golden spear and stood over my fallen brother. Tommy's arms were stretched toward him, palms out in a futile attempt at defense. Or mercy. I struggled for my holstered gun, and when I finally got it out it fell apart in my hands before I could fire. The Archangel thrust the spear four times into Tommy's chest, opening him wide and spilling an impossible amount of blood—vivid, red, spurting blood. Then he turned to me. His face was oddly calm. No anger, but still just as frightening. The look was identical to the one he had shot me when I was a kid and we lived in Beirut, and he had found me inspecting the .38 revolver I had found in his satchel. He flung the spear. I woke up before it could strike my chest.

The dream rattled me so much that I had to turn the bedside light on. That was rare. I've had cop dreams and nightmares on multiple occasions, but never one this personal. I don't know what the hell it meant, but I didn't want it in my head. It took me a few minutes to regain myself and feel comfortable enough to turn off the light again.

I turned to Elena's urn and said, "Come visit. Please."

When I woke up the next morning, the nightmare had faded to something less vivid and shocking.

Elena did not show. I looked at the photo of her to keep her image in my head.

Tommy had gotten up before me. Starting my day on the deck with him was my new routine. It was nice. I wondered if it had been my father's routine too. I believed it was.

I had two cups of coffee. Tommy scrambled a few eggs and toasted some wheat bread for us. He offered me fresh milk, but I didn't accept. Never been a milk person.

"It's from a local farm," he urged. "Not raw, so don't worry."

"Nah," was all I said in response.

"You going to the police station again?"

"Yeah, it sorta feels good to get back in it."

I don't know why I invented sentiments like that. Was I trying to convince myself?

"I'm heading upstairs to work."

"I'll see you this evening—maybe sooner, if there's nothing for me to do at the station. Let me know if you need anything."

"I won't need anything, but thanks."

"I can give the back of your head a shave, if you want."

"That'd be good. Appreciate it."

Tommy had been in his room when I got home last night. I hadn't wanted to bother him then, but now I realized he might be able to satisfy my curiosity about Ada.

"I talked to this woman last night at the pub—Ada. She owns a bakery in town. I saw her at Dad's funeral."

"Sweet Tooth. I don't know her. I love the custards."

"Did he ever talk about her?"

"No. Why?"

"Just curious. She said he went in there every week. Figured he might have mentioned her to you."

"Nope. Just what he bought there is all. He'd been going since it opened. You think Dad liked her or something?"

"I don't know. Maybe," I said, half-joking.

"If he did, he never told me about it."

"Probably because she would've been a bit too young for him."

"That wouldn't stop him."

"Okay, then," I returned. "I like pastries with my coffee sometimes. Maybe I'll go there in a day or two. Get you some custard treats, and I'll try the bourbon biscuits she said Dad liked."

"He did like those a lot. You got eyes for this woman, or something?" Tommy winked.

"No, man—I just like the thought of having a good treat with my coffee."

"Okay, big brother."

Damn his intuition.

At the Charontown police station, an older officer with a head of thick white hair approached the window when I buzzed. His name tag read D. KING.

"Can I help you?"

"Hi, Officer. I'm Graham Sanderson—"

"Oh yeah," he said before I could finish introducing myself. "The retired DC detective here to help Gottert."

"That'd be me."

He walked around and opened the door to let me in. I stepped in, shut the door behind me.

"Dana King," he said as he extended his hand to shake.

"Good to meet you," I said, offering mine.

"The chief said you'd be dropping by. He went with Gottert to the mayor's office. They'll be back shortly."

"That can't be good."

"Two murders in a row—and in a small town like this—will stir things up."

"I can imagine."

"Chief was my captain when I worked patrol at NYPD."

"You guys go back, then."

"We do indeed. I retired there as a sergeant three years ago. Came up here to work for him after I realized I wasn't done with the job yet. Or it wasn't done with me." He smiled.

"Much slower pace than you're used to."

King chuckled and said, "Just a bit."

"You had to go through an academy again, right?"

"Hell yeah. Six months, brother. Just as tough as the larger-department academies, but my class had recruits who scattered to other small towns around here after graduating, not a single big class all going to the same city. I was the oldest recruit in their history, but I still kicked ass over some of those young guns."

"You're a bigger man than me. I sure as hell wouldn't want to go through that a second time. Volunteering is more than enough."

"At least you got your brain working again. You want some coffee or something?"

"No, I'm good, thanks."

"You can have a seat in the break room until they get back."

"Sounds good."

I followed him there.

"Sit anywhere you like. I've got to finish writing up an incident report. Let me know if you need anything."

"Appreciate it, Dana."

* * *

I heard Bill and Mike entering the station about twenty minutes later.

I got up and walked out to greet them.

"What a nightmare," Bill said to me.

"Sorry to hear that," I said.

"Well, no different than the city—but at least there it was easier to keep a handle on, and we had more manpower. Damn, I need at least five more officers, another sergeant, and an investigator here. Bad as it sounds, maybe I'll get it approved now."

"As long as you don't take my overtime away," King chimed in.

"I'll make sure to always have that available for you, Dana."

Dana smiled and shot him an upward nod in approval.

"We got an image back from my boy at the sheriff's office," Gottert told me.

"Oh yeah?"

Gottert pulled a printout from the case jacket he was holding. The suspect's face was not identifiable, just as I had thought, but the logo on his cap was: STEELERS.

"That's good there," I remarked. "How many Steeler fans you got in this town?"

"I have no idea," Bill said. "I know it's mostly Bills."

"I mean, it's good, but not so uncommon that it'd make it exceptional. It's good, though."

"I want to get it on the local social-media page here—see if anyone comes forward with information."

"I'm not so sure about that, Chief," I began. "If the suspect sees it, he'll probably trash the cap—and right now it's all the evidence we have."

"I can hold on to it for a while. I didn't let the mayor know, so that should buy me some time."

Gottert broke in: "My guy said based on the height of the truck's cab and the suspect's image, he can put him at about five foot ten."

"That's good too," I said.

"Yeah, it's a very good start," Bill added.

"I'd better get back to it then, Chief," Gottert said.

"Let me know if you need anything, Mike—and thanks again. You too, Graham." Bill gave me a gentle slap on the back of the shoulder.

I followed Gottert into his office.

He plopped himself on his swivel chair and leaned back. Looked toward the ceiling, like he didn't know where to begin. I thought he'd let out a big sigh, but he didn't.

"Gotta catch a break on this," he said as if to himself.

"Keep working it. Follow everything through, and it'll happen. Shit—you already caught our suspect on camera."

"But they won't be able to enhance it enough to identify him, right?"

"No, I doubt it. At least you have a slight description: male, approximately five-eight to five-ten, average build, Steelers ball cap. Appears not to have any facial hair."

"Can't even identify a race in that footage."

"No, but at least we have something to work on. Granted, it's not much, but it's a good start. Most homicide cases don't even have that."

"You're one of those positive thinkers, huh?"

I huffed out a little chuckle. "Not really. Just trying to make you feel better."

"Ha! Good luck with that. I'll always find something to worry about. Oh, and I meant to show you: I searched *three-edged knives* a while ago and came up with these."

He turned his monitor screen to face me. It showed several images of dagger-like knives. Several of them appeared to be antiques.

"Nice. Any spots in town where you might be able to buy something like that?"

8
Chasing Leads

The gun-and-tackle shop was on the east side of Charontown, across the street from a lumber store. A large U.S. flag was mounted on a pole affixed above the display window. A tall, older man stood behind the counter.

"Officer Gottert," he said indifferently.

"Bob, how's it going today?"

"Same ol', same ol'."

Gottert shut the door behind him.

"This is Graham Sanderson. He's helping us out with an investigation."

"You related to Carl Sanderson?"

Had to smile to myself, because Dad sure seemed to get around. For some reason I always figured my father as more of a recluse.

"Sure am. He was my dad."

"I'm sorry for your loss. I got to know him through the years. He used to come in during fishing season from time to time for bait and gear."

"He did enjoy fishing. Thanks."

We stepped over to the counter. Several handguns, different makes and models, were displayed in the counter on the right side and on the left along with four hunting-type knives, none of them tri-edged.

"What can I do for you boys?"

"We thought you might be able to help us out with something."

"I can try."

"Looking for some information on a kind of knife."

"My business is primarily guns, ammunition, and tackle. Not many knives, as you can see here."

"We're looking for a knife that would be more tactical—specifically, a tri-edged one."

"Like a tri-edged dagger, something like that?"

"Yeah."

"This have to do with the two murders?"

"No, no."

"Well, I never did good with stuff like that here. If you can't butcher a deer with it, most of my customers don't want it. Knife like that is tactical—good for only one thing, really—"

"Killing," I jumped in.

"Mostly. Also collectors into military hardware, or just custom."

"I didn't know the military used that kind of weapon," I said.

"I don't know if they do anymore. World War Two or maybe Korea, or even further back."

Damn—my dad had served in Korea.

"Anywhere else in the area where you might be able to buy one like that?" I asked.

"I have no idea. Hell, online you can get just about anything."

"Okay, Bob. Thanks."

"Sure thing. You boys stay safe. And again, I'm sorry for your loss, Mr. Sanderson. Your dad was a good man."

"Appreciate it."

When we got outside I asked Gottert, "What are the state laws about selling tactical knives in New York?"

"They're not illegal, unless your intent is to use them to commit a crime. Ballistic knives, knuckle knives, and maybe a couple of others are illegal. I don't know about something that might be collectible."

"Chances are, if a weapon like that was used, like the man said, it was probably bought on the internet."

"Whatever kind of a weapon, it was meant to be up close and personal. Like you mentioned before, maybe someone trained. Former military?"

"Could be."

"But again, why those two men?" he asked.

"That's the question to keep asking yourself, because there is a connection. You interview all the family members of both decedents?"

"Yes, but the first vic's oldest daughter was a tough one. She never got along with her father."

"Yeah, I got that in your running résumé. How about we try again, but don't call? Let's just show up at her home."

"Sounds good. Seems like your father got around in this town."

"Appears that way."

We crossed an arched bridge made of iron that looked designed for a horse and carriage. It was so narrow you'd have to wait for an oncoming car to cross before you could. Still there after all that time. Well maintained.

Most of the homes in Tina Scott's community, by contrast, were not well maintained. Many had peeling paint or dry rot, with dandelions and other overgrown weeds assailing the front yards. They cried out for attention.

"You get a lot of calls to this part of town?"

"Yeah, mostly domestic and disorderly."

"It's kept hidden from the rest of the community."

"Isn't it always?"

"Not everywhere. A lot of areas in DC are gentrified, but still a lot of bad spots. There was a time, not so long ago, when you could walk a couple of blocks almost anywhere in the city and suddenly find yourself in one of those drug-infested bad spots, with homes that were just empty shells. Not so easy to hide. Now those homes are going for over a million."

"Damn, you could buy a shell of a home here on some good land for something like thirty-five thousand."

"Maybe I should invest."

"Don't waste your time. We'll both be dead and gone by the time most of these neighborhoods get better."

Tina's house was one of the few exceptions to the other homes. The tiny front yard was mowed and edged. Three nice potted flowering plants embellished the front patio. Still needed new paint, but it looked cozy enough.

We parked and stepped up to the patio. Gottert knocked. No answer. He knocked harder. We waited, but still no answer.

"You think she's home but not answering?" I asked.

"No, I don't see her car. She's probably at the Tim Hortons where she works. Back to the other end of town, then."

He said that like it was a drive. To get from one side of DC to the other could sometimes take up practically a whole shift.

We drove back toward the bridge.

"Shit," Gottert said.

I noticed a young guy ahead of us on the right. He was crossing the street at the corner.

"That's Tucker Barnes. I got a warrant out on him for felony assault."

"Let's light him up."

Gottert slowed as we neared him.

"Shit, I can't do that with you in the car."

"You think I'm some damn civilian ride-along you have to watch over? I can't count how many times I've had to jump out on someone."

"Dana King told me that exact same thing! I don't know, though. He's probably too drunk to run. You just stay in the car. I'll roll up behind him."

"A felony warrant is a felony warrant. I'm your backup, and I can handle myself. Plus I promise not to sue if I do get a scratch."

"I don't want to let him go. He'll make us by the time King gets here."

"Let me out here. Then you roll up a little ahead of him."

"Fuck. Okay."

Reluctantly, he stopped the car. I got out and quietly closed the door. Walked to the sidewalk and toward Gottert's boy. He was less than a quarter of a block ahead of me. Gottert drove past him and parked at the curb. Spotting Gottert, he made an awkward pivot, then bolted in my direction. Gottert was quick and got right on his heels. Walking fast—I didn't even have to run—I moved swiftly toward him. He was right on me in a couple of seconds, and thought he had the footwork to make it around me.

He didn't.

I laid one on him with the base of my right palm against the xiphoid area of his chest. He lost all his wind and curled. I took his right hand and twisted it behind him, then kicked him behind the right knee. Down he went.

"Shit," said Gottert upon reaching us a second later. "Impressive, old man."

9

Information for a Deal

Tucker Barnes sat on a metal chair in the interview room of the police station. His head was down. I was sitting on a chair with rollers in front of a cubicle across from the room. I could see him on a monitor secured to the wall. A digital recording system was on a table below the screen. Bill walked out of his office followed by Gottert, who was carrying a bag that contained the prisoner's property. He dropped the bag on the cubicle's desk. Bill leaned against the divider wall.

"Maybe we need to fit you for a uniform," Bill teased me. "Get you back on the street."

"Hell no. I'm not gonna suffer through the academy again."

"Well, good job—but don't do something like that again."

"Copy that, Chief."

"Keep me informed," he said to Gottert.

"Yes, sir."

Bill headed back to his office.

"I get you in trouble?"

"Not really," Gottert told me, then walked toward the interview room.

"Have fun," I said. "I'll listen in."

"The audio switch is to the right of the monitor."

"Got it."

He pulled a can of Coke from a small refrigerator near the cubicle and disappeared into the interview room. Tucker looked up as he stepped in. Gottert sat across from him, set the file on a small table between the two of them. Then he pulled a small notebook from his rear pocket and placed it on the table as well.

"I got you a cola," he said, then handed the cold drink to him.

"Thanks," Tucker said.

"I wanna let you know you're being recorded."

"I know."

"Okay. I'm Investigator Mike Gottert—"

"I know who you are."

"Tucker, I'm saying that for the recording, not to you."

"Oh, got ya. Sorry."

"I'm Investigator Mike Gottert with the Charontown Police Department. Seated across from me is Tucker Barnes."

Almost comically, Tucker nodded toward the camera. *Nothing like a cooperative defendant.*

"The time is 11:47 a.m. Tucker, I read you your rights when I placed you under arrest, and you waived them and agreed to talk. Is that correct?"

"Yeah, I have nothing to hide."

"That's good. Do you have any questions about your rights?"

"Naw."

"You've been arrested for assault in the third degree."

"That asshole tried to pick up my wife when she was sitting at the bar, just like I told you." Tucker looked defiantly at the camera.

"You knocked out his two front teeth and broke his nose."

"Yeah, I did—but I was defending myself."

"Several witnesses at the Birdhouse say different. They say you walked over with your pool cue and smashed him in the face with it without provocation."

"No, he stepped up to me first. It was self-defense."

"I have to be honest with you, Tucker. It doesn't look good for you. The only witness you have is your wife—"

"Are you saying my wife's not good enough?"

"Not at all—just that there are several witnesses to your single witness who say something different, and your wife couldn't even keep her story straight. The best thing you can do for yourself at this point is to be honest about the whole thing. Let the prosecutor and the judge see that. This is a serious charge. Up to seven years."

"Listen, Officer—"

"Investigator," Gottert corrected him.

"Investigator, I can't do that kinda time. And he did step up to me; I thought he was going to attack me."

"You have a history of getting into fights, Tucker, and drunk and disorderly. Be honest now and tell the truth. I have a lot of evidence, so the last thing you want to do is get caught up with all these lies."

"I'm not lying."

"Alright, I tried to help you. I walk out of here and the only thing the judge is going to see from you is lies and someone who is not remorseful. Is that what you want?"

Tucker bowed his head like he was thinking about it. That was always a good sign.

Then he looked up and said, "What if I had some good information for you? Could you make the charge go away?"

"What kind of information?"

"About the murder here. That dude Pauly."

10
A Person of Interest

I can't recall how many cases I've closed thanks to information provided by a defendant who was trying to get a deal. Gottert handled it well. He had obviously been down that road before, but probably not with a homicide investigation. He told Tucker Barnes that he couldn't make any promises, but that based on his experience, if the information was good and it helped to close a homicide, it could lead to a nice plea deal for him in the end.

"The only one who can make that happen is the prosecutor. But I'll need to know what information you have."

"I want something in writing first."

"You know I can't do that. I've locked you up a couple of times, before I got promoted to investigator. I ever treat you wrong?"

"No, you been good."

"That's right, Tucker. I ever mislead you?"

"No."

"Well, I'm not messing with you now. I will personally go to the prosecutor if what you have is good. But I can't do that if I don't know what kind of information you have. You understand me?"

"Yeah."

"Okay, so what information do you have about the homicide?"

Tucker did that bowing-his-head thing again for a few seconds.

"I was sitting with a couple of boys at the bar," he began. It sounded like the opening to a stale joke.

"At the Birdhouse?"

"Yeah."

"Go on."

"Just having a few beers, you know. One of them asked if we heard about Pauly—that the police found him dead."

"When was this?"

"Couple of weeks ago. Honestly can't remember the day, but it was like maybe three days after I heard you guys found him."

"Okay."

"One of the boys said that Pauly got himself in trouble with the wrong guy after Pauly was caught trying to sell fentanyl to some people at an NA meeting. He said the guy kicked Pauly out and they got in a fight right there in the parking lot. He heard the guy tell Pauly after kicking his ass that if he ever tries that again, he'll take care of him for good—or something like that."

Gottert finished writing in his notepad.

"The guy who saw all this was at the NA meeting?"

"I'm assumin', but I never asked."

"He ever tell you who the guy was?"

"Naw."

"What's your boy's name?"

"You'll keep me out of it, right? I don't want my friend to know I got him caught up in this shit."

"Sounds like there were a few witnesses there. He won't know who it came from."

"His name is Jak."

"Last name."

"Avery."

"I know him," Gottert said. "He still work at the Dollar General?"

"Far as I know, yeah."

"Any idea where the NA meeting was held?"

"He said it was out of this church, but I didn't ask which one. So . . . is that information good enough for you?"

"If it pans out, sure. You probably won't get held for this and get released tomorrow. If you hear anything else that might help us, get in touch with me here and let me know right away. Okay?"

"Yeah."

Gottert finished processing Barnes. He had an officer transport him to the jail at the Sheriff's Department.

"He'll get released in the morning," Gottert told me. "No one gets held here anymore, unless it's for something like rape or murder. Even then, there's a chance they'll get out on bond."

"Same everywhere, really."

"I know this Jak dude. I locked him up for a DUI when I was in patrol. I saw him a few days ago when I went to the Dollar General for a shoplifting."

"Small town has its benefits."

"Yep, you get to know pretty much everybody—even the ones you don't wanna know."

"Hell, I don't know why the chief thinks you need *my* help. You're doing pretty damn good on your own."

"It's nice to have someone around."

"Like an older sidekick?" I smiled.

He chuckled. "I didn't say that. But really, man, when it comes time to draft up an affidavit or two, I *will* need your help with the language. I've done simple drug stuff, even a couple of burglaries, but never anything this serious."

"You got it, brother. You should get the interview with Tina out of the way first, and then Jak. I'll go with you."

"Sounds good, Doctor Watson."

It took me a second. I spit out a chuckle.

"Funny guy," I said.

Tim Hortons was outside town, near Seneca Lake. It was one of the larger Finger Lakes. I wondered if my dad had ever fished it.

"When I first tried to talk to her," Gottert told me in his police cruiser on the way over there, "Tina was pretty uncooperative. She's probably not going to be good for anything, but I still have to try."

"You never know."

Tina Scott was working behind the counter along with a couple of other people. My brother Tommy, a local-history buff, once told me that the restaurant chain had originally been founded by a Canadian hockey player, Tim Horton. It eventually found its way to our country.

Only a handful of customers were seated inside. Tina looked toward us as we entered. She appeared to be in her early twenties with dyed blond hair and dark roots. She seemed to recognize Gottert because she shook her head immediately.

"You can see I'm workin'," she said before Gottert could say anything.

"Tina, I'm sorry for having to bother you here, but I have some more questions—"

"You're going to get me in trouble."

A male co-worker—Tina's manager?—glanced our way with concern.

"Just a few questions and we won't bother you anymore."

"Either that or we'll come back with a subpoena," I volunteered. "That would take you away for half the day."

Gottert studied me but didn't seem pissed. It was more like he hadn't expected me to say anything.

Tina turned to her manager and announced, "I have to take a short break."

He nodded.

"I need a cigarette. Meet me out back, near the dumpster. I only have a few minutes."

We walked out and around to the rear of the restaurant. Tina was already outside, lighting a cigarette.

After a long first drag she said, "I already told you I don't know anything."

"Just a couple more questions," Gottert said.

"It's not like I don't care that my father died. It's just that all he ever cared about was getting high."

"I'm sorry you had to live through that as a child."

Her eyes got red. Looked like she was about to cry. She wiped her eyes with the back of her left hand. No tears.

"You never told me when it was that you last saw him."

"It was over a month ago, after my mom kicked him out of the house. Again. He needed a place to stay, but I told him no."

"Did he ever mention any of his friends to you?"

"No. They used to come around when he lived with us. That was years ago, though, and I don't remember their names."

"You get along with your mom?"

"Better than him."

"When was the last time you saw her?"

"A couple of days after she learned he was killed."

"Did she tell you anything that you think might help us?"

"I don't know if this will help you, but she said he was trying to get clean. He'd started going to meetings."

She teared up again but didn't bother to wipe them away this time.

"Did your mother say where he was going to meetings?"

"No, just that some other guy got him to go. He had a weird name—*Deal* or something."

"Del?" I asked.

"Yes, that's the name."

11
At the Dollar General

So NA is what Del Thomas and Pauly Savell had in common," I said as Gottert and I walked to his cruiser.

"Looks like it."

"It shouldn't be too difficult to identify the guy who beat up Pauly. Oh, and sorry for jumping in with that subpoena thing—I couldn't help myself."

"I'm not worried about that shit. It got her to talk."

"From Tim Hortons to Dollar General. I don't know if I can contain myself."

A cashier at the Dollar General informed us that Jak Avery was mopping up in the toy section. He was just finishing up when we got there. Was surprised to see Mike Gottert, like he was about to get in trouble again. He looked at me after and seemed even more apprehensive.

"Don't worry," Gottert said.

"I ain't worried 'cause I ain't done nothin'."

"You looked a bit worried for a second there."

"Naw, just didn't expect to see your face here. You need a toy for your kid or somethin'?"

"I don't have kids. I need to ask you a couple of questions."

Avery looked at me again.

Gottert didn't introduce me. I wondered if that was on purpose because sometimes it was a good thing to keep them off-balance.

"I gotta work here," Jak said.

"This won't take long, unless you'd rather I subpoena you and then you'd probably miss a whole day of work."

I smiled.

"I don't want that shit."

"If you give us the information we need, then I won't have to do that."

"What kind of information you need?"

"It's about a fight you witnessed in a church parking lot."

"I didn't witness any fight."

"I got several people who put you there, so don't play that shit with me, Jak. I will subpoena your ass every day."

I started thinking that Gottert should take it easy with the *subpoena* shit.

"Tell me who the guy is that got in a fight with Pauly, and we'll be on our way."

They always bow their heads.

When Avery looked up again, he was clutching the mop handle with both hands like a crutch.

"Who was it?" Gottert asked again.

"Dude named Jeffrey."

"Last name."

"Sikes."

"What was the fight about?"

"You said if I told you his name, you'd be on your way."

"Yes, I did. Just a couple more questions. What was the fight about?"

"Some shit about Pauly slinging dope at the meetings."

"He dealt drugs?"

"On occasion. At the Birdhouse, mostly."

"Did Sikes threaten him?"

"Don't get me caught up in this murder shit. I ain't goin' to court and I don't know if Jeffrey had anything to do with that anyway. I known him since high school."

"I'll keep you out of it."

"That's what all the police say."

"If I say it, I mean it. Did Jeffrey Sikes threaten Pauly?"

"Yeah, he said he'd fuck him up bad if he ever came back."

"What church did this happen at?"

"Wait, I thought you already knew all that?"

"I need to confirm it with you."

"The Presbyterian church right behind the high school."

"Okay. Now where does Sikes live?"

"He used to have an apartment at the Tenley building on Rose Street, but I think he moved."

"Where does he work?"

"Damn, man."

"Just tell me where he works, Jak."

"Kwik Fill."

"The one here in town?"

"Yeah."

Gottert looked at me and said, "You have any questions?"

Jak was shaking his head, obviously frustrated.

"Jeffrey get in a lot of fights?"

"He been known to, but usually only with the ones who deserve it."

"How well did you know Pauly?" I asked.

"Only at the NA meetings. That's all."

"You ever see Del Thomas at the meetings?"

"That shit supposed to be confidential."

"Not when it comes to homicide. You know Del?"

"Yeah, I know him. I mean, *knew* him."

"Were Del and Pauly friends?"

"I'm assumin' so. They came to meetings together sometimes. You thinkin' his murder had somethin' to do with Pauly's?"

"Right now we're looking into everything. Was Del there during the fight?"

Avery had to think about that one for a moment.

"Naw, I don't think he was."

"Thanks. That's all I have for now," I told Gottert.

"Appreciate your time, Jak."

"By the way, NA supposed to be confidential. I'd appreciate you keepin' it that way. I'm trying to do somethin' good with my life here."

"That's a good thing, Jak. Don't worry."

We turned and walked away.

"And now Kwik Fill," I said.

When we got to the parking lot Gottert said, "Those were good questions. Not sure why I didn't think to ask them."

"It'll become natural with time. I'd be willing to bet that most of the guys Jeffrey got in a fight with never reported it to the police."

"We'll find out soon enough when I run him."

12

The Old Church

Sikes had a couple of arrests in the system. Typical shit for this town—driving while drunk and criminal mischief. That was over two years ago. No assaults, though. There was an address. It was a rental on Rose Street, like Jak Avery said. We drove there, but Sikes no longer lived at the apartment. The current resident didn't know anything about him.

The church that Avery had mentioned was on the way to Kwik Fill, so we went there first. An old stone structure with a soaring bell tower, it occupied the corner of a residential neighborhood behind the high school. The building had to be over a hundred years old. Still stood strong. The Associate Pastor for Youth Programs let us in. The large stained-glass windows did not admit much light.

"Pastor Simon is in his office."

We followed him down a wide corridor to the stairs that led to the bottom floor, then through a large community-type room to an office in the back.

He knocked on the door. Pastor Simon answered, immediately looked at me, and then at Gottert.

"Graham," he greeted me and extended his hand.

We shook.

The associate pastor said, "They told me they were with the police department."

"I'm Investigator Gottert."

"Good to meet you, Investigator," the pastor said with a mildly confused look.

"I'll be on my way, then," said the associate pastor.

"Thanks, Stan," Pastor Simon told him. "Well—come in, come in."

We entered.

"We're here about a fight that occurred in your parking lot during an NA meeting," Gottert told him.

"A fight here?"

He seemed genuinely puzzled.

"Yes, between two men who were attending the meeting."

"This is the first I've heard of something like that happening. I should tell you, though, that the church does not run those meetings. The previous pastor allowed a member to use the community room on Wednesday evenings to conduct them. That's about it. I personally never get involved—unless, of course, one of the folks wants spiritual guidance."

"I understand. I'd still like to ask you a couple of questions."

"Of course. You didn't tell me you were working with the police here, Graham." He said it almost like he was concerned. That struck me as odd, but I didn't make anything more of it.

"I'm just volunteering. Needed to get out of the house more. Feel useful again, you know?"

"Good of you to give your time and energy for something worthy. What questions do you have?"

"Can we get the name of the person who runs the meetings?"

"I'll have to call Beth, in administration. She will have that information. Would you like to sit down?"

"I'm fine," I said.

"No, thank you," Gottert said.

He went to the desk, picked up the phone, and tapped an extension. After a moment he said, "Hi, Beth—Pastor Simon here. Can you give me the name of the gentleman who runs the NA meetings? Thank you."

He grabbed a notepad and a pen on his desk. A few seconds later, he wrote down the information.

"Thank you, Beth."

He hung up, tore the top sheet from the pad, and handed it to Gottert.

"Thank you, Pastor," Gottert said. "Also, what time are those meetings?"

"Seven o'clock in the evening."

"Thanks for your time," Gottert said.

We all shook hands.

"The last thing we want is to bring trouble to the community. I'm going to bring this up at the deacons meeting and see about having that group removed."

"This is an isolated incident, Pastor Simon," I began. "And you haven't had any calls here for other incidents, have you?"

"None."

"I'm sure everything will be fine," I told the pastor.

"I'll make sure someone keeps an eye out, then. Good to see you again, Graham. Maybe next time will be under different circumstances—like a beer at the pub or something."

"Sounds good to me, Pastor."

"You boys take care—and stay safe."

"We can find our way out," Gottert told him.

We walked out, heard the door close behind us.

Gottert displayed the sheet of paper Simon had given him. "Yet another name to follow up on," he said.

"The daily grind of the hardworking detective."

"That'll be the death of me."

"Hell, I'm still alive and kicking."

"You a churchgoing man, then?"

"Not really. My father went there. The pastor's just trying to recruit me now. By the way, I think you should call Kwik Fill to see if Jeffrey Sikes is working today—but don't say you're the police. If we just show up and he's not there but he's your guy, he might disappear."

"I know."

We got in the car. Gottert googled *Kwik Fill,* then dialed the number. He put it on speaker.

"Kwik Fill," a woman answered.

"Hey, this is Joey. How are you today, sweetie?"

"I'm fine. How can I help you?"

"Is Jeffrey working today?"

"No, it's his day off."

"Damn, when will he be working?"

"He starts tomorrow at nine in the morning."

"Okay. Appreciate it."

He disconnected.

"Gotta be honest. If you ever tried that kinda call with a drug thug in DC, you wouldn't have got far."

"Good thing it's just a simple small-town gas station. You got time for one more stop?"

"Yeah—but then I should head home."

Truth was, I wanted to stop by Sweet Tooth on the way home. Ada was probably still open.

Mike Keleher was the name the pastor had written down, along with his address. We drove to his home. It was a nice place on the south side of town, and he looked like a nice family man. Gottert explained why we were there. I got the feeling Mike wouldn't have a lot to offer.

"How did you get my name?" he asked politely.

"It came up during the course of the investigation," Gottert said.

"Well, Paul wasn't hurt badly, and he didn't want to make a police report. I mean, I had no idea Paul was trying to deal drugs in there. I never would have let him attend if I had known what he was doing."

"How long has Sikes been attending the meetings?"

"Investigator, with all due respect, those meetings are confidential. You'd need to ask him that."

"I'll do that. Have you had any other problems with those guys in the past?"

"No, not at all. I'm sorry, but I don't know how I can help you. Don't get me wrong—it's shocking what happened to those men. I mean, do you have any reason to believe anyone else who attends is in danger?"

"At this time, we don't."

"I wish I could be more help."

"You seem to be a very decent man, Mr. Keleher," I said.

"I try."

"I don't believe you're the type of man who would withhold information that might help with a homicide investigation."

"Of course not. If I heard anything about that, I'd tell you."

"Two men who belonged to your group—Paul Savell and Del Thomas—have been murdered. You wouldn't be breaking confidence with respect to them anymore."

"You're right."

"Did the two of them appear to be friends?"

"I mean, I think so. They came to the meetings together a couple of times and left together."

"How long have they been attending?"

"Del started coming about four months ago, then Paul showed up with him around two months ago."

"Was Del there when the fight happened?"

"I don't really remember. I think so."

"What did Del do when his friend and Sikes started fighting?"

"It all happened so fast. I don't think anyone got involved. We were all stunned."

"Have you ever witnessed an argument between Del and Jeffrey Sikes?"

"Not in front of me. Personally, I don't think anyone at the meeting could murder someone; the fight totally took me by surprise. It's terrible what happened to those two men. I think it had everything to do with what they were involved in outside the group, though."

"Have there been any problems with them in the past?" Gottert asked.

"Not at all."

"Okay, sir," Gottert said. He fished a business card from his wallet and handed it to Keleher.

"Call me if you do hear anything that might help us with the investigation."

"Of course—but I doubt I'll hear anything."

A dead end. But I knew that at the beginning.

13
Another Nightmare

Sweet Tooth was a charming pastry shop in a small one-story red-brick building. It was wedged between a mom-and-pop pizza joint and a hair salon.

I hesitated before I entered. Almost changed my mind.

The little bell on top of the door chimed when I entered. The rich smell of goodness made me smile. Two large glass-front counters stood on the far side of the shop, with four small round tables and a few wooden chairs arranged near the front window. A second door behind the counters led into another room. I couldn't see Ada, so she was probably working in the back room. Two women sat at one of the tables, sipping coffee and eating some kind of pastries. Nice landscape paintings depicting the Finger Lakes region dotted the walls, along with well-placed floating shelves that held books, vintage baking utensils, and tins labeled *Baker's Delight* and *Magic Baking Powder.*

I looked at the large chalkboard on the wall to the right of the door that led into the back. It highlighted several coffees and coffee-related drinks, along with the pastry specials. I stepped over to the counters. They were filled with all kinds of pastries, cookies, and a handful of cakes. My eyes caught sight of the bourbon biscuits.

"Hi there," I heard.

I looked up to see Ada behind the counter. She was wearing an apron over a sunflower-yellow casual V-necked dress. She looked lovely.

"Hi," I smiled.

"You decided to come by."

"Yes. Everything looks delicious."

"That's because everything *is* delicious."

She picked up a pair of tongs and slid open the back of one of the glass counters.

"Here."

She grabbed a bourbon biscuit, put it in a paper baking cup, and handed it to me over the counter.

"Thank you."

I bit into the biscuit.

"Wow. That is something."

"Happy you like it."

"I'll take half a dozen."

"Sure thing."

"You make all these yourself?"

"I sure do."

"Impressive. And what kind of custards or other things did my dad buy?"

"He liked the cinnamon-roll bites and the peanut-butter bars. And the custards for your brother."

"Okay. Load me up. I'll take a half dozen each of those too."

Ada shot me a nice smile, got a pastry box from a table against the wall, and filled it up with everything. She placed it on the counter.

"There you go."

I took a credit card out of my wallet and handed it to her. She ran it. I signed the receipt.

"Thank you, sir," she said in fun.

"Appreciate it, Ada."

"Are you getting to know our town?"

"Slowly, but I am."

I didn't want her to know I was getting to know the town through a homicide investigation.

"Well, thank you," I said.

"Maybe I'll see you around."

"You will. Take care."

I took the box and walked out. I should have asked her out for a drink, I thought after. At the least, kept the conversation going a little while longer. But then no—too soon. An image of Elena popped into my head. I went straight home.

Tommy was excited about the custards.

"I'll have a couple after dinner for dessert," he said.

"By the way, did Dad still have his Korean war mementos stashed somewhere?"

"I'm sure he does. Why?"

I kept the *why* to myself, but it was the possibility of the knife that I was interested in. And if I didn't find something like that, then what?

"Just feeling nostalgic. I remember when I was here last, him showing me some of what he managed to sneak out of Korea."

"Maybe his closet."

"I'll check it out sometime."

Tommy simply nodded his head. Looked like the thought of Dad's room made him sad, so I didn't pursue it.

"I can hit the back of your head with the shaver."

"Okay, but I'd rather you be gentle." He smiled.

I chuckled at that.

He went upstairs to get the electric shaver and a large bath towel. He carried a stool from the kitchen into the laundry-room bathroom and set it in front of a large mirror, then draped the towel around his front and over his shoulders and sat on the stool facing the mirror.

"Just the back, okay? I can get the rest."

"I got ya."

I was slow and careful about it. I smiled at Tommy in the mirror, but he stared straight ahead with a dead face. He was somewhere distant, so I didn't talk. I felt bad for him. I couldn't imagine living the kind of life he lived. It saddened me.

It didn't take long to finish. I slapped him gently on his right shoulder when I was done. He nodded a couple of times. No expression and that was that.

We had a late dinner. Grilled hamburgers and red bell peppers from his garden out back. We basically lived on the deck. I had to admit, it was relaxing. No sirens or horns honking. Birds chirping and all that shit. I'm sure I lengthened my lifespan by moving here, but then I started to worry about Tommy. It didn't help when he brought up the second murder.

"I read online about it. I know that's why you're volunteering. Right?"

"It is."

"What are your thoughts about it? I mean, two back-to-back murders here. That's unheard-of."

"I don't know what to think about it. I'm sure the two are related. Probably drug related. I don't think it's anything more."

That wasn't all true.

"You think?" he asked.

"Yeah. I'm going to have some scotch. You want something?"

"Grab me a beer."

I didn't want to have this conversation with my brother, but there were things I needed to know, like where he had driven that night. But like I said, I was afraid to ask. I couldn't stand the thought of his condition being a false front.

And then there was the puzzle of the Steelers ball cap. I'd never known Tommy to be into football—or into any sports, for that matter. The thought was ridiculous.

I handed him the bottle of beer, sat down, and sipped my scotch. Peaty—very nice. Our dad had loved scotch. I'm sure the bottle I poured this one from had been sitting around here for a while. Tommy didn't like hard liquor—just beer or wine, on occasion.

"Did you know Bill's nephew, Del Thomas?" I asked him.

"No. Was he the one who was killed? There was no mention of who it was online."

"It was him."

"I feel bad for Bill. Henry was the only close friend I've ever had here. The old pastor, too—the one before Simon. Dad had him over for dinner a lot, and drinks. Pastor Simon is okay, but he won't be around for long. He'll leave soon after they find another one."

"What happened between you and Henry?"

"He couldn't take my condition anymore. He's a social guy, likes to get out. Wanted to travel—which is the last thing I want to do, of course."

I could understand Tommy's reluctance to travel after his spine injury in Arlington.

Damn.

"You guys still talk at all?" I asked.

"No. He completely broke it off."

I had a feeling it was Henry who I'd heard him arguing with over the phone, but all I said was, "Sorry, man."

The two of us were so different. But hell, what kind of man might I be today if I had gone through the shit he did as a kid?

"How you holdin' up now?"

"I'm fine, big brother. No need to worry."

"It's good to be here with you," I told him.

He looked at me with a quirky half-smile.

"It's good to be here with you too."

I felt better.

After dinner we watched television. Reruns of *American Pickers,* one of Tommy's favorite shows. I found that a little unusual, especially since the two pickers were all about traveling. Maybe that's why he liked it, though. I'd never been into the show. In fact I'd never really gotten into television at all. Elena and I used to watch *Monk,* but the show drove me crazy. The things they did with respect to evidence. My God, get a better fucking police consultant! Graham Sanderson was not the man you wanted to sit down beside and watch a crime show. Few cops are.

After a couple of episodes of *American Pickers*, I excused myself and got ready for bed. But before I hit the sack I went into Dad's room, turned on the light. Drop a quarter on that tightly made bed and it would bounce. Framed photos on his dresser of me with Tommy when we were little kids, and one photo of Dani smiling big. She must've been around five. He had a built-in bookcase on the other wall across from the dresser and to the side of the bed. Mostly paperbacks. An abstract floral painting was on the wall above the bed. He'd had that since we were kids too. It felt odd being in there—almost like he was still alive.

I opened the door of his walk-in closet. Seeing his clothes was even harder, and the space smelled musty; I'd have to air out the room soon. His shoes were on the floor under the hanging clothes. The shoes were lined up according to style. I didn't know if it was his military training or if he had OCD. Probably a combination of both.

Dad's green wooden army trunk was on the floor across from the door and under his sport coats. It had a latch, but no lock. I remembered it always having a lock. I got down on one knee and opened it.

The left half of the trunk was stacked to the top with papers, binders, and manila folders. The right half had a lot of what I remembered him showing me years ago—a couple of training grenades with inert fill, a field shaving kit, and countless other odds and ends from whatever wars he'd been in. No weapons. I closed the trunk and stood up. Then, hoping to find a safe built into the wall, I slid the hangers toward the far end of the rod. Nothing.

I knew he had guns, so I searched the rest of the bedroom, including his dresser and nightstand drawers. His Colt .45 was in the nightstand drawer on the right side of the bed, where he slept. His M-1 carbine rifle lay under the bed. No knives—but then there was the rest of the house and the garage, too.

I didn't want to think about it anymore. I sat in Dad's leather recliner in the corner by a window and looked around the room. Everything had its place.

I went back to my room, said good night to Elena. Stared at the ceiling, just like I always did—for how long I don't know, but the dream I dropped into was sudden.

I was driving and spotted a sign that read ESTATE SALE, with an arrow pointing in the direction I needed to go. I drove until I saw the same sign in front of a Victorian bed-and-breakfast. I found myself walking from room to room inside, looking at all the items someone had put up for sale, until I came to a table topped by Elena's urn. *How had it come to be there?* Mystified, I picked up the urn and started walking toward the front door. Wasn't going to pay for it. Tommy and Ada were in the hallway. It started to look a lot like our hallway. He held a large dagger that had a brilliant red blade. He charged at Ada and thrust it into her chest. It came out the other side. There was no blood, but I felt the pain so acutely in my own chest that I dropped the urn. I had a sense of great loss. It was the same sort of intense feeling I'd experienced after the doctor told me Elena had passed away. It's like I wanted to cave into myself. Again.

I woke up. My pillow wet with sweat.

I turned it over.

Those feelings of dread and loss stayed with me for most of the night. It felt like I was trapped.

The next morning after coffee—Tommy had gone to his room to work—I went to the garage. I felt I had to search the car. The driver's door was open. I looked in the center console but found nothing of interest. I searched the glove compartment and then under all the seats. I stepped out and opened the hatchback. Still nothing. You'd think that would have made me feel a bit better, but it didn't.

This property furnished plenty of hiding places. *Tommy wouldn't be stupid enough to hide a murder weapon somewhere easy to find, would he?* I felt disloyal for thinking such a thing. He was going through something, but murder? That was nonsense.

14
Kwik Fill

Jeffrey Sikes was stocking the Kwik Fill Mini-Mart coolers with soda. A young woman with purple hair and a nose ring was behind the counter, working the register.

Sikes did not match the basic description of the man who had exited the truck on the surveillance footage. He was a short, sturdy man with a lumberjack beard who looked like he could take a punch. He did not seem worried about our presence.

"I figured you'd be showing up to talk," he said after Gottert introduced us.

Gottert didn't respond, so I did.

"Why do you think we're here?"

Gottert looked at me like he should have thought to ask that. It was a strange, awkward glance.

"The fight I got into with him, right? I'm assuming you think I had something to do with Pauly getting killed."

I knew right away that Sikes hadn't done it, but I sensed that Gottert was still on the fence, so I kept my mouth shut.

"What do you know about the murder?" Gottert asked.

"I don't know shit. I did get in a fight with him, though. Pauly was nothin' but a piece of shit, and you two shouldn't be wastin' your time with me. That's a fact."

"What were you two fighting about?"

"He was tryin' to peddle drugs to me in the bathroom at the NA meeting. I told him to get the fuck out of the building and don't come back, so I followed him out. Fool had the nerve to step up to me outside. That's how that happened."

"Was Del in the bathroom?"

"No. He the other one that got killed?"

"Why do you think Pauly was killed?" Gottert asked without answering Sikes.

"I don't have a clue, but probably 'cause he was a piece of trash. Maybe got hisself involved with the wrong people. I ain't heard nothin' about it, though. I don't run with people who would do something like that. Like I said, you're wastin' your time with me. And now I'm done talkin', so if you're gonna arrest me, then do it. Otherwise just let me get back to my job."

Sikes turned away from us.

"I *should* fucking arrest you," Gottert said.

That was a mistake; Mike had nothing to charge Sikes with. Pauly hadn't reported the fight to the police. *Never put something out there that you can't or won't follow through with.* That's how you lose credibility.

Sikes faced Gottert. He knew that Gottert was bluffing.

Gottert looked at me. I shook my head with an expression that suggested it was a waste of our time.

"Thanks for your time," I said, and we walked away.

That was a bit embarrassing.

"He's not your guy," I said as the two of us left the mini-mart.

"I know he doesn't match the description, but he's the only good suspect I have. I should have made him come in to question him further."

"Trust me, Mike—Sikes is not your boy. The one you want is the guy from that surveillance camera, with the Steelers cap."

"How can you be so sure it's just one guy?"

"A sixth sense," I said facetiously.

Gottert's cell rang before he could reply.

"Gottert," he answered. "Yes. Great. Be there in about ten minutes."

He slipped the cell back in his pocket.

"The navigation info on Del Thomas's truck came in."

We met Sergeant O'Born back at the station. He gave his report to Gottert.

"The navigation system is an older model; it stored only recent geolocations. But if his cell phone was synced to the car's system, it might show more. I hope this is useful."

"Thanks, Sarge. That helps."

We went to Gottert's office to look over the report.

"Bunch of latitude and longitude shit," Gottert said. "Addresses after a couple of them."

He handed it to me. I looked it over.

"The addresses aren't always accurate," he said. "One of them is close to where Del lived, so it's probably where he parked the truck."

"Yeah," I said. Then, pointing to a set of coordinates that lacked an address: "This one here might be where his body was dumped. And then you have a couple of other physical addresses some time before that."

"Those are all in town here. We'll have to check them out."

The dispatcher suddenly came over the radio with, "Available unit to respond for an unconscious female."

"That can't be good," I said.

Officer Dana King answered the call. Gottert wasn't worried. He told me they often got calls for that, or calls to check the welfare of, and they usually amounted to nothing.

The dispatcher came over the air with the location.

A few minutes later King came back on the air with a priority, requesting an ambulance. He also asked Gottert to respond to his location.

Definitely not nothing.

15
Jean Marie

The young woman's body was in the passenger seat of her car, parked in the lot on the side of the Birdhouse. The cleaning lady saw her through the rear window when she took out the trash. Thought she had passed out, but when she approached the car, she noticed the blood spatter on the windows and then her body. She screamed, ran back inside, and called 911.

The young woman had shoulder-length brown hair and was wearing a revealing pink blouse and tight blue jeans. The front of the blouse was blood-soaked; so was the waist area of her tight jeans.

Her purse was in the car.

Jean Marie Evans.

Twenty-seven years old. She had a Charontown address. A known prostitute who mostly worked out of the Birdhouse. Gottert arrested her a few months ago for credit-card fraud.

Inside the wallet kept in her purse there was four hundred and thirty dollars in cash, as well as a credit card.

Further examination of the body revealed that she had what

appeared to be several small puncture wounds in her chest. The puncture wounds looked very similar to the other two bodies.

"We have a damn serial killer," Bill said.

"You won't know for sure until the ME examines the puncture wounds. No apparent exit wounds, so it still could be a small-caliber gun," I said, like I was trying to comfort them, but knew it wasn't a gun.

I felt like a jinx. Three bodies in a row. So, a serial killer—or killers. What a way to break in a fucking rookie. What a way to be welcomed to a new town.

O'Born finished taking photographs and the body was placed on a gurney and transported to the County Medical Examiner's Office.

Her car would be towed and dusted once it had been secured.

We huddled close to the victim's car.

"The other two crime scenes were clean," I began, "and neither one was where they'd been killed. This one's different. He killed her here and left a mess. Seems impulsive—like he was angry and went off on her."

"A lot of blood," Officer King said.

"I don't think he's done," I continued.

"I get that feeling too," Bill said.

"Her body should be thoroughly examined. Inside her mouth too," I advised.

"The ME here is good."

"A drug dealer/addict, a town drunk—" I looked at Bill after saying that.

"It's okay," Bill told me.

". . . and now a prostitute," I continued. "If she knew the other two, it'll be on her cell. If not, the only thing she had in common with them was criminal activity."

"Del wasn't a criminal," Bill corrected me.

"I didn't mean for it to sound like that. But he *had* been arrested for DWI, and he was associated with Pauly."

"So you're saying some petty-crime vigilante is stalking our town?" Gottert asked half-jokingly.

"Dealing drugs isn't petty, but the other two—I guess?" I said. "You might want to reach out to surrounding jurisdictions and ViCAP to see if there's anything similar."

"We have access to ViCAP. I'll get on that at the station."

I was hoping there would be other similar cases, maybe in a state far from here. That'd make me feel a lot better about my brother. Seeing him drive away in the dark that morning, around the same time that Bill's nephew Del Thomas had been killed, was discomforting to say the least. But still, there was no way. I had to believe that.

"I'll call my boy at the crime lab and see about getting a rush on her cell and the vehicle's navigation system," Bill said.

"Thanks, Chief," Gottert said.

The owner of the Birdhouse was not happy, but not because a young woman had been murdered. He was upset because he couldn't open the bar until Bill cleared the scene, and that included the interior of the bar.

There were two security cameras in the front. Nowhere else.

"This place has been nothing but a nuisance property," Bill told me. "Maybe now I'll get the damn place shut down."

"Any security cameras inside?"

"Hell no," Gottert advised. "You think he wants to give up what goes on in there?"

"We'll look at the footage for the front," Bill said.

I had a strong feeling this guy wouldn't let himself be caught on camera.

"Our guy was in there," Gottert said, half to himself. "I know it."

"Maybe," I replied. "Or maybe he was somewhere outside, waiting for the Birdhouse to close. Approached her when she was getting into her car. Not as many witnesses and no surveillance cameras, but we'll see once we look at the recording."

We reviewed the digital recording and saw Jean Marie Evans walk up alone at a little after eight o'clock. She ambled out about three hours later with a fat older man. He didn't look anything like the man we'd seen exiting Del's truck, but still, you never know. We'd have to try to get him identified.

Jean Marie went back inside the Birdhouse about fifteen minutes later and didn't leave again until the bar closed at one in the morning. Must have been a slow night for her, unless she used a back room or a restroom to do what she was paid to do. It was a busy night, though—a lot of folks entering and exiting. Any of them could be the one we were after. Gottert had the recording uploaded to the department's secure file.

16
Notification

Jean Marie lived alone. No pets. The place looked more like a crash pad than a living space. Several take-out food containers were stacked on the kitchen counter or tossed in the garbage. There was one sofa and a flat-screen TV, both too big for the cracker box–sized living room. About an ounce of weed had been left in a baggie on the coffee table, alongside a liter of cheap vodka and a smudged glass. A pile of dirty laundry spilled out of the clothes hamper in Jean Marie's bedroom. In fact the only things suggesting a comfortable life were the stuffed animals that cluttered the queen-sized bed and the Bible on her nightstand.

She didn't have a laptop or a landline, just a cell phone—and we already had that.

After a couple of hours there, we returned to the station to find a few local reporters crowding the small parking lot. Two of them were from the network-news stations in Rochester.

"There's your welcoming committee," I said, like it was no big deal.

I'm sure it was a very big deal for Gottert and Bill, though.

"Damn," Gottert said. "That happened fast."

Officer King was there to keep an eye on everyone. He was a seasoned officer and I'm sure that's why Bill trusted him to watch over everything without answering any questions.

Several of the parking spaces were allocated for police vehicles. We parked in the one nearest the door. As soon as we stepped out, we were assaulted with questions. Gottert did the right thing by not acknowledging any of them.

Bill called in the off-duty officers. The tiny crew would begin rotating shifts of twelve hours or more. Thanks to a social-media bulletin that Bill had released when we were still at Jean Marie's apartment, the police station was being inundated with calls. The bulletin urged anyone with information about the three victims or their murders to contact the department. The name *Jean Marie Evans* was withheld, however, because her family had not yet been notified. The only information disclosed about her was that a female victim had been found inside a vehicle parked at the Birdhouse.

Two officers were assigned to answer the phones, which were mostly calls from concerned citizens asking if they were safe. A few others were people who had known Pauly Savell or Del Thomas, but the scant information they provided was not worth following up on.

My cell rang.

It was Tommy.

"Hey," I said and walked into the community room.

"There was another murder?" he asked.

"Yeah. You saw it on TV or online?"

"Charontown has a community group on Facebook. I read about it there. What the hell's going on in this town?"

"He'll get caught. They usually do."

"I hope you're right."

I hoped for that too.

"Are you coming home for dinner?" He asked the question like Elena used to. It made me smile.

"No, I'll grab a sandwich at the pub. Want me to get you something?"

"Naw. I'll just stick a frozen dinner in the microwave."

"Alright."

Dead air.

Did he disconnect?

"Everything good?" I asked.

"Yeah—I should get back to work."

"I'll see you later, then."

Tommy had a habit of getting quiet like that, both on the phone and in person. Been like that for as long as he could talk. It wasn't like he was confused—more like suddenly detached. I never saw him punch a hole in the wall out of anger, though.

Gottert walked in before my brain got worked up again.

"Hospital records listed the decedent's mother as an emergency contact. She lives in Syracuse, about forty minutes from here. Wanna take a drive?"

That was the last thing I wanted to do, but I said *Sure* because I sensed he was nervous.

Notifying parents about the death of their child was my least favorite part of the job. It's something that had to be done and I've never had one go easy. I wouldn't be the one making the notification this time, though.

"This gonna be your first time having to do this?" I asked.

"Yep. Not looking forward to it."

"Best thing you can do is be a comfort if needed. Don't say you understand unless you have personally been through it."

"I won't."

Jean Marie's mom lived in a small home in the Berkeley Park

Historic District of Syracuse. I would not have imagined her daughter coming from a cozy neighborhood like this, or such a well-kept home on a hill.

We pulled to the curb. Gottert looked like he was trying to gather his thoughts, maybe find the words to say. I decided against going up to the house with him. I would have just stood there silently. Uncomfortably.

"I should wait in the car," I told him.

"Yeah, you should, I guess."

He smiled awkwardly and then stepped out.

A good cop.

Mrs. Evans answered the door shortly after Gottert knocked. She appeared to be in her mid-fifties. And from this short distance, I could tell that she was an attractive woman.

I could not hear them.

Gottert showed Mrs. Evans his ID folder. A moment later she dropped to her knees, her face cupped in her hands. Gottert knelt down and placed his hand on her shoulder. After a few seconds he helped her up and they walked inside. He closed the door behind him.

I felt bad about not being there with him, but I wasn't a sworn officer anymore. Plus it just didn't feel right to be there when he broke such terrible news to Jean Marie's mother.

Gottert returned about thirty minutes later and climbed heavily into the car.

"She's divorced and lives alone," he began. "She thought her daughter was a clerk at a medical office. I didn't tell her what she really did."

"That's a good thing."

Mrs. Evans didn't have to know how her daughter had lived. Let the life her daughter had made up for her be the life she knew. Let her find rest with those memories—even if they were a lie.

17
Sweet Tooth Revisited

Dead bodies have a way of staying with you, like unwelcome guests. I had always believed that once I retired I wouldn't be burdened with them anymore. I was wrong. Don't misunderstand, I didn't mind the work, and I especially loved the chase. The pursuit was what kept me going for most of my career, and it had a lot to do with why I agreed to help out with the investigations in Charontown. It was all about the chase and eventually, hopefully, getting them in the box. That was where I thrived.

The fucking box. I loved it.

I was exhausted when I got home. Sounded like Tommy was up. I heard him shuffling around in his room but didn't knock. I just wanted to fall into bed and lose myself in nothing. I knew that wouldn't happen. It was getting to the point where I feared sleep. Nightmares—*lucid* nightmares. But after I got in bed, it wasn't long before I allowed myself to fall.

I woke up a couple of times during the night, but not from terror. I was a fairly light sleeper, and this was an old home that liked to moan and groan. Once o-dark-thirty rolled around, I didn't even bother trying to sleep again. Daylight eventually seeped in through the window, and with it my new routine.

Tommy made bacon and eggs. He loved to cook. I was happy about that. Cooking was something I had done with Elena. After she passed, I fell into the habit of eating out most of the time and on occasion getting something to go. The kitchen had lost the comfort it once held.

I decided to stop by Sweet Tooth on the way to the station and pick up some goodies for the crew there. Mornings were a busy time for Ada. All the tables were taken, and a couple of people were already standing in line at the counter ahead of me.

Ada smiled when she saw me. I shot her a wave and smiled back. I went to the counter to select what I wanted her to box up. Cops were easy: mostly anything that's bad for you. I'm sure everything Ada made here was prepared with love and good ingredients, so it wasn't like buying a dozen donuts at Dunkin'. Not that that'd be a bad thing.

"Hi there," she said after finishing with the other customers.

"How are you?"

"Doing well."

"I thought I'd buy some assorted stuff for the guys at the station."

"That's nice of you. Chief Finn stops in occasionally. Do you know what you want, or do you need a little help?"

"A little help would be nice."

"Well, the chief usually buys the mini-cannoli or the raspberry Danish."

"Danishes are always safe. How about a dozen assorted Danishes and half a dozen of the bourbon biscuits?"

"Drinking on duty?" Ada asked.

"Come again?"

"I'm kidding. The alcohol has all cooked out."

"I'm a little slow lately, so that one went right over me." I smiled.

"I understand."

She had a lovely smile. Guilt set in after thinking that. Once again.

Ada boxed everything up and set it on the counter.

"So sad about that young woman," she said.

"It is."

"Everyone is worried and scared. Is her murder related to the other two?"

"I don't know." I couldn't be honest with her because of the nature of the investigation.

"That place is nothing but trouble. I don't know why they don't just shut it down. I'm sorry. I didn't mean to blast you with questions."

"That's alright. I can understand. They'll get whoever is responsible. I'm sure of it."

I regretted sounding so sure of myself, but I wanted to comfort her.

"I hope so."

I paid and was about to leave but abruptly turned back. No other customers were at the counter, so I went for it.

"I was wondering," I began. "I was wondering if you'd want to go to the pub for a drink, or maybe another spot, but I don't know where because I'm still getting to know the place."

Another lovely smile and she said, "That'd be nice. I close up at six."

I didn't expect her to suggest this evening. I hesitated for a second.

"Or another evening if tonight isn't good," she said.

"No, this evening works. That'd be great."

"You can pick me up here a little after six, then."

"Okay. I'll see you then."

"Bye."

"Bye," I said and walked out.

Wow. I was actually going out on a date. I got nervous all of a sudden, then felt overwhelmed by guilt.

Damn.

18

It's All About Following Leads

The parking lot was clear of the news reporters.

King let me in after I buzzed. His eyes were on the box I was holding, so I opened it for him.

"Picked these up this morning. Grab one."

"Don't mind if I do."

He picked up a cannoli and said, "Thank you, sir," and took a bite.

"Looks empty in here," I said.

"Gottert's in his office. I'm manning the phone, and the chief and everyone else are out on patrol."

The phone rang.

"I gotta get that."

I walked into Gottert's office.

"Mornin', Mike."

He looked up from his computer screen.

"Hey, Graham."

"I brought these for you guys," I said, setting the box of pastries on his desk.

"What do we have here?"

He opened it.

"Oh yeah." He grinned. "Sweet Tooth?"

"Yep."

"Thanks, man. I'll take one of these."

He grabbed a Danish. Took a bite.

"These are dangerous," he said while chewing. "I might just keep them all to myself. Naw, I'll put them in the community room. They won't last."

"That's what they're here for."

I sat on the swivel chair beside his desk.

"Looks like all hands on deck today," I said.

"It is."

"I can't count how many times we've had to do that in DC."

"I can imagine."

"Anything new?" I asked.

"Not a damn thing. I'm doing a little catch-up right now with a couple of cases I've been neglecting."

"You need help with any of them?"

"No, thanks. I just got off the phone with a lady who was a victim of a burglary. She was more concerned with the murders than her stolen property. I guess that's understandable."

"For most people, losing the comfort of safety in your own environment is worse than what was stolen. Having that happen and then the murders can be a lot for some."

He took another bite of the Danish, wiped his fingers on his pant leg after.

"I tried to reassure her."

"That's all you can do. How long you think before the chief hears back from his contact at State Troopers about the forensic search on the cells and the internet?"

"I'll get with him on that."

"Three victims. Their shared relationships can make all the difference. That is, if they have any."

"Let's hope for the best, then."

"You have to ask yourself—why these three? The only thing that keeps coming back to me is what kind of lives they led."

"Drugs, alcohol, and sex. Everything they drilled us to stay away from in the academy."

"You got that right. And I believe it was the sex that pissed him off. I don't think he liked how it made him feel. Killed her right there. Didn't even move her after."

"And didn't clean up. Maybe we'll get lucky and discover that he left something behind. But then, she's probably had a lot of men in that car; it'll be filthy with DNA."

"I don't know about that," I began. "Most girls like her are professionals. The client's car or a hotel room, not in her car or where she lived. She didn't have anything in her apartment that would suggest otherwise."

"It's crazy, because this town is so small that we know who most of the bad guys are. You'd think someone like this guy would stand out—that I or one of the other officers here would know who to take a hard look at. I'm racking my brain, but I don't have a clue."

"Like I said, I don't think this guy's an amateur. With three murders in a short span, I'm pretty sure he's killed before. And I'm thinking a predator like this wouldn't hunt where he beds down—too risky. Maybe he's just passing through."

"That'd be easy enough to check if we had a hotel or a motel in town, but we don't. Closest one is twelve miles away."

"We know he more than likely met Jean Marie at the bar. But what about the other two?"

"At the NA meetings?"

"Possibly."

"That Keleher guy—the one who runs the meetings—said they don't keep any kind of records."

"They aren't required to keep membership records. I'm sure he knows everyone there, but he's bound by AA and NA standards, so he probably won't give you any information about anyone."

"I'll subpoena his ass, then."

"You might as well subpoena a priest. I've been there, but do what you gotta do. It's all about following leads."

Gottert's cell rang, and he looked at the screen.

"It's the chief," he told me before answering: "Hey, Chief . . . yes sir . . . copy that."

Gottert disconnected, then slipped the phone back in his pocket.

"Finn got the results back for all the cells."

"Including Jean Marie's?"

"Yep."

"Damn, that was quick. He must have called in a big favor."

"You up for a nice drive?"

"Always."

19
Digital Forensics

It was almost a three-hour drive from Charontown to Albany. Despite its being the state capital, I had never been there before. The State Police Investigative Center was in a large building in an area that looked more like a college campus. Once inside, we met Sam Beck, a civilian computer-forensic analyst. He was a heavy-set older guy with a salt-and-pepper goatee and round wire-rimmed glasses. We followed him to the office where he worked.

"We appreciate the quick response," Gottert told him.

"I was a detective assigned to the computer-forensic unit at NYPD," Beck informed us. "I went to the academy with your chief."

"I never knew," Gottert said.

"Yeah, we go back." Then, to me: "Bill told me you're a retired homicide detective from DC police."

"I am."

"You couldn't get enough there, so you had to come all the way up to Charontown to volunteer?"

I puffed out a chuckle and said, "I'm not *that* crazy. Family brought me up here."

"I see."

Beck led us to a large cubicle whose counters were crowded with computers, with larger equipment underneath. On a table in the center were the victim's phones, along with a thick folder full of papers.

"Pull up a chair. We'll go over what I got."

We rolled up a couple of chairs and sat.

Beck grabbed the folder.

"I printed this out for you guys," he said, handing the file to Gottert. "This contains everything I was able to extract. I know it looks intimidating, but the last few pages break down the relationships and the geolocations for the time frames Bill requested. It also includes several conversations I extracted from WhatsApp between your first two victims."

"That's great," Gottert said, "but I thought that app deleted all conversations after a certain amount of time?"

"It does," Beck acknowledged. "But one of your victims had an iPhone with Biome and KNowledgeC databases on them. Those are system databases from Apple, capable of tracking and recording the device usage. Even something like the flashlight app, as silly as that sounds—every time it's used, it gets recorded. Anyway, the first two male victims apparently knew each other well; they had several chats I was able to extract from the one iPhone. It's all in there. A lot of good stuff about buying and selling illegal narcotics, mostly fentanyl. There's a lot of pages to go through."

"I've been there before. Our computer guys at MPDC have done the same thing with WhatsApp, Telegram, and Instagram. Some of those cases went RICO because of what they found."

"That's what we're here for. And I got the shared geolocations from the phones because they were synced to their cars' navigation. That's about it."

"Thanks a lot, Sam."

After we all shook hands, Beck showed us out.

"You mind if I look through everything on the drive back?" I asked on the way to the car.

"Not at all. I was hoping you would."

"It'll take a bit longer to go through everything, but at least I'll get an idea of what we have."

"Sounds good."

There was a lot of information to sift through. Beck had printed out years' worth of the digital lives of Pauly Savell and Del Thomas: phone numbers, emails, internet search history, and more, plus the WhatsApp chats between the two men. Most of it was too much for my brain to take in.

Leafing through everything, I stopped when I got to the printout of the geolocations. I scanned it. Looked like all three of our victims had only one location in common.

Birdhouse.

20

Dinner at the Pub

We stopped for lunch along the way and got back about twenty minutes before I had to go pick up Ada. We were in Gottert's office going over some of what I found.

The station was empty. Bill and the officers working that shift were out on patrol.

The WhatsApp conversation between Pauly and Del was interesting but didn't really tell us anything we didn't already know. Pauly did mention a contact for the narcotics, but not by name, just "my guy." The only other WhatsApp conversations Pauly had were with a couple of women who liked to share revealing photos of themselves.

Del and Pauly did have one person in common. Her name was in Pauly's contacts as *Alice* and in Del's as *Alice Winters*. She was in the system, but not for anything bad: Almost eight months ago she had reported a theft from auto in front of her residence. We would still have to go through the rest of their contacts, though, especially Pauly's. Maybe find his dealer.

"We know the killer has been to the Birdhouse," I began. "Maybe it's his hunting ground."

"What do you suggest we do?"

"You guys don't have the manpower to sit on the location for an extended period of time, and all your faces are too recognizable to hang out there on the weekends in plain clothes. So I don't know."

"I'll talk to the chief, let him know where we are."

"Yeah, we should also go to the next NA meeting. After all, two of their companions were violently murdered. You'd think they'd want to help."

"Sounds reasonable."

"Yes—but unfortunately most people aren't reasonable."

"There are some good folks in this town. Most of them even pro-police."

"That's nice to hear. Maybe this Alice Winters will be, too, and have something good to offer."

"We can go tomorrow, see if she still lives at the location she gave in the report."

"Okay. Listen, I have to run. I'm getting together with a friend for drinks."

"Alright. Thanks for going with me to Albany."

"I'll roll with you anytime, brother."

"I'm going to go through all the geolocations and then try to get some sleep tonight."

"Get it while you can."

It didn't take long to get to Sweet Tooth. The door was locked, so I knocked. I saw Ada walk out of the back room.

I convinced myself not to feel guilty about that smile.

She unlocked the door and said, "Right on time."

She stepped out, locked the door, and politely leaned into me for a peck on the cheek. I stumbled.

"I wasn't trying to knock you off your feet."

"I can be an awkward kinda guy," I said, then immediately wondered if it sounded too . . . *awkward.*

We walked to my car.

"Nice car."

"Thanks. I didn't own a car in DC. I had a take-home cruiser, but when I retired and decided to move here, I realized I would need a car. So I got this."

"Audi makes a nice SUV."

"They do."

I opened the door for her. Ada slid in with a gracious "Thank you, sir," then exclaimed, "And an all-leather interior."

"I splurged."

I shut her door, walked around to the driver's side, and climbed in.

The pub was only about a four-minute drive.

It was busy at the bar. There were a few open tables.

"Hi, Ada," said a nearby waitress. "You can sit anywhere."

Ada waved an acknowledgment.

"How about a booth?" I asked. "We could get dinner too, if you're hungry."

"I could eat."

The waitress brought her a Manhattan and a Guinness for me.

"Are you ready to order?" the waitress asked.

Ada looked at me. I shrugged.

"I'll have the fish and chips," she said.

"I'll have the same."

"Be right up."

Ada lifted her glass, stretched it toward me. I lifted mine. She had a sincere smile and dark, comforting eyes. If she were a cop, I'd hate to be the guy sitting across from her in an interview room. I'd give it up just to make her smile.

"Cheers," I said.

"Cheers."

We clinked glasses.

"Did you help out at the police station today?"

"I did."

"Don't worry, I'm not going to inundate you with questions."

"I don't mind. I just may not be able to answer some of them."

"There's peace of mind in ignorance, so I'd rather not know."

"Maybe that's what my problem is, then," I joked, before realizing there was some truth to that. "So, you grew up here, in one house."

"Yes, I did. You say that like it's something unimaginable."

"It sort of is. We grew up around the world, never in one place for more than four years."

"What countries?"

"Lebanon, India, a few in Africa. Finally settled in Arlington, Virginia, with Tommy and my mother after our parents divorced."

"That must have been quite the childhood."

"It was, and I wouldn't trade it for anything—except maybe for my parents' divorce. I ended up living with my dad after he returned from Saigon."

"How old were you when they divorced?"

"Thirteen. My mother's in Florida now. We don't talk."

"I'm sorry."

"Nothing to be sorry about. It happens. How long have you been divorced?" I asked in an effort to change the subject.

"Seven years. We still talk. Sophie, my daughter, stays with him every other weekend. He lives in Syracuse now."

"That's good she's a part of his life."

"She is."

"How old is your daughter?"

"Thirteen going on thirty."

"I don't know if that's good or bad."

"It's mostly good. She's a smart kid."

When the waitress showed up with our food, we ordered another round of drinks.

"The fish and chips are good here," she said.

"Been a while since I've had them. I used to go to this spot in DC, Murphy's, with some of the detectives in my squad. That was a few years ago. Always ordered the fish and chips."

"I've only been to Washington once, with my daughter. We went for the cherry blossoms—and the Smithsonian, of course."

"That's the best time to go. Where'd you stay?"

"The Embassy Suites, downtown."

"I was a kid last time I went to the Smithsonian. My dad took us to the Air and Space Museum."

"We went there too."

She cut into one of her fillets with a fork. I did the same.

"What does your brother do for a living?"

"He works remotely for a large insurance company. Customer assistance, something like that."

"Usually in a small town you eventually get to know almost everyone. I've never seen or met your brother, though."

How to explain this without falling back into something distressing?

"It's complicated," I said.

21

A Bit about Tommy

Tommy has PTSD and agoraphobia."

"I don't know what to say. Your dad never mentioned anything like that. I'm sorry. I wasn't trying to be nosy."

"No reason to be sorry. It came on him late in life, about 11 years ago, probably the result of a lot of childhood trauma."

"How terrible."

With all the possible dangers that existed in the foreign countries we grew up in, it was Arlington, Virginia, where the storm in his life hit. And it hit hard.

I kept it simple and just said, "He was emotionally abused by our mother when he was a kid."

"That's horrible."

"It was. I was living with my dad at the time. A lot of baggage in my family."

"Every family has baggage."

"To make a long story short, when Tommy was in his mid-thirties he was shot in a robbery gone bad, then had to spend a couple of weeks in the hospital because of complications. When he got home, he never left. Lost his job—everything. My dad drove down, helped him pack up his life, and Tommy moved in with him."

"That's a lot for anybody to go through," said Ada. "Thanks for sharing it with me."

"It's a little much on the first da—" I caught myself before saying it. "Get-together, or whatever this is." I smiled awkwardly.

"I think it's a date."

I couldn't think how to respond to that, so I just smiled and took another sip of my Guinness.

"You don't do this much, do you?" she asked.

"I actually don't do this at all."

"Wow, I guess I'm flattered, then. I think."

I puffed out a chuckle.

"This town doesn't offer much in the way of restaurants," I told Ada, "and I do love to eat out."

"I do too. Canandaigua has a lot of nice places, depending on what you like. Rochester has even more."

"I'm game for most anything."

"One of my favorite spots is in Canandaigua. It's more high-end, but very authentic Mexican food."

"I do love Mexican food. I'd like to check it out. We should go."

"Are you asking me out again?"

"I guess I am."

"I'd love to."

"Is Friday or Saturday too soon?"

"It's not. My daughter will be with her dad this weekend. Not that she can't take care of herself at home, but it does make it easier on me."

"You mean not having to explain to her that you're going on a date?"

"No, nothing like that. I tend to worry a little too much about her. Especially with everything going on here lately."

"I can understand that."

"So how about Friday around 6:30? You can pick me up at the shop."

"That works. Do I need to make reservations?"

"It wouldn't hurt."

It was a nice evening at the pub. We talked for over two hours. I liked her, but for some reason that made me nervous. I hoped it didn't show.

After we'd both had coffee she said, "I had a wonderful time."

"I did too. Is your car at the shop?" I asked.

"No, I walked. I don't live far from there."

"I'll give you a ride home."

"I don't live far from here either, but I'll take you up on that."

She lived in a cute white-brick colonial home with a light-blue front door. A large Japanese maple grew on the left side of the patio, with a rosebush and colorful flowering plants and shrubs on the right. A redbrick walkway stretched from the sidewalk up to the small porch. In the driveway, a dark blue Toyota SUV.

"You have a lovely home," I said.

"Thank you. I'd invite you in, but I'm a lightweight when it comes to drinking and I have to get up early."

"No worries. I am too, actually. Sleep well."

"You too."

She leaned my way and planted a quick but nice kiss on my lips.

"Good night, Graham."

"Good night, Ada."

She opened the door and stepped out.

I watched her walk to the door and unlock it. Before opening the door, she turned and waved a goodbye, then entered.

I drove toward my dad's house, but then changed my mind and pulled to the curb in front of an antique store on Main Street. I tapped the Maps icon on the iPhone screen and then the Birdhouse for the location.

Two and a half miles.

I made my way there. I had a sudden burst of energy and wanted to take a look at the thorn in Bill's side.

22

Watered-Down Whiskey and Crystal

The Birdhouse had a dense, musty odor, like rotting wood in an abandoned building. It was a small but crowded dive. Most of the round wooden tables were taken. Everyone else was either sitting or standing around the bar. Two flat-screen televisions were attached to the wall over the bar. I noticed two unoccupied stools. A few people looked at me skeptically as I headed for them. I sat on the stool at the end, next to a fat-fingered man, riddled with tattoos that had lost their luster over time. He looked at me with a weird grin meant to be a smile. I shot him back a half-smile.

It took a while for the waitress to show—not because she was busy with a customer, but because she was chatting with a woman at the far end of the bar.

"What'll ya have?" she growled.

"Powers on the rocks."

"We only have Jameson."

"That works."

She returned with my drink.

"That'll be seven dollars."

I looked in my wallet. I had about eighty bucks. I handed her a twenty. She took it without saying a word and returned with my change a couple of minutes later.

I sipped the whiskey. Tasted watered down.

I was seated in a spot that offered a good view of the surrounding room. *What the hell am I trying to accomplish sitting here?* I wondered. It did bring back memories of my younger days on the job, when I was working plain clothes and out looking for trouble. I wasn't trying to find that here, though. I only wanted to get a sense of the place where the suspect had his last kill and Jean Marie the last moments of her life.

Before I knew it I had nursed my way through my whiskey, so I asked for another. Fat Fingers settled his bill and left. The barstool was quickly taken by a bony older woman who smelled like a full ashtray dipped in cheap perfume. As with Fat Fingers, time had had its way with her, making it hard to determine her age. Her hair was a whiteish blond with gray roots. Both her short, lime-green skirt and her revealing black halter top were a bit too tight for her figure. Looked like she came alone. She turned to me briefly with an irregular smile, then tried to get the bartender's attention.

"Rum and coke, Liz."

"Right with ya, sweetie," the bartender said.

I had another sip of the whiskey-flavored water and went back to eyeing the crowd. Their loud voices mixed together. The occasional laugh or expletive broke through the wall of sound.

Gray Roots turned back toward me and asked, "You looking for someone?"

It took me a moment to register that she was addressing me.

"A friend of mine. Why do you ask?"

"I been coming here since they opened, about twenty years ago, and I've never seen you around."

I started to feel like I stumbled into a social gathering run by some kind of secret society. That was okay—so long as they weren't hunting for an outsider to sacrifice.

"I'm just here to meet a friend. This place is open to the public, right?" I said in jest.

She snorted an odd laugh and said, "Of course it is, honey. Who's this friend of yours? I might know him."

Gray Roots was the nosy type, but I sensed that could be a good thing. So I said, "Her name is Jean."

She looked startled.

"You okay?" I asked.

"Yeah, I'm okay. You talking about Jean Marie?"

"Yes. You know her?"

"Damn, mister—don't you read the news?"

"Why would you ask that?" I played along.

"If you're talking about the same Jean I knew, then I'm sorry to say, but she's dead."

"What the hell are you talking about?"

"Murdered."

"No, I just talked to Jean a couple of days ago. She said she'd meet me here today."

Gray Roots pulled a Samsung phone from her purse and said, "Hold on there for a minute." She swiped through some pictures, then held the screen up for me to see. "This is who you're talking about, right?"

It was a photo of Jean sitting on a stool at this bar and giving the finger to whoever took the picture.

"I took this picture two weeks ago."

"That's Jean," I said in my most concerned voice. "I don't know what to say."

"Sorry, mister."

"What the hell happened?"

"She got murdered. She was found in her own car, parked in the lot here."

"But I just talked to her a few days ago."

"You mind me asking how you know her?"

"We met at a party on my last trip here and hung out. Exchanged numbers. Talked on occasion. Damn, I can't believe it. Did they catch the person responsible?"

"You kiddin'? Police here couldn't catch a rat in a trap."

That was a new one.

"We've had three murders so far. No one's been caught by the police. Everyone's on edge around here."

"Three murders? And I thought this town was safe."

"It is, mostly. The occasional fight, but that's about it."

"Was Jean friends with the other two victims?"

"I seen her hang out here with them, but just for drinks—nothin' more."

"Sounds to me like it might be the same guy."

"That's what people are saying."

"This is a small town. You'd think someone would have an idea, you know? Of who's responsible?"

"You sure ask a lot of questions," she said, "and you sorta look like a cop. But I know all the cops here. You're older, so . . . maybe a fed?"

"No, I'm not a fed," I smiled. "And would the feds get involved with murders in a tiny town like this? They got bigger problems to deal with. The fucking world's falling apart."

"Yeah, maybe."

I downed my whiskey, got the attention of the bartender

"What are you drinking?"

"Rum and coke."

"Another Jameson, and the lady here'll have another rum and coke."

"I'm Crystal," she said. "Appreciate the drink."

"Sure thing. I'm Joe."

I was still nursing my drink when Crystal ordered her third on my tab. It had been obvious from the start that she was a prostitute, and that I was being worked. I played along, to get her feeling comfortable so I could pry a bit more. She was agreeable as long as the drinks kept coming, but it wouldn't last. Soon she'd figure out I wasn't planning to step out with her, and then she'd move on to a better prospect.

"How long have you known Jean Marie?" I asked.

"I've known her for a bit."

"I'd love to get my hands on the guy who killed her."

"You a killer too, Joe?" she asked with that irregular smile again.

"I could be, with him. Do you remember who she left with the night she was killed?"

"Wish I did, but I was at a club in Rochester that night. Funny thing is, she told me a couple of weeks ago that she wanted to get out of what she was doing—said she found God or some shit like that."

"What? She never told me that."

"Of course not, because she still needed money. I'm assumin' that was your arrangement with her."

I raised my brow and shrugged, like I agreed.

"She wouldn't want to scare you off with that kinda talk. I mean *finding God* and all." Crystal shook her head. Chuckled. "You know how those people get after they come to Jesus—all preachy and in your face and wanna get you to believe what they believe, or you'll go to hell."

"I've met a couple in my lifetime."

"Jean Marie got a little pushy at first, tried hard to recruit me, get me to go to church with her."

"Did you go?"

"No, I don't believe in all that *come to Jesus* and *eternal life* shit. We live and then we die, and that's the end of that. Get the most you can while you're here, you know?"

"What church did she go to?"

"I don't know the name. She said it was Presbyterian, though."

23
Matters of the Soul

There was only one Presbyterian church in Charontown. That would make two things all three victims had in common: the church and Birdhouse. But why hadn't the church location been found in the forensic search of Jean Marie's phone?

A storm was blowing in. Tommy was asleep. I went straight to bed. The steady wind outside my window was like a comforting white noise. The rain soon followed, and it didn't take long to fall asleep.

The rain was steady through the night and into the morning. Tommy had the awning up over the deck. He was rocking in his chair drinking an orange soda, looking out toward the pasture.

"Good morning," I said.

"Mornin'. What time did you get in?"

"A little after midnight. Went straight to bed."

"Pub's not open that late. Did you go to her house or something?" He winked and grinned.

I sat down, sipped my coffee, and said, "No, I dropped her home and felt like having another drink. Birdhouse was open, so I stopped there."

"That's where that girl was killed. That place is a pit. You shouldn't go there."

"I felt restless is all."

"Yeah, you need to stay away from that place. It's nothing but trouble."

Tommy said that like he had been there before, but then again, most folks in this town knew Birdhouse to be a bad spot. I went with the latter. Made me feel better.

"Won't happen again, little brother. Don't worry."

"So, you like this woman?"

"Yeah, I guess. She's a nice person."

"You going out with her again?"

"We're going to have dinner on Friday. Now enough with the prying."

"I'm just curious is all. Happy you met someone."

"Appreciate that, but it's only been one date."

"Soon to be two."

"Yeah, okay. Hey, I was meaning to ask you about the church Dad went to."

"Mine too," he jumped in. "Just because I don't physically attend doesn't mean it's not my church. I listen to the sermons online."

"I know, sorry. I'm just thinking about going. I used to go with Elena. Our church in DC was nondenominational, and super-casual. What's your church like?"

"It's casual but follows some traditions. It's biblical, but nothing like fire and brimstone, if that's what you're wondering. You just get fed the Word of God, you know? Some good contemporary music, too."

"Sounds nice."

I did wonder if they knew Tommy was gay. If the pastor knew, and how he felt about it. I personally wouldn't want to be part of a church that judged like that.

"Do they welcome all kinds of people?"

"You mean people like me?"

"I didn't mean you specifically, but now that you bring it up, yeah."

"They are very welcoming. The doors are open to everyone who is searching. You can watch with me if you want to. See if you like it."

"I might do that. I'll let you know. Is it the kind of church where they send members out to knock on doors?"

"That's an odd question."

"Just curious about the ministry."

No, I was fishing.

"They're not in your face like that, but they do have a few ministries that reach out to people in the community. Not really knocking on doors—more in-house events like concerts, picnics, and things like that."

"Sounds like a good church."

"It is. Dad loved it too."

"I know he did."

"I'm gonna have to sign in for work in a bit, so I'd better go get ready. I was thinking of grilling some burgers tonight."

"Sounds good. I'm going to head over to the police station in a few."

"Okay, Graham."

"Call if you need anything."

"I have everything I need, but thanks."

* * *

When I met Gottert at the station, I told him about the interesting conversation I had with Crystal at Birdhouse, and how I'd pretended to be there expecting to meet Jean Marie.

"I'm sure she doesn't know anything substantial about the murders," I began, "but she told me that Jean Marie had known the other two. She said Jean Marie wanted to get out of what she was doing because she *found God.* And guess what church she went to?"

"The Presbyterian church."

"Yeah, so now we have *two* places that the vics have in common."

"But it didn't show up on the geolocations. Her apartment is three or four blocks from the church, so maybe she walked?" Gottert questioned.

"More than likely. Or she went with someone. So, we know the suspect was either inside the Birdhouse with Jean Marie, or waiting for her outside. Whichever it was, other people were probably in the parking lot too because it was closing time, so I don't think the suspect would risk struggling with Jean Marie outside, or even inside her car. I think she allowed him in her car because she knew him. They probably sat in there until the parking lot was clear."

"That's good. Sergeant O'Born said he'll take the image of that older fat guy Jean Marie was seen leaving with to the crime lab in Albany because he has to go there anyway. He'll see if it's good enough to put through their facial-recognition system. I know he doesn't come close to the description of the guy we saw exiting the truck, but we still gotta interview him."

"Definitely." I agreed.

"I spoke with the ME, and he said the puncture wounds are a match to the other two bodies. Also, they did get some good DNA off Jean Marie's body—looks like pubic hair—and it's being analyzed now. Hopefully, whoever it belongs to will be in the system."

"That's possible—but I don't think this guy had sex with her."

"Why not?" Gottert asked.

"Just a feeling. If two men hadn't been murdered before her, then I'd think otherwise. But like I said before, her murder was different. He went off on her—like a crime of passion."

"May be someone she met who got jealous because of what she did for a living?"

"Could be. Crystal did tell me Jean Marie wanted to get out of that lifestyle. The church and Birdhouse are the two places they all had in common. I'm thinking our suspect too."

"One concerns matters of the soul and the other the flesh," Gottert said.

"Now you're getting profound."

24
The Pastor's Son

Alice Winters invited us into her home. She looked to be in her early thirties. A pleasant woman. A stay-at-home mom of two young children. Her boy was away at his kindergarten class. Her daughter was two and was sitting on the sofa in the living room, watching some kind of educational program for children. Her husband was at work. Gottert introduced us and explained the reason for our visit.

"Would you like to sit down?"

"We're fine, thank you," Gottert said. "This shouldn't take long."

"I don't know how I can help you," Alice said.

"You were a contact on Paul and Del's cell phones. This is just routine. We have to talk to everyone."

"I was deeply saddened when I heard they were killed. It's awful. And now that poor young woman. How could that happen here?"

"We hope to find out soon, ma'am. How well did you know them?"

"I'm assuming you know about the meetings held at the church?" she asked.

"Yes."

"That's how I knew them. I'm almost five years clean."

"Good for you," I said.

"Thank you," Alice replied. "I only knew them from there."

"Did you ever get together with either of them outside of the meetings?" Gottert asked.

"No. The only reason they had my phone number was because I was their sponsor. I was devastated when I learned that Paul had been trying to sell fentanyl, though."

"Was Del involved too?"

"I don't know. They were friends. I do know Del was trying hard to stay clean while Paul had us all fooled for a while."

"Were either of them close to anyone else in the group?"

"We all talked and shared at the end of the meetings. I don't know much more than that."

"Were you there when the fight happened in the parking lot?"

"Yes, but I didn't witness it. I was inside."

"As their sponsor, did they share anything with you about other people they knew?" I asked. "Anything about any trouble they might have been having?"

"No, and I didn't talk to Paul much. Del called me a few times in the beginning when he first started to go, but then his calls stopped. He still attended, but he looked high on a few occasions. I tried to talk to him about it, but he denied he was using."

Gottert showed Alice a photo of Jean Marie that he had recovered from her apartment.

"By any chance do you know this woman?" Gottert asked.

"Is that the woman who was murdered?"

"Yes, ma'am," Gottert said.

"Dear God. No, I don't know her. She looks familiar, though."

"Maybe one of the NA meetings?"

"Not the NA meetings. I'm sorry, I just don't remember. Should I be worried too?"

"We have no reason to believe that you are in danger," Gottert said.

"I wish I could be of more help."

"We appreciate your time."

"Mrs. Winters, do you also attend the church?" I asked.

"Yes, I do. Why?"

"I was wondering if any other members from the church go to the meetings?"

"Do you think someone from my church is responsible?"

"We're looking into everything," Gottert said.

She hesitated, clearly unwilling to break the confidentiality rule, so I said, "I understand the meetings' confidentiality, and that it's called *Anonymous* for a reason. But this is a homicide investigation. One of the victims attended your church."

"That young girl? Wait, yes—I think that's where I've seen her before."

"At your church?" Gottert asked.

"I think so, but I can't be positive."

"So, who from your church also goes to the NA meetings?"

"As a sponsor, I don't have to give you any information about our members. Even the court has ruled that, but if it will help you find whoever is responsible, then I feel I have to." After a long sigh she said, "A young boy. Matthew. He's a very nice young man. I can't imagine he'd be involved in something as terrible as this."

"Do you have his last name?"

"I assume it's the same as his father's. I can never pronounce it—*Guyerra,* or something like that."

"*Guerre?*" I asked. "The interim pastor's son?"

"Yes, that's it."

25

Keep the Memories

We knew Matthew Guerre's approximate age, and his last name was unique, so we ran him through the system. Nothing came up on him locally, but he did pop up on NCIC—for a 2016 arrest in Pottstown, Pennsylvania. The charge was possession of a controlled substance: heroin. He was nineteen years old, which would make him around the same age as Jean Marie. Didn't do time. They rarely do for something like possession, especially if it's a first offense.

Gottert and I both found it intriguing that Pastor Simon had not revealed his son was in the group. Respecting his privacy, I suppose—or possibly concealing the fact that the pastor's son was an addict in his twenties who still lived with his father. Tommy came to mind, so maybe the kid had his problems too and I should be applauding the fact that his dad was there for him. It did make me curious, though.

The police department in Pottstown emailed us an arrest photo of Matthew Guerre. Good-looking kid. Probably hadn't changed that much since then. I told Gottert I would meet him at the NA meeting after having dinner with my brother.

"I'm starting to feel guilty for taking up too much of your time," he said.

"Not even. You're doing me a favor, brother. You brought me back to the chase."

"You ever have to go to an AA or NA meeting to interview anyone?"

"Couple of times. A church is private property, and without a search warrant he can ask us to leave—especially if it's a closed meeting. I'm sure he'll do that before the meeting begins; no one wants to share their personal struggles with two cops hanging around."

"So why waste our time?"

"Because maybe we'll get an eye on Matthew."

Tommy was close to being a grill master. He really enjoyed it. I'm sure that's why he was so good at it. The burger was cooked medium and was juicy, but not dripping-down-your-chin juicy. He also cut a couple of bell peppers in half and grilled them until they got a nice char. I understood now why he and our dad spent so much time outside on the deck. There was nothing like the smell of grass and dirt after a good, soaking rain. That was something I didn't get in DC. Rain-drenched pavement and buildings smelled a helluva lot different.

"Do you ever think about Dani?" Tommy asked out of nowhere.

Our sister Dani had been older than me. She died in a terrible car accident when we were kids. Our dad was driving at the time. Dani was in the front seat, and I was in the back. Tommy was somewhere else, with our mother. It was before their great divorce. The image of Dani after the accident would always stay with me, but stored in a different part of my mind than all my homicide victims: I kept Dani with Elena, where the image of my sister became less horrific over time. I hadn't seen my dad after he died, or he'd be with them too.

"Of course I do," I said. "All the time. Why do you ask?"

"Because we rarely talk about that. I can understand why Dad wouldn't want to, though."

"If you need to talk, I'm here."

"I feel like I'm losing my memories of her."

"She'll always be there, like Dad, and like Elena is with me—always a part of our lives. The memories are there, and they'll come to you. For me it's at night in bed, before falling asleep. My mind is clearer then, and they just show up."

"Dad does for me sometimes, but lately I can't quiet my brain, so it's hard."

I was afraid to ask, but I did. "Something else going on that you want to talk about?"

"No, nothing," he said shaking his head slowly.

"You still doing online therapy?"

"Yeah, it helps a bit."

"I look at old photos too. Sometimes it's painful, but then you see one that brings you back and fills you with joy. Dad had those shoeboxes full of photographs, remember?"

"Yeah."

"Do you have them here?"

"They're somewhere in his room—maybe his closet."

"We should dig them out sometime."

"I'm not ready to go in his room just yet."

"I will, if you want."

"I don't know. I'll let you know."

"I have some photos too, but most of our childhood photos are in my storage."

"Where the memories should be kept, huh?"

"Not on purpose. I just had so many boxes to pack that I forgot what was where. I don't even have some of my police memorabilia that I used to keep on a couple of shelves in DC. I liked having that stuff around."

"I don't know why, but lately I've been thinking about Dani a lot, and Dad . . . and Mom."

Mom was a sore subject for me, but I kept that to myself.

"I understand, man."

"It's not normal for a family to experience so much loss, and so much damn pain. To say that *Time heals all wounds* is such a crock. They only fester with time."

How should I respond to that?

"If you wanna hang out tonight, I'll cancel what I have to do," I said.

"No, man. I'm good. Really. I just miss Dad."

"I do too."

I stood up, leaned toward him and placed my hand lightly on his shoulder. He smiled and patted the back of my hand with the palm of his own like everything would be okay.

26

"This Is a Closed Meeting"

I arrived at the church parking lot about fifteen minutes before the NA meeting began. Mike Gottert was already there. A couple of other cars were in the lot. I parked next to Gottert, stepped out, and sat in the front seat of his car.

"You get a chance to go home?" I asked.

"No. I had a few new cases I had to catch up on, then I hit the Burger King drive-through."

"Be careful with that fast food. It'll catch up to you."

"I was desperate."

"I can help you with some of your other cases if you want."

"No, you're doing enough."

"Keep it in mind anyway."

"I will. Thanks."

"Keleher might be in there now," I said.

"Let's go inside then."

"Goes without saying but I'll say it anyway—if you see that Winters lady, I wouldn't act like you've talked to her."

"Yeah, I got that."

The church doors were open. We walked back to the community room. The NA group leader Mike Keleher was there already, setting up some folding chairs.

"Good evening, Mr. Keleher," Gottert said.

"Detectives?" He seemed surprised.

He unfolded another chair, set it down, and walked toward us.

"This is a closed meeting."

"We understand—but I'd like a chance to talk to the group before the meeting begins," Gottert said.

"You have to be an addict to be here. I take it neither of you has a substance-abuse problem?"

"Of course not."

"Some of the people here might have a problem even walking into the room when they see two police investigators. It's intimidating."

"We're not trying to intimidate anyone," I began. "We have to do our due diligence to investigate these murders."

"The courts respect this organization's anonymity, so you should too. And if I had any information about the murder, you'd be the first to know. We all have to feel safe in this environment, investigators."

"I can respect that," said Gottert. "But you need to take it very seriously that two of the people who attended these meetings were brutally murdered."

"I know. How about you let me talk to everyone? Leave your business cards with me, and I'll put them on the table over there where the coffee is. I'll let everyone know, and they can discreetly pick up a card if they have anything to offer."

Gottert looked at me. I didn't know why. I was only a volunteer. I gave him a slight nod.

"Let them know that if they do reach out it will be kept confidential," Gottert said.

"Of course."

He pulled a leather cardholder out of his front pocket, opened it, and handed Keleher the small stack of business cards it contained.

"Appreciate your time," Gottert told him.

"Thank you for your service."

I almost blew out a chuckle after he said that. I exercised restraint, though.

We walked back toward the front entrance.

"How about we hang out at the parking lot?" I proposed. "See if a familiar face shows."

27
Meeting Matthew

Gottert and I were leaning on the hood of his car with eyes on the front entrance. Several people parked and entered the church. We didn't bother approaching them because it was Matthew Guerre we wanted to talk to first.

"If he does show and agrees to talk," I suggested, "I wouldn't hit him with Jean Marie right away. Sometimes you want to catch them off guard, see how they react."

"Makes sense."

A couple of minutes before the meeting was supposed to start, a black, older-model sedan pulled in.

Matthew Guerre stepped out of the sedan and walked toward the front door. His hair looked longer than it had in his Pottstown arrest photo. Other than that, he looked the same. We cut him off at the lot. He stepped back a bit.

"Didn't mean to startle you," I said.

"What do you want?" he asked defensively.

"I'm an investigator with the Charontown Police Department, Matthew," Gottert said. "We'd like to talk to you."

"How do you know my name?" he asked suspiciously. "And talk about what?"

"We're interviewing everyone associated with the meetings here. It concerns the murders of Paul Savell and Del Thomas."

"Why would you want to talk to me about that? And again, how do you know my name? These meetings are supposed to be confidential."

"Your name came up during the course of our investigation, outside the meeting." Gottert's version was sort of the truth.

"Came up? How?"

"Well, that would be confidential."

"Can you spare us a couple of minutes?" I interjected. "You're not in any trouble, Matthew."

"The meeting is starting."

"It won't take long," Gottert said.

"I really don't want to miss it."

"You won't."

"Just for a couple of minutes, then."

Gottert began.

"Thanks. Your last name is *Guerre*? Am I pronouncing it right?"

"Yes, it is."

"Did you know Paul and Del?"

"No, not really. I don't hang out with anyone at these meetings. I just go for me. That's it."

"Did you ever talk to them?"

"Yeah, of course I talked to them. We all talk on occasion."

"Were you here when Paul got into a fight?"

"Yeah."

"Do you know what it was about?"

"That Jeffrey guy got pissed because he found out Paul was using, or trying to sell drugs at the meetings. Something like that."

"Did Jeffrey threaten Paul?"

"Just that he'd kick his ass all over again if he ever came back."

"So did Paul ever come back?"

"No. Neither did Del."

"You live here with your dad, the pastor?"

He hesitated for a second before replying, "What does that have to do with anything?"

"Just in case we need to get in touch with you again."

"Yeah, I do. And I think you've taken over two minutes now."

"Did your friend Jean Marie go to any of the meetings here?" I jumped in.

That seemed to rattle Matthew; he hesitated for more than a second this time. Gottert, on the other hand, maintained a straight face, so I couldn't tell if I'd angered him by jumping in like that. I had to keep in mind that these were his cases, not mine.

"Did she?" Gottert pressed.

"No, she didn't."

Gottert looked at me with a downward nod like he wanted me to continue.

I took up the thread: "How long have you known Jean Marie?"

"Not long."

"How long is *Not long*?"

"Not even two months. Listen, I'm going to miss my meeting, so I really need to go. I can't help you with any of this. I liked Jean, and I was torn apart when I heard she was the one who got killed. I don't know what else to say. I have to go."

He started walking away.

"We'll need to continue this conversation, Matthew," I said.

He stopped and turned toward me.

"Can you come into the station tomorrow?"

"Am I being charged with something?"

"No. Should you be?"

"No," he said defiantly. "Of course not."

"Then help us out and come in tomorrow," I said. "Or we can always come to your house."

"Don't do that. I can be there in the morning—about eleven o'clock."

I looked at Gottert, and he nodded.

"We'll see you then, Matthew. Just one last question, though: Where did you and Jean Marie first meet?" I asked.

He waffled, then said:

"At the Birdhouse bar."

28
The Morsville Murders

The next morning as I was waiting in the community room for Gottert, Bill stepped in and said, "Mike told me there's a good suspect coming in for an interview."

I was thinking he was more *a person of interest* than *a good suspect*, but I didn't want to make Gottert look bad, so I didn't mention it.

"He fits the profile," I said.

Gottert had built up Matthew to be more than he was. I didn't believe that it was an effort to make himself look good; it was probably nothing more than a rookie mistake. He just wanted to give his boss enough to put him at ease, or maybe get him off his back. I didn't put in the hours that Gottert did, so I wasn't around enough to know if Bill was pressuring him, but I got the impression he was not: Bill didn't come across as the type of supervisor who would do that. Unless, that is, Bill was getting pressured in turn by the mayor's office.

"I'd like you to sit in on the interview," Bill said.

"Mike is very capable."

"I know he is. I'm not asking you to take the lead, just sit in. I already talked to Mike last night about it. Am I asking too much of you?"

"It does put me in an awkward position. Like I said before, I don't want anyone here feeling like I'm *that guy* from the outside, coming in thinking he knows better."

"I understand, but trust me—Mike is all about learning. This is his first time in the room for a homicide investigation, so I want someone with experience in there with him."

"Alright then. I'm here to help."

"Appreciate it. As bad as it sounds, if it was just one victim I'd be okay with Mike being in there solo. But we're looking at three victims with the same MO."

"Understood."

Matthew showed up on time. Gottert led him into the interview room and advised him where to sit.

"Do you want a soda or anything?"

"No, thank you."

"I'll be right back."

"Can you leave the door open?" he asked.

"You're not under arrest, so yes."

Gottert walked out and left the door open.

Bill came out of his office and leaned against the front of the cubicle.

"I got some information back from ViCAP," he told us.

"Anything useful?" Gottert asked.

"Well, our country's plagued with similar crimes, but only two appear identical to ours."

"How so?" I questioned.

"Four times in the chest with a tri-edged knife. Now, I'd believe that to be coincidence if they were three separate victims spread out across the country, but they both happened in the same small town—Morsville, Pennsylvania—within a two-month stretch."

Gottert got out his cell, started tapping his index finger on the screen.

"When?" I asked.

"January 2017."

"Okay," Gottert began, like he had something. "Morsville is about three hours from Pottstown, according to Google Maps."

"It's a bit of a drive from Pottstown," I said, "but doable in a day for a motivated killer. We need to find out if Matthew was still living in Pottstown at the time."

"Morsville is a small town like ours, with a small department. I'll contact the chief and have him get me whatever they have on those two cases."

With that we walked into the interview room and sat down across from Matthew Guerre, our prime—our only—suspect. Gottert had his notepad and pen at the ready.

After he'd introduced us, Gottert said, "Appreciate you being here. Want to let you know that we like to record all our interviews."

"What if I don't want to be recorded?"

"That's your right," Gottert advised.

"Matthew, you're here voluntarily and not under arrest," I pointed out, "and I don't think you have anything to hide. I'm not suggesting you would ever do something like this, but certain people have claimed the police coerced them, or made things up that they never said. So it protects all of us to record the conversation, and it's a helluva lot easier than having to take notes." I smiled.

"I guess. And no, I don't have anything to hide."

"Okay then," Gottert said. He glanced at his wristwatch. "It's 11:37 a.m."

29
No Alibi

"You and your mom and dad moved up here from Pottstown, Pennsylvania?" Gottert asked Matthew.

"My mom died."

"I'm sorry for your loss. Do you mind me asking how she died?"

"I don't mind — she had liver disease."

"I lost my wife to ovarian cancer," I cut in. "I know how hard it can be."

"How did you know we moved here from Pottstown?"

"We ran your name to make sure you didn't have any warrants on you," Gottert said.

He looked nervous, like he realized we knew about his heroin arrest.

"You can do that?"

"Of course. It's for our safety."

"Not that we're worried about you, Matthew. It's just routine."

"Yeah, nothing to worry about," Gottert added. "How long did you live in Pottstown?"

"What does that have to do with Jean Marie's murder?"

"Just getting a little background on you is all."

"Why?"

"To get to know you," Gottert said.

"Why do you want to get to know me? I only agreed to come here because you made me feel like if I didn't, you'd think maybe I was involved or something."

"I'm sorry you felt that way," I told him. "It's good to get a bit of background on a person being interviewed, though, because you want to make sure they're credible and telling the truth. We're not trying to trick you, but there might be certain things we ask you that we already know the answer to. Again, to ensure your credibility."

"Credibility?"

"In case you have some good information that we can use. Your credibility is important for court purposes," I said.

"I told you that I don't know anything about these murders, and that's the truth."

"We still need to talk," I said. "It's looking like you might have been the last person to see Jean Marie alive."

"Why do you call her *Jean Marie* like you know her?" Matthew asked me the question as though the very idea offended him.

"I was under the impression she went by *Jean Marie*."

"Okay, fine."

I glanced at Gottert with a slight upward nod. He understood that to mean I didn't have anything else.

"How long did you live in Pottstown?" he asked again.

"Five years or so."

"Where did you and your dad live before that?"

"Alexandria, Virginia. That's where I was born."

"What kind of work did you do in Pottstown?"

"Construction."

"A company?"

"An independent contractor."

"Is there a lot of construction work in Pottstown? I mean, it's a pretty small town, right?"

"It's small, but there's plenty of work."

"Ever get any jobs in other towns outside Pottstown?"

"Yeah, of course."

"I've driven through that area. Mostly tiny towns, but Morsville is bigger. You ever work there?"

"Morsville? That's like hours away." His comeback amounted to *Why the hell would you bring up that town?* After that, Matthew's face assumed an odd look.

"I just figured you might have been through there and done some work."

"No," he said with a curious blank expression.

Feeling the conversation needed to move away from that, I asked, "How long have you known Jean Marie?"

"I told you yesterday evening. A couple of months."

"And you first met her at the Birdhouse bar?"

"Yeah. I was having a beer at the bar, and she sat down next to me."

"Was she there alone?"

"Looked like she was."

"Were you there with her on Monday night?"

Matthew had to think about that for a moment, but finally he shook his head: "No."

"Where were you Monday night, then?"

That question seemed to throw him.

"That's when she was murdered?"

"Yes," Gottert said.

"So I'm a suspect?"

"I'd like to rule you out," Gottert told him. I let him take over from there.

"You mean like I need an alibi?"

"That'd help," Gottert replied evenly. "So where were you?"

At that Matthew tightened his lips, but I got the impression it wasn't voluntary. It was more like a tell.

"I was at home."

He was lying.

"Was anyone with you?"

He did that compression thing with his lips again, but this time he shook his head lightly.

"No," he said, resigned.

He was hiding something.

"I know how that looks," he acknowledged.

Gottert appeared to be debating what to say next.

In my mind, if Matthew was guilty he would make something up. *So why didn't he?*

We needed to keep the ball rolling, so I asked Matthew, "What were you doing at home?"

He was giving it a little too much thought.

"It was only a few days ago," I urged.

"I was watching TV."

"What were you watching?"

"I can't remember. You're getting me all confused and treating me like I'm guilty. It's making me nervous."

"We're just asking simple questions, Matthew. Like Investigator Gottert said, we need to rule you out."

"I just can't remember is all."

"I understand. Let's move on, then—work your brain a bit to help you remember. Did Jean Marie attend church with you?"

"Yes, she did. Well, not *with* me. We met there. She liked to walk from her home."

"You've been to her place?"

"Couple of times."

"Was she at church with you this last Sunday?"

"Yes."

"Did she go regularly?"

"Mostly. I mean, she missed one or two Sundays because she overslept."

"Did she make any other friends at church?"

"Not that I'm aware of."

"How about outside of church? Do you know any of her friends?"

"She never talked about friends. I think she was a loner."

"No one at all?"

"She never talked about anyone, and I never met anyone she knew."

"You didn't find that odd?"

"No—why would I? We only knew each other for a short time."

"What about your friends? She ever meet them?"

"I don't have any friends here. I keep to myself."

"Jean Marie was a friend, though."

"I'd like to think she was becoming a friend."

"Did she know Del or Paul?"

"I'm pretty sure she did. She knew about the fight Paul got into."

"How did she hear about that?"

"I think she heard it from someone at the Birdhouse. She hangs out there a lot—I mean she used to."

"Did she tell you how she heard about it?"

"We were just talking about things. I told her I went to NA meetings, and she said something about hearing a couple of people at the bar discussing a big fight involving Paul. I didn't ask further."

"Did they all hang out together?"

"Who?"

"Del and Paul with Jean Marie."

"I have no idea."

"And you never hung out with Del or Paul?"

"No. I told you I didn't."

"What kind of vehicle did Del Thomas drive?"

"A pickup truck, I think. I don't know what kind."

"When did you last see Del in his truck?"

"I don't know. At a meeting, in the parking lot there. I can't remember."

"Did Jean Marie ever talk to you about anyone she may have been having problems with?"

"No, never."

"Did the two of you do anything after church last Sunday?"

"We hung out."

"What did you do?"

"We went to the park by the canal. Talked. We made plans to go out this week . . . tonight . . . the drive-in in Newark."

He looked sad. It seemed real.

"Do you know what Jean Marie did for a living?"

That took him by surprise.

"Yeah, I knew what she did. What does it matter? Jesus showed kindness to women like her, so why can't I be friends with her?"

"I never suggested you couldn't be friends."

"There is no condemnation for those who believe in Christ Jesus," he told me.

"A good Bible quote. One to live by."

"I'm paraphrasing, but it is, yeah."

"It didn't upset you, what she did?"

"I was a heroin addict, but I think you both know that. Jean Marie didn't judge me. I didn't judge her. I'm not saying I agreed with her lifestyle."

"It made you angry?"

"Not angry—I just didn't *agree* with it. I mean, she has the right to do whatever she wants. I mean, had the right. It's her body, but it's not something I could ever condone. And she did tell me she wanted to get out of that life and find a real job."

"What kind of job?"

"She mentioned wanting to go to nursing school."

"That's admirable—but how would she support herself through school? That can be expensive."

"Get something part-time, I guess. She said she had some money saved up."

"She was in a cash business. In my experience they don't open a bank account for that, so it's more than likely she stashed her cash somewhere in her home. Do you know where?"

"Of course not. Why would she tell me where she kept her money?"

"Maybe she trusted you."

"I don't know if she had a bunch of cash stashed."

"The only reason I asked is because it's possible that whoever killed her was out for the money."

"I don't think she had enough money for someone to kill her over."

"You'd be surprised what someone would murder for."

"I wouldn't know."

"What do you do for work?"

"I'm working for a mason here in town."

"You like working with stone?"

"Yeah, cement, stonework—whatever. He keeps me busy."

"What's his name?"

"I'd rather you not call him. I like the work I do."

"Is it Rob Whitlow?" Gottert asked.

The abashed look Matthew gave us suggested it was.

"He's the only good mason in town. He did some work for me a while ago. A walkway."

"Yeah, but don't call him, okay?"

"I don't think there's a need for us to call him," I noted. "So you do okay financially?"

"I'm saving up, living at home, learning a good trade."

"Good for you." I paused for effect. "Matthew, you and Jean Marie were more than just friends, weren't you?"

"We weren't anything more than friends."

"Because she was a prostitute."

"Was that a question?" he asked with a trace of anger.

"I'm assuming that's why you couldn't be more than just friends. I can't think of another reason. She was very attractive."

"Well, you're assuming wrong."

"Why am I assuming wrong? I'd definitely have a problem with what she did if it was me. I know a lot of other men would too. How about you, Investigator Gottert?"

"I'd have a big problem with it."

"What are you insinuating? You think I killed her because she sold her body?"

I didn't answer, just shot him a bit of skepticism.

"I could never do something like that."

"I have to tell you, Matthew, we're having a problem with a couple of things here."

"What things?"

"Your lack of an alibi, for starters. Your poor memory. I would definitely remember what I was watching a few days ago, especially if my life depended on it—and I'm much older than you are."

"I feel like you played me and now I'm a suspect."

"You weren't played, Matthew."

"You said I'm free to go, right?"

"Yes," Gottert told him.

"Then I'm out of here."

30

Cause for a Search Warrant

Matthew walked out.

"That was a *little* revealing," said Bill Finn, "but still disappointing."

"I've had a lot of interviews like that one, Chief," I began. "There's always something useful you can find to pull out of them."

"He doesn't have a good alibi, for one," Gottert added.

"No, he doesn't. But I don't believe you have enough for a search warrant for the home. There's more than enough for his phone, though."

"That would be a good start," Bill said.

"It could reveal a lot," Gottert added.

"I can help you draft the affidavit if you want, Mike. The fact that he had a relationship with the decedent—and may have been the last one to see her alive—should be more than enough. But you can strengthen it by adding that his physical description matches the description of the subject getting out of Del's pickup truck, and that he has no alibi."

"And you don't think that's enough to search his home?" Gottert asked.

"In DC? No. I wouldn't get circumstantial evidence like that past an AUSA. I don't know what your DA is like here, or what kind of judges you have. If they're fairly permissive they might issue one for his home, but your chances are thin."

"It's hit-or-miss with them here," Bill said.

"I'd write it up just for his cell phone," I added.

"I've got to get to a meeting. Keep me informed."

"Copy that, Chief," Gottert said.

I helped Gottert write up the affidavit in support of a search warrant. I advised him again that including the home would make a prosecutor unlikely to sign off on it, so Gottert agreed to go for the cell alone. When we finished, he walked the affidavit up to the DA's office; if it was sound, Gottert would then take it to the judge in chambers. I waited in his office.

Dana King and Jimmy O'Born were the only two officers on duty for daywork, and they were out on patrol. I was left at the station alone until Gottert got back. I sat on the swivel chair and got lost staring at the paint-peeled, water-stained ceiling until Ada popped into my head. It was a nice feeling. Much better than the ceiling. I was looking forward to dinner with her tomorrow.

About an hour later, Gottert returned with a warrant in hand.

"That didn't take long," I said.

"Not much going on today. You were right, though: The ADA said there wasn't enough here for the home."

"Maybe the cell will give you what you need to add a bit of language for the home."

"Let's hope."

"You want to go serve it now?"

"Hell yeah."

* * *

The old colonial stone house sat on a small lot beside the church. The dwelling was provided free of charge by the presbytery to Pastor Simon and his son. Officer King was parked at the curb in front of the house. The chief had insisted on his being there: After all I was still a civilian, and he felt I no longer qualified as backup in case something went bad. Didn't hurt my feelings—I knew I was capable—but Bill was by the book, so I kept my mouth shut.

Gottert pulled up behind King's marked car.

"I don't think this kid'll do anything stupid," I told him, "except possibly try to run if he's your guy, or just plain afraid. Might be a good idea to have King take the rear. I'll go with you to the front."

"The chief never said you have to stay in the car, so that's fine with me."

We stepped out and huddled briefly with King behind his cruiser.

"You take the back," Gottert told him.

"Copy. Don't go up until I'm in place. Go to Tac 3 and I'll let you know."

They switched their handheld radios to the channel.

King walked around the front yard and disappeared through the cut between the house and the church.

Seconds later he came over the radio quietly with, "I'm in position."

"Copy."

We walked to the front. Gottert knocked loudly on the door.

Pastor Simon opened it. Looked at us evenly.

"Graham . . . Detective. What brings you here?"

"We need to see your son, sir," Gottert said.

"I don't know what kind of information you have, but it's insane to think my son had anything to do with this."

"He's not under arrest, Pastor Simon. But Investigator Gottert does need to see him."

"What's that paper you have in your hand, Detective?"

"It's for your son, Pastor."

"Graham, why are you involved in all this?"

"I'm just consulting, Pastor. Is Matthew home?"

He seemed reluctant, but then said, "What is it for?"

"Your son is an adult, Pastor," Gottert said politely. "We'll tell him the nature of the document. Please have him come to the door if he's home."

"This is ridiculous," the pastor said.

Nevertheless he left the door open and walked to a stairwell at the end of the hallway.

"Matthew," he called up the stairs.

"Yeah," came the muffled reply.

"Come down here, please."

Footsteps hitting a creaky wood floor and stairs. On the last step he noticed us and stopped. For a second, I thought he was about to bolt.

"You're not under arrest, Matthew," I assured him.

"Come here, son," the pastor said.

He approached, but kept his distance.

"They said they need to talk to you," his dad said calmly.

"About what? I already told them everything I know."

"I have a search warrant for your cell phone, Matthew," Gottert told him.

"What?!" An angry bark from Pastor Simon.

"We'll need to take it now."

"But why?" Matthew replied. "I don't understand."

"Why are you harassing my son? He's got nothing to do with any of this."

"If he truly doesn't, then he shouldn't have a problem surrendering his phone."

Pastor Simon was visibly riled, his son, shaken.

"It'll be okay, Matthew," Pastor Simon said in a resigned voice. "They have a job to do."

"But I need my phone."

"Just hand it over to them, son. You've got nothing to worry about."

Matthew grudgingly pulled his cell phone from his pocket, paused like he had to think about it, then walked over and handed it to Gottert.

"We'll be in touch," Gottert said.

"When can I get my phone back?"

"As soon as we can."

"You're doing all this just because my son was friends with the woman who was killed?" Pastor Simon demanded. "Matthew was only trying to help her."

I didn't know what to say to the pastor. He was the man who had buried my father.

31
A Surprise Visit

Bill called in another favor with his boy, Sam Beck. Sam told him he'd get on it right away if we could get the cell to him by the end of day, so we made our way to Albany again.

Beck met us in front.

"Really appreciate this, Sam," Gottert said.

"No problem at all. I haven't had something like this come my way since my days at NYPD."

"How long do you need?"

"Depends on what you want."

"How far back can you go to include mapping?" I asked.

"Cell-phone records are usually kept for around seven years—sometimes longer, depending on the carrier. This is an iPhone, so it should be good. I can work it a couple of hours today, but unfortunately I'm out of town this weekend; I can't get it for you until early afternoon Monday."

"That's good enough. Thanks," Gottert said.

He handed the cell over to Beck, and we made our way back to the car.

"That's a lot of driving."

"I'm used to it," Gottert sighed. "Gives my brain time to rest."

I got home in time for dinner. The shedding cottonwood around Dad's property looked like dust bunnies blowing in the wind. That kept Tommy inside because it was hard on his allergies. After dinner we sat in the living room for drinks. He had his usual beer or two and I nursed a single malt.

"*No one ever told me that getting therapy felt so like fear. I am not afraid, but the sensation is like being afraid.*" Tommy recited the words as though reading them.

"You come up with that?"

"No, it's C. S. Lewis, from *A Grief Observed*. I've been reading it. Pastor Simon gave me a copy."

"He did? When?"

"He brought it over earlier today."

"Why'd he do that?"

"He recommended I read it. It's good—*really* good. It puts so much of what I'm going through into perspective."

"I'm happy to hear that. Did he come in and visit?"

"No, just dropped the book off and said to tell you he said hello."

"You two talk about anything else?"

"Not really."

"About what time did he come over?"

"Why does that matter?"

"It doesn't, really. I'm just curious."

"Around four o'clock, I guess. Feels like you're grilling me here."

Damn, that was after we served Matthew. But he'd been counseling Tommy since before all that shit with his son, so I moved on from the negative thoughts.

"Didn't mean it to sound like that, Tommy."

"Alrighty then, detective. You should read the book when I'm done. It'll do you good."

"Maybe I will."

Truth was, I probably wouldn't. I used to read a lot until Elena got ill. Haven't picked up a book since. Too hard to focus on things like reading. Work was something different. That's why I decided to help out Bill. I needed the work to occupy my mind in a different way and free me from myself—take me out of myself.

"I'll give it to you when I'm finished," Tommy said.

"Alrighty then," I teased him.

He spit out a chuckle like he remembered how the phrase used to drive Dad crazy.

"What's going on with those murders?"

"Following a lot of leads."

"Got any suspects?"

"Now you're grilling *me*."

"Yeah, right. It's called having a conversation. Maybe you've forgotten how," he said jokingly.

"I still remember how to have a good conversation," I smiled.

"So?"

"So, what?"

"Any suspects?"

"Not really."

"Sounds like you can't or won't talk about it."

"I just don't want to think about it until I have to."

"I can understand that. I bet I know something you want to talk about, though."

"Yeah? What's that?"

"Aaadah." He grinned like he had when he was a kid.

"Get outta here with that."

"C'mon, I know you gotta be looking forward to dinner with her tomorrow."

"Maybe I am. That make you happy?"

"Make me happier if you got laid."

"Shut the fuck up," I said lightly.

"No, really—you need to. You're fucking wound up tight."

"I am not."

"Oh yeah you are, brother."

"I thought you'd come back with something better than that, like *wound up tighter than* . . . I don't even know."

"I got nothin'."

"That's probably a good thing. And yeah, I like her, but I'm not about to rush into anything."

"I hope I'll meet her soon."

"We'll see how it goes."

A couple of single malts later and I was down for the count. I wasn't much of a drinker.

Sleep came easy. The dreams, not so much.

I woke up before daylight. That was happening too often lately. I wanted to be rested for the next evening, so I closed my eyes and hoped for the best.

32
Getting Cozy with Ada

It was about a twenty-minute drive to the restaurant in Canandaigua. There was still an hour or so before sunset, but the sun was making its descent, painting the sky a pale blue, yellow, and pink. As beautiful as some of the sunsets were in DC, they couldn't compare to the sun setting over farmland and rolling pastures. It felt like we were sailing into it.

I glanced toward Ada. She had a tranquil, slight smile and dark, vibrant blue eyes. It was refreshing. I looked away before she could notice but kept her profile in the corner of my eye. I was afraid of the feelings I was having—they felt like disloyalty to my wife—but maybe it was time for me to take a chance, even given the possibility of getting hurt. I meant what I said to Tommy about not wanting to rush anything. Rushing into a relationship was not something Elena and I had done. Instead it had felt natural—not something we discussed doing. If there was a chance with Ada, I wanted it to be like that too.

The restaurant was in a residential area off Main Street. If not for the nearly full parking lot out front, you'd think it was just another home in the neighborhood.

When the waitress arrived with our menus we ordered two aged sipping mezcals and the signature guacamole to start. For our main course I went with the glazed pork belly and Ada the short-rib tacos. Our conversation was pleasant. It felt unforced, like we'd known each other longer than we actually had. I learned considerably more about her—some significant, some trivial: Her parents were still alive and together; she didn't like crab; she wasn't a huge sports fan; she wasn't afraid of spiders but couldn't bear accidentally walking through web; she loved to travel but had not been able to in a while; and she didn't care for beer. Just a few details to file away for safekeeping.

"You've led an interesting life," she mentioned.

"Most of it not of my own doing."

"I imagine as a child you wouldn't have had much of a choice."

"That's right—I didn't. But I did have some great childhood adventures growing up in other countries, so I'm not complaining."

"I'll bet you did. So why a cop?"

"I'd like to say it was a calling, but it wasn't. I mean, I did it for all the right reasons: I was naïve enough back then to think I could make a difference in the city I loved."

"And you don't believe you've made a difference?"

"Not in the way I originally thought I would. I did to a certain extent, though."

"I think you're being too modest."

"No. You can't bring back the dead."

"But you can provide closure."

"True. I think *you're* making a difference, though."

"Me? In what way?"

"You put a smile on the face of everyone who takes a bite of those sweet creations of yours."

God, was that corny!

"Now I think you're just trying to sweeten *me* up."

I smiled and downed the rest of my mezcal. Sometimes the best response is no response at all.

The evening ended too soon.

I drove Ada home.

"Would you like to come in for a nightcap?" she asked when I pulled to the curb. "I don't have scotch, but I do have some Irish whiskey."

"Sure. That'd be nice."

Her living room smelled like cinnamon. It was dimly but comfortably lit. No television—maybe in another room? Framed original artworks on the walls. A couple of them looked like outsider pieces—local artists, perhaps. Dark wooden built-in bookshelves lined the far end of the living room, past an arched opening to what appeared to be the dining room. A top shelf displayed items of pottery and primitive American folk art, spotlit by accent lights on a track secured to the ceiling. The remaining shelves held books. A lot of books. Ada appeared to be a reader. I liked that. Elena had been too.

For God's sake stop comparing, Graham!

"Lot of books."

"Yes. I confess I haven't read them all, but I picked them up at flea markets or garage sales with every intention to. Have a seat."

There was a sectional sofa and two nice leather armchairs, the latter separated by an accent table. I was being polite, so I chose the armchair nearest the sofa. Probably the wrong move, but in my awkward mind I didn't want to give the appearance of suggesting anything. I was rusty as hell.

"I'll get us drinks. Do you like ice, or neat?"

"Just a tiny bit of ice. Thanks."

Ada disappeared into the dining room, then returned a minute later with a drink in each hand. She handed me a tumbler that had only a few cubes in it and then sat at the end of the sectional to my left, but still close enough for warm conversation.

Ada lifted her glass to me and said, "Cheers."

I did the same and had a sip before setting it down.

She scrunched her face in a cute way after she sipped hers, like she wasn't used to drinking straight whiskey.

"Your home is cozy."

"Thank you. I've put a lot of work into it over the years. Still more to do, though."

"I imagine it never ends. My father was always working on his place."

"I've driven by your dad's place, but I've never been inside. It looks lovely. The property is beautiful. He took great care of everything."

"He did. So does Tommy. Tommy loves working the land. My dad loved to make things. He could build anything. Me, on the other hand, I'm hopeless; about all I'm good for is keeping things clean and tidy."

"Feel free to come over any time you get the urge to clean," she said with a half-smile.

"Doesn't look like you need much help with that." I grabbed my drink like it was a life preserver.

"It's not always this put together."

"That's what you have a child for."

"Good luck with that—she's a teenager. Walk into her room and you might not come out alive."

I chuckled.

"I've been in a few places like that. I have a feeling your daughter's room isn't anything like some of those places."

"Well, there's no dead bodies that I know of." She shook her head a couple of times and came back with, "That was bad—sorry."

"I'm an ex-cop, Ada. I'm used to gallows humor, most of it much worse than that."

"Well, she's a good girl. Just likes her organized clutter."

"I hope to meet her one of these days."

"I can arrange that. I think she'd like you."

"I think I'd like her too."

The conversation went on mostly like that for another hour and a few more drinks. She showed me around her house, even a through-the-door view of her bedroom, which felt awkward because I wanted to take her and kiss her right there. We ended up back in the living room, where I found myself sitting beside her on the sofa. I was pleasantly surprised and pleased when she made the approach and kissed me. Her lips were warm and moist, and she tasted good. I wrapped my right arm gently around her shoulders to pull her in closer. I don't know how long we kissed for, but it came to a comfortable end. By that I mean there was no hint of awkwardness. I caressed the back of her neck with my hand. She smiled. It was lovely.

"I like you," I said.

"I like you too, but you said that like a *but* should come after."

"Not at all. I guess I'm just not used to drinking this much."

"I understand. I feel the same way."

"I should go. Let the both of us get some sleep."

She took me in with that same lovely smile. I wanted to stay, but managed to resist the temptation; I wanted to be at my best when and if that happened.

"I really do like you," I said again, and kissed her softly on the lips.

"I'm glad you do."

"Are you busy tomorrow?"

"I'm getting together with a couple of girlfriends in Rochester."

"Sometime next week, then? You could come over for dinner. My brother loves to grill."

"That sounds wonderful—I'd love to."

"Tuesday?" I asked.

"I think that'll work."

"How about I give you a call on Monday to confirm?"

"Okay."

I forced myself to stand.

She did likewise, and walked me to the door.

"I had a great time," I said.

"Me too."

She leaned into me for a good night kiss.

"Good night," I said.

"Sweet dreams."

That was something I was hoping for.

33

New Details Come to Light

I met Gottert at the station Monday afternoon after he returned from Albany with the results for Matthew's cell. Bill also gave him the case jackets from the Morsville murders: Joseph Timons and Vernon Houston. The two murders were eerily similar. Both men had been stabbed in the same manner. Although the investigators believed that the second victim had not been slain where his body was found, the first victim had a messy crime scene that allowed DNA to be recovered. Not only that, but both victims had a criminal history.

Gottert had already spoken to one of the lead investigators while driving to Albany. The other investigator, since retired, was now living in Florida.

Much like Charontown, the Morsville police department was shorthanded, so the lead investigator did not have the time to drive over. But he'd be willing to on his own time if an arrest was made, he advised us. Gottert assured him he'd be kept in the loop.

Equally revealing was the search of Matthew's cell phone.

Over the course of a couple of months, several calls had been made to Alice Winters.

Geolocations also showed that his car had been on the same block as her home. Most of those instances were in the daytime, and once it was even on the same day and time that Matthew had claimed to be home alone, watching television. The data also showed his car parked back at his house later on that day, though—after he had probably been with Alice—but it did not remain there for long: A little before midnight, it had been driven and parked within a couple of blocks of the Birdhouse, just a few hours before Jean Marie's body was discovered.

All that is what fucked Matthew and gave Gottert enough to search his home.

"Couple of things I'm curious about, though," I said. "If Matthew was going to the Birdhouse to meet Jean Marie, why wouldn't he call her before going there? There's no record of him calling her."

"I don't know."

"And second, why didn't we see him on the exterior surveillance footage?"

"Maybe 'cause he stayed in his car in the parking lot? Never went in?"

"Possibly. Before we draft the search-warrant affidavit, though, we should re-interview Alice Winters—see if you can nail down the timeline."

Gottert agreed and off we went to Alice's home.

Her husband was at work. She admitted that she spoke to Matthew often, but always about their mutual struggles with addiction.

"But he came over, too," Gottert stated.

That threw her off. I sensed they were having an affair, but this was not an adultery investigation.

"We know he was here quite a lot," I added.

"So, what's wrong with that? We talked in person, too—and why does any of this matter anyway? Is Matthew some kind of suspect?"

"We just need to know when he was last here, Mrs. Winters," Gottert said firmly.

"Do you believe he was involved in Del and Paul's murders? Is he using me as an alibi or something?"

Smart lady.

"Right now we're looking into all possibilities, and all we need to know from you is when Matthew Simon was last here. So please tell us."

She thought about it for a moment, then said, "The Sunday before last."

"How long was he here for?"

"I don't remember—a couple of hours? We had a long conversation."

I felt she wasn't being truthful, and that she and Matthew were romantically involved.

"About what time did he leave?"

Alice Winters clearly didn't want to answer that question, but after a couple of seconds of hard thought she said, "Maybe around eight o'clock."

"Obviously the evening?" I asked.

"Yes."

"And your husband can confirm that?" I asked even though I knew the answer.

The question obviously got to her.

"Mrs. Winters, we couldn't care less about your personal life. We're investigating three murders—possibly more—so it's important that we have this information."

"My husband was out of town. Please don't tell him. I broke it off with Matthew that evening because I just couldn't do it anymore. Did he already tell you all this? That's how you knew he'd been here?"

"Did you talk to him again after he left?" Gottert asked.

"He *did* tell you," she assumed. "And no, I made it clear to him that it was over."

"How did he react to that?" Gottert asked.

"He was hurt, of course, but Matthew is a decent young man. He was never violent or anything like that, if that's what you're thinking. You won't have to talk to my husband, will you? This would kill him."

"We don't have to talk to him," I assured her.

34
Something Found

It didn't take long for Gottert to walk the affidavit through and get the search warrant. And we wasted no time once we had it in hand. Bill called in everyone. It was all hands on deck again. Two officers were kept on routine patrol. Everyone else was with us.

In DC the entry to the home would have been made by the emergency-response team. It was a little different here. There were only five members, excluding myself. We had a briefing at the station led by Gottert. A photograph of Matthew was handed out, as well as items of interest that should be seized, especially a Steelers ball cap. Gottert made it clear to the other officers who would be involved in the search that they could search only Matthew's bedroom, as well as any common areas of the home shared by Matthew and his father.

"I'll be the only one searching his bedroom," Gottert advised.

I wouldn't be making the entry with them. I'd have to wait until the scene was cleared.

Even though they had a ram, they started with a knock-and-announce. In DC we wouldn't give a shit if it was a pastor's home. We usually just tore the place up. A little more relaxed here.

I was standing out front beside Bill's cruiser. Gottert knocked hard on the front door and announced, "Charontown Police! We have a warrant to search the residence!" Pastor Simon promptly opened the door. Even from where I was standing, I could tell he was surprised as hell. He had no choice but to let them in.

After a few minutes, Officer King stepped out and called to me, "It's clear. You can come in."

Matthew and his dad were sitting on a sofa in the living room. Matthew was not in handcuffs. It looked like a cushion on another chair had been lifted up and set back in place, so I assumed the rest of the sofa had been checked before they were seated. I've been involved in some search warrants—thankfully not one I was responsible for—where a weapon was later discovered right beneath the cushion on which a suspect had been sitting. Even if the chances were low, as in a pastor's home, you still had to follow the same procedure for every search warrant.

Pastor Simon watched me when I entered. It was an odd look, like he was okay with what had to be done, but still displeased. Made me feel both bad and puzzled at the same time. I'm guessing the pastor had already had something to say before they were seated, but I missed all that.

I met up with Gottert in Matthew's bedroom on the second floor.

"Just getting started," he said.

"I always took my time too. Looked around at everything before I began."

"Yeah, the only time I like to dive right into tearing something open is on Christmas."

I chuckled.

"Good comparison. A search warrant always did feel sort of like Christmas to me. I can't really do much here except look around—maybe point you in the right direction if I spot something."

"I don't think anyone would object if you searched."

"Probably not. Except if I found something that could be used at trial, I'd probably be called to court. I don't like going to court. Happy to be done with that part."

"I can understand that."

Not much of a life was kept in this room, it appeared, perhaps because Matthew didn't consider it his home. Probably wouldn't be long before the Simons were leaving. Less to pack up. No laptop, but a lot of guys and gals his age didn't have one. All they needed was a smartphone. Certainly made it easier on us.

I searched with my eyes while Gottert went through Matthew's closet. He began to pull out the clothing on hangers, checking each item closely for possible blood or hair. The shoes came after that.

"No ball cap in here," he said after.

I got down on one knee and looked under the bed. Nothing there.

"This kid keeps a clean fucking room," I said.

"Yeah—both good and bad."

The dresser was next, then under the mattress and through every drawer of the desk. We left Matthew's bedroom with nothing more than a couple of pieces of junk mail that would corroborate his name and address for court purposes.

The only other rooms upstairs were the pastor's bedroom and a shared bathroom. Officer King had just left the bathroom. He walked down the stairs and approached us with a wide smile.

"Found something in the hallway closet," he said.

We followed. The door to the closet stood open. Clothing and winter boots were piled on the hallway closet floor.

"On the shelf."

Gottert pushed his way in as far as he could.

"Nice work," he said. "Get O'Born here to take a picture before you recover it."

"Copy that," King said, then went to the other room to get the sergeant.

"What do you got?" I asked.

"Steelers ball cap." He grinned from ear to ear.

35

The Chief Decides

Bill Finn stepped into the hallway, followed by Sergeant Jimmy O'Born.

Officer Dana King pointed out the cap on the shelf in the closet.

Bill looked at Mike Gottert.

"Arrest him," Bill ordered in a quiet but firm voice.

I was surprised when I heard him say that; Gottert looked a bit surprised too.

"I don't think it'll hold up in court," I advised him quietly. "If a tri-edged blade was recovered here and you had prints in the truck or in Jean Marie's car, it would be a slam dunk. But you don't, so it's not."

He looked at me directly.

"Then get a confession."

I was quickly reminded of one of those cases I had left open upon retiring—and why my head was no longer in the game—so I said:

"Pretty tough spot there, Chief. I mean, some good circumstantial evidence. But in my experience, not even close to enough for an arrest. If the baseball cap wasn't so common—"

Bill cut me off: "Graham, I understand what you're saying, but I want him in custody. There are identical murders in close proximity to where he used to live, and then what we have here shortly after he comes to town. He's good to go. I'll deal with the DA and see if we can at least get a 48-hour hold on him."

I had been in Gottert's position before. Not a good position to be in. I was under intense pressure from my commander to close that case I left open. It involved the murder of a city councilman's son. I had a good suspect, a shady witness, and some strong circumstantial evidence, but the AUSA I was working with said I needed more: "At the least another witness," he advised. I told my lieutenant, who in turn told the commander, who then came directly to me and ordered me to make the arrest: "Get a damn confession," he demanded.

It hadn't worked out so well. Pissed the hell out of the AUSA, for starters. He rolled with it, but as much as he tried, the case never even made it past the preliminary hearing. The suspect was released—and, so far as I know, is still out there. So this new chief's insistence on arresting a questionable suspect hit too close to home for me.

"Let's get him cuffed and out of here quick," Bill ordered. "King, you stand by at the station with him until we finish the search. Maybe we'll get lucky and find that knife, too."

"Copy that, Chief."

I waited in the hallway while Gottert and King entered the living room.

"We're placing you under arrest, Matthew," Gottert told him.

"What?" Matthew replied in disbelief.

The pastor stood up, faced Gottert.

"Are you joking, Investigator? What are you arresting him for?" He looked at his son. "Did you have drugs in your room, Matthew?"

"No, Dad," Matthew snapped back.

King helped Matthew up, had him turn around.

"Hands behind your back," King ordered.

Matthew did not respond, but he was not actively resisting arrest either.

"What are you arresting him for?" his father demanded.

"Sit down, Pastor," Bill advised him.

"Did he have drugs?" Pastor Simon pleaded. "Did he?"

"Sit down," Bill said again.

The pastor stared at him blankly before grudgingly sitting back down.

"There's absolutely nothing in this house," the pastor said with conviction.

King grabbed Matthew's right hand but not with great force, handcuffed it. Then he did likewise with his left hand.

"I'll get you a lawyer, son. Don't talk to them. Don't say a word."

Matthew gave his dad a strange, sad look, filled with either disbelief or quiet resignation. In all my years, I can honestly say I'd never seen an expression quite like it.

A small crowd (but no reporters, I was relieved to see) had gathered on the sidewalk outside the house. They watched as O'Born walked Matthew to King's cruiser.

We finished our search of the Simon home but recovered nothing else of value. This would be a tough one.

"We can play off each other," I said to Gottert on the drive back to the station. "It makes it seem more natural. Plus I'm not comfortable thinking I'm jumping in on you all the time."

"I'm good with that."

Back at the station, Gottert contacted the investigator with the Morsville PD. Although the investigator couldn't make the three-hour drive to Charontown on such short notice, he would arrange to question Matthew Simon in jail. Gottert told him that they would try to get a hold on him, and he'd be in touch later.

I watched Matthew on the monitor, seated in the interview room. The look on his face had changed to an odd, distant gaze. He sat erect in his chair, hands resting on thighs.

Good thing he didn't listen to his dad: After Gottert read him his rights and advised him what he was being charged with, the younger Simon didn't request a lawyer. He simply said, "I'm innocent."

36

Chasing the Wind

That's not my hat," Matthew said after Gottert showed him a digital picture of the cap in the closet.

I felt it was too soon to bring up the hat, but now we had to roll with it.

"Then it's your dad's?" Gottert questioned.

"I've never seen him wear it. In fact I've never seen him wear a ball cap at all. What's that cap got to do with anything?"

"What would you say if I told you we have surveillance footage of someone who looks a lot like you wearing this hat when Del Thomas was murdered?" Gottert told him.

Matthew, looking honestly confused, shook his head and said, "No. I'd say it's not me."

"Last time we talked, you said you didn't hang out with Del. Remember?" I brought up suddenly.

"I did."

"So why would your fingerprints be in his truck?"

I was taking a real chance with that one. Gottert himself looked surprised, but it was a risk I was willing to take. I worried the interview might end like the last one we'd had with Matthew in this same room, except this time he might lawyer up rather than walk out. That look he shot me after I asked about the prints told me everything I needed to know. Still, it'd be nice to hear it from him.

"Matthew?"

"I sat in his truck once in the parking lot before a meeting. I was just being friendly." He smiled indifferently. I found that odd.

"But last time you said you never hung out with Del. I'd consider sitting in his truck and being friendly as hanging out together, wouldn't you?"

"I thought at the time you meant like he was my friend or something. That's why I didn't mention it. It was no big deal."

"All the evidence against you is going to the prosecutor and then the judge," I advised him. "It doesn't look good for you. As you know, this is being recorded. Getting caught up in lies will hurt you even more."

"I'm not lying. I agreed to talk to you because I have nothing to hide. I just misunderstood what you meant by *hanging out* with Del."

I hated to admit it to myself, but in that moment I believed him. It wasn't looking good for him here, but something about him didn't fit the man in the surveillance footage. Also, most serial killers are pretty full of themselves. They love the chase just as much as we do. Matthew seemed too passive, but it could be a game. I've been fooled before, so we had to play this out. However, I sensed that getting a confession would be like chasing the wind.

"Let's back up a little bit," I began. "You've said you were home watching TV around the time Jean Marie was murdered, right?"

"Yeah."

"Now that right there is a prime example of you getting caught up in lies. It won't go well for you. I'm not going to beat around the bush, Matthew: We already know you were with Alice Winters."

That time he didn't look so confused. He knew he'd been caught.

"You talked to Alice?"

"Not only that, but there was a forensic search of your phone, and it sure as hell revealed a lot. Listen carefully: We might ask you questions we already know the answers to, so the best thing you can do for yourself is to be honest."

"Then I got my alibi, right?" he asked unemotionally. "I was with Alice."

That sort of turned me around from what I was previously thinking. The smug look he shot my way was not the same kid.

Had he been fooling me?

"Well, it doesn't really help with an alibi. Did you even hear what I said?" I looked at Gottert. "What did all the geolocation stuff reveal?"

"That Matthew did come home after his visit with Mrs. Winters, but then later that night he drove to the Birdhouse."

"Pretty damning. Did you go to the Birdhouse later that night to meet Jean Marie because you were depressed after Mrs. Winters broke up with you?"

"No. That never happened."

"You're lying. The evidence is all there. Your cell is synced to your car, so it showed us where you were. You want to try to clear it up? Now's your chance."

"Yes, Alice and I had something going. But it was tearing both of us up, because we both knew it was wrong. I was depressed when she broke it off with me. I went home and started getting bad thoughts about using. I obviously couldn't talk to Alice. The urges got really bad, and I just wanted to be numb, so I drove to the Birdhouse. I parked for the longest time, but never went in. I knew if I went in that it wouldn't end with just drinks: I'd find someone there who had what I needed. I didn't go, though. Go *in*, I mean. That's the truth."

"You knew Jean Marie would be there," I told him.

"That thought came up, but I didn't know for sure. If she was there and saw me this way—I mean, I didn't want her to, so I drove home."

"Why weren't you straight up with us from the beginning, then?" Gottert asked.

"Why do you think? I knew you wouldn't let me leave if I told you. I was scared to death. And look at me now."

What Matthew was saying would explain why he'd never materialized on the Birdhouse surveillance footage. But then, as Gottert had suggested before, maybe he'd simply waited in his car for Jean Marie to show.

"There's nothing I can say that will convince you that I didn't kill anyone, is there?"

"We're not your judges," I began. "But if it goes to trial, you'll have twelve people you can try to convince. Our job is to present the facts and circumstances."

"So the smartest thing for me to do is stop talking and get a lawyer."

"It's your choice," I said.

"I want a lawyer. My dad said he'd get me one."

And that was the end of that.

37
Little Monster

On the short drive home I remembered I had to call Ada to confirm our dinner tomorrow night. It was only about 7:30—not too late. I called her on the way. She was still good with it. I was freed up with helping Gottert out for the time being. He said he'd give me a call in the morning to let me know if Matthew had been held. I almost hoped he wouldn't be. I was fairly confident he was not the one we were looking for.

I floundered through the evening and went to bed early. I was startled out of sleep when it felt like someone—or some*thing*—had lightly brushed my forehead. Was it a dream? It felt so real.

I forgot to close the curtains, and the gentle moonlight seeping in through the windows admitted enough light for me to scan the room.

Something whooshed across my face. Noiseless.

I snapped up to a sitting position.

"What the fuck?"

I sat still, taking in the entire room, and spotted a small shadowy figure flitting erratically from one side of the room to the other.

Quiet and fast. *A bird makes noise,* I thought to myself. It didn't seem to hit anything, like it could see clearly. Then I realized it was a small bat.

I turned on the light on my nightstand; startled, the bat flew behind a curtain.

I hopped out of bed and dashed out the door, slamming it behind me to contain the damn thing.

Fucking bat! What the hell?

I'd never dealt with such a thing. I thought about calling Animal Control, but then realized my cell was in the bedroom, and the county department was probably closed anyway. *What time was it?* I wasn't about to go back in there to retrieve my cell; *don't bats carry rabies?* I had no choice but to wake Tommy up.

I knocked on his bedroom door and opened it.

"Hey, Tommy?"

He sat up in his bed.

"Graham?"

"Sorry, man, but there's a bat in my damn room and I don't know what to do."

"A bat?" he asked. He was still half-asleep.

"Yeah, a bat. Flying around the room. Hit me in the head and woke me up."

"We get bats in here on occasion. It's no big deal."

"It'll be one if it gives me rabies."

He chuckled, rolled out of bed, and stretched his arms.

"Did it attack you or bite you?"

"Like I said, it hit my head when I was sleeping. I didn't check if it bit me."

"I haven't gotten rabies yet, so I'm sure you'll be okay too."

He turned the light on. He was wearing flannel pajamas as though it was winter.

"What do we do?"

"I'll take care of it. Big-city cop afraid of bats." He snickered.

"Haven't you heard? There's no cure for rabies," I told him.

He walked up to me, studied my face, then combed my scalp with his fingers like he was hunting for lice.

"Nothing I can see on your face or your head. Let me see your arms."

I showed him. He grabbed my hands one at a time and looked everything over like it was a medical exam.

"Nothing. You're good."

"I've heard that their excrement, or saliva, or whatever it is can transmit rabies too."

"Big Brother, Dad and I survived countless bat encounters. They're usually cute little harmless things. Yeah, they carry diseases, so you don't go trying to grab one with your bare hands. But I got this — don't you worry yourself."

He moved around me, turned the hall light on, and opened a closet door. He stretched up and grabbed a medium-sized clear-plastic container from a shelf, then a thin piece of cardboard that looked cut to the size of the container opening.

"You'll be safe here," he teased.

"I think it flew behind the window curtain across from my bed."

Before he opened the door, he turned to me and said seriously, "If I'm not out in five minutes, call for backup."

"Shut the hell up."

A short time later he came out again, holding the cardboard in place over the top of the container. I could see the little creature inside through the plastic.

"I'm going to let it go on the deck."

"So it can get back in again?"

"I'm not going to kill this guy."

He walked up to me and held the container a bit too close to my face for comfort. I backed away.

"Look at him. See how cute he is? You really want him dead?"

"Little monster is what he is. How'd it get in?"

"They can slip through the tiniest opening, or down the chimney if the flue cap was left open. I'll check."

"What about the attic? Maybe there's a whole nest of them up there."

"Dad had the entire attic sealed. Nothing up there now but cobwebs. Damn, you're scared of a harmless little bat."

"Not the critter—only the disease it carries."

He brandished the container and said in a bad Dracula impression, "I vant to suck your blood!"

"I'm fucking sleeping on the couch," I told him.

Tommy laughed, and mocked me all the way down the stairs.

38
Something About the Walk

They got a three-day hold on Matthew. Gottert needed the morning to catch up on his other cases. I'd meet with him after I returned from Wegmans. He said he'd like to get my help figuring out how to strengthen the case they had on Matthew. I confided my doubts about him as a suspect. Gottert disagreed, saying all signs pointed to Matthew. We agreed to work it hard and see where it led—hopefully not to a cold case like those two victims in Morsville.

I wiped down the furniture in my bedroom, vacuumed the curtains and the floor, and changed my bedding. I didn't want to find anything related to the bat in my bedroom later. I took a long shower after.

It was clear to me that I'd have to find something to do to occupy myself once the volunteer work ended. Having nothing but my own thoughts to occupy me during the day was not a scenario I relished. I needed a hobby, but nothing I could think of appealed to me. Having Ada over for dinner, by contrast, definitely appealed to me. *Maybe I should take up cooking.*

I had a list of what Tommy needed from Wegmans for the dinner. He wanted to grill rib-eye steaks and zucchini and bake some fingerling potatoes with rosemary. Sounded good to me. I stopped by the liquor store after the grocer and picked up a bottle of whiskey, some bitters, and a bottle of sweet vermouth; I wanted to make Ada a proper Manhattan. I dropped everything off at home. Tommy came downstairs from work and insisted that he put it all away, so I headed to the station.

Gottert was on the computer in his office. The bags under his eyes were telling.

"How's it going?"

"All good. Just finishing up this report entry for a burglary while armed that occurred last night."

"At night? And they were home at the time?"

"Yeah. Just one guy lives there."

"I worked burglary when I first made detective. When someone's brazen enough to burglarize a house at night or at any time when the residents are home, they're either really desperate or it's something more."

"*Something more* like what?"

"I had a guy who would always stake out homes and hit the ones where single women lived. He'd rape them, then steal their jewelry after. Another guy was always armed with a gun: He'd hit a home, tie up the victims, and steal their bank cards, then threatened them into giving him the PIN numbers. *I'll be back if these numbers are fake,* he'd threaten them."

"Damn. You got them both?"

"Of course. What did your victim report?"

"He was asleep but woke to the sound of someone walking up the stairs. They were old, creaking stairs, he said, and he was a light sleeper. He went into his closet and got his shotgun. He opened his bedroom door to find the suspect at the top of the stairs, holding something 'sharp and shiny.' After he pointed the shotgun at him, the suspect ran down the stairs and escaped out the back door."

"He get a good look at him?"

"No, he said he was wearing a ski mask, a long-sleeved, plain-looking shirt, and gloves. The only good description he could give was that he was average build."

"How did he get in?"

"Open kitchen window."

"Anything missing?"

"Not that he could tell, but he told me he'd do a more thorough check today. Sergeant O'Born dusted for prints and all that, but probably just got the victim's prints. Nothing on the window or trim. No witnesses, no surveillance cameras—nothin'."

"And you've never had anything like that here before?"

"Never. We did have a robbery knife about six months ago at the liquor store, but that's it. He was arrested shortly after, though, and he had backup time, so he's still in jail."

"The victim have enemies or any threats?"

"I asked him that and he said he didn't. It's like our town is being plagued with violent crimes all of a sudden. Last thing we need now is some fucking sicko busting into homes while armed."

"And he didn't describe the weapon?"

"Not even that. His 'sharp and shiny' description made me assume it must have been something like a hunting knife. What are you thinking?"

"I don't know, but there's something more there. You might want to look harder at the victim."

"That's what I've been doing. I just started a background check on him."

"Need anything from me?"

"Not on this. Maybe get back on Matthew. I can give you access to one of the other computers and show you how to access the write-ups we have. Take it from there."

"Okay. I'd like to look at the surveillance footage for the pickup truck, too, if you can."

I followed Gottert to a vacant office. He logged into the computer and gave me a brief tutorial on how to get everything I needed, including how to run a suspect's name. It didn't give me access to NCIC or anything national. It was all local, but enough for me to work with for now.

I reread the running résumé for all the murder victims, then rewatched the surveillance footage of the suspect exiting Del's truck. I watched him emerge and walk out of frame several times. I was trying to picture him as Matthew, but somehow I couldn't—and I was at a loss to explain why not. There was something about the way he moved. Walked. Nothing so distinctive as to identify him; it was just an unsettling feeling I had.

I spent most of my time looking into the victims, including the two cold cases from Morsville. The three victims from Charontown had more in common, but the only thing all five of them shared was a criminal history. Morsville was three hours from Pottstown. If Matthew was the killer, why would he have traveled all the way there to murder those two?

Despite my misgivings, I longed to throw the names of the two Morsville victims at Matthew once we had him in the box, just for shits and giggles.

39

Sit-Down with the Pastor

Pastor Simon showed up at the station a few minutes before I had to leave. I'd been hoping to get out of there by 4 p.m. so I could grab a shower and get things ready for Ada's visit. Sergeant O'Born answered the buzzer, came into Gottert's office, and told me the pastor wanted to talk to me. I found that odd, so I asked him point-blank: "Why *me?*"

"He didn't say," O'Born reported. "Just that he wanted to see you."

"He probably figures he has a connection with you because of your dad," Gottert said.

"He didn't know my dad. He just buried him. But you're probably sort of right, because my dad was a member of his church. He's more than likely ferreting out information. I'll be diplomatic, but not too forthcoming."

"You can use the community room," Gottert said.

O'Born showed Pastor Simon into the room. I let him sit there and stew for a couple of minutes before I entered.

He stood from the chair he was sitting on, extended his hand to greet me. I offered mine.

"Graham, thank you for seeing me."

"Of course, Pastor."

"Can we sit? I'm still a little shaken."

"Please."

I sat in a chair across from him.

"What can I do for you?"

"Is my son being held here? I tried calling, but each time it just went to voicemail."

"They're short-staffed and they don't have overnight cells, so he was taken to the Sheriff's outside of town."

"Have you seen him?"

"Only when he was first arrested."

"So you interrogated him?"

"I wouldn't call it that."

"What did he say to you?"

That was peculiar.

"Matthew is a very sensitive young man," he continued. "But he can also act very distant at times, especially when he's frightened. It's how he copes. What I mean to say is—he can sometimes come across as uncaring when he gets that way. I don't want you to get the wrong impression of him."

"Pastor, I know how hard this must be for you, but I'm only a volunteer here. I have no say in the investigation."

"But you're assisting that young investigator, aren't you? Because of your experience?"

"I'm helping out however I can."

"My son is not a murderer. I'd like to know what evidence you have?" he asked directly. "I *have* to know."

"That's something you should ask his lawyer. I'm not trying to be difficult here, but that's not something I can share with you."

"Matthew has gone through some very tough times in his life. He should not be in jail. He should be home with me."

Did he realize the extent of the charges against his son?

"I was sorry to hear that he lost his mother. He said she had liver disease."

"He said that?" He acted surprised.

"Yes. Was that not how she passed?"

"It was." He seemed reluctant, but then continued with: "She was an alcoholic. Unfortunately, Matthew inherited . . ." He shook his head slowly, like he couldn't find the words or had decided against finishing the thought. "He's been sober for a number of years, now back to his church home and faithfully seeking God again. He is not what you think, and whatever evidence there is has to be wrong. This is a mistake. A very serious mistake."

"He said you were getting him a lawyer."

"Yes. A member of the church is a very good lawyer. His offices are in Rochester."

"That's good. So you've talked to the lawyer?"

"Yes, he should have seen Matthew by now and is supposed to get back to me by the end of the day. I assumed I would find Matthew here, though. I don't know why I came to see you. I was just hoping . . ." He shook his head in the same manner as before. "God is merciful."

I had nothing to say to that.

"I know you understand what it's like to lose your wife," he told me sincerely. "I don't want to lose my son, too."

He stood from the chair, rested his palms on the table, and looked at me directly.

"The Lord is just." He straightened himself up. "I'm sorry."

I stood.

"Make sure Matthew doesn't leave town when he gets out."

"He has no place to go. He's safe with me."

40

The Urn

Ada brought a box of goodies from her bakery and offered them to Tommy.

"Great to finally meet you," she told him.

"Likewise," he returned, opening the box to take a peek. "Wow."

"Guinness chocolate cupcakes."

They had white creamy frosting.

"They look wonderful," I said.

"I know Graham likes Guinness. Hope you do too."

"Definitely," he lied and made a smile. "I'll keep these safe in the kitchen."

He walked out.

"You look very lovely," I told her.

"You do too."

She leaned into me, and we kissed. A short kiss, but nice.

I gave her a quick tour of the house, including a glance through the open door into my bedroom. The urn was not visible from where we were standing. That was good, because I didn't want to have to explain it. We went back to the kitchen. The box of cupcakes was on the center island. I made her a Manhattan.

"Mmm."

"It passes inspection, then?"

"Yes. Thank you."

I poured myself a scotch on the rocks and we went out to the deck, where Tommy was dumping pellets into the grill's bin.

"Hickory," he told us.

"I can't wait," Ada said.

"I like to get the Traeger going for a little while before putting everything in. Build up the smoke."

"Thank you so much for cooking, Tommy. Graham says you're a master on the grill."

"I wouldn't go that far," he said seriously, then sealed what was left of the pellets in the bag and placed them in the storage bin on the deck.

He sat on his rocker, lifted his beer toward us.

"New friendship," he toasted.

"Cheers to that," I returned.

"Cheers," Ada added.

We sipped our drinks in unison. Tommy came out with a long "Ahh" after.

"I always loved what Dad brought back from your bakery. It was sort of a weekly tradition here."

"That makes me happy. I'm glad I got to know your father. He was an interesting man."

"He is," said Tommy, as though Dad was still with us.

"This is a lovely place you have here."

"It is nice," I agreed. "It's growing on me."

"Well, that's a good thing," Ada came back.

"Yeah, it's your home now too," Tommy said.

"I guess it is."

"I should get the meat up to room temperature," Tommy said, standing from his rocker. "Be right back."

We sat silently for a moment. A comfortable silence. That was a good sign.

"It's so peaceful," Ada said, looking out over the pasture.

"Yes. It's become something of a morning and evening thing for us too."

"Better than television."

We had dinner in the dining room. That was the first time for me since moving in. The last time was a few years ago when I was visiting. Our dad loved having dinner at the dining-room table. He was a quiet man around us but would on occasion get caught up in good conversation. Mostly about current events.

Ada was a good conversationalist herself. I enjoyed hearing her talk, and most of my responses were more questions in an effort to get to know her better.

"What's going on with the investigation?" Tommy asked during a comfortable pause in the conversation.

Didn't he know an arrest had been made?

"Trudging along," was all I said. It was the last thing I wanted to talk about.

"I heard there was an arrest made," said Ada.

"Yes—they have someone in custody. Still a lot of work to do, though."

I looked at Ada with a tilt of my head and an uncertain smile. She smiled like she understood.

"The steak is wonderful, Tommy. The smoke flavor really does make it."

"Thanks—it's the only way to cook, as far as I'm concerned."

Tommy was the perfect cohost. He cleaned up after dinner,

brought the box of cupcakes out with dessert plates. Even refreshed our drinks. He had two cupcakes, then said he was going to his room to read. He gave Ada a quick hug and was off. Ada and I went back to the deck, sat and watched the sun go down. Our second sunset together. I was sentimental that way. I was also a bit buzzed.

I should have stopped after the last drink. I had never been much of a drinker. Ada was nursing her third Manhattan when I poured my fourth scotch on the rocks. I hoped I wasn't giving her the wrong impression. At least I wasn't staggering or slurring my words.

Ada and I were cuddling on the living room sofa by the end of the night. We kissed. A lot. It stirred me inside. Hadn't felt that in a bit. I didn't want to look at the time, but I knew it was late. I didn't want the night to end. I wanted her to stay, but I feared what would happen. I'd had too much to drink, so it just didn't feel appropriate. Last thing I wanted to do was rush into it; the timing had to be right. I was thinking too fucking much.

"Can you stay?" I asked quietly after we kissed.

She didn't answer right away. That worried me, but then she didn't look away from me either.

"We've both had a lot to drink," she said softly.

"I know. I'm sorry. I don't usually drink this much."

"You're cute when you're tipsy, though."

"Don't get used to it. Stay. You shouldn't drive anyway. I'll sleep on the sofa."

That smile.

"We could just cuddle in bed. Fall asleep together. Wake up together." She kissed me lightly on the lips.

"That would be lovely."

We headed for my bedroom, sneaking past Tommy's closed door like guilty teenagers. When we got to the room she asked for a T-shirt. I pulled one out of the dresser, along with another for myself (I didn't want to sleep in the polo shirt I was wearing). I felt shy as I stripped down to my boxers and put on the T-shirt. I got in bed first, then watched Ada slipping on the T-shirt. A beautiful body. She got into bed, slid close to me. I rolled to turn off the light on my nightstand.

"That's a gorgeous vase on your nightstand. Was it your dad's?"

I didn't think of moving it before because I hadn't expected her to stay the night. It made me feel remorseful again.

"No. It's actually an urn. I hope that doesn't alarm you."

"Oh—your wife's ashes."

"Yes. I've always kept it beside my bed. I'm used to it being there now."

"You keep her memory beside you. That's adorable. Why doesn't it have a top?"

"She had claustrophobia," I said. I was trying to hold back a chuckle, but it came out sounding more like a feeble grunt.

"That's sweet."

"I'm not some kinda weirdo," I said with what I hoped was a sincere smile.

"I know."

"Do you want me to move it?"

"Of course not."

I cradled her head under my arm, and she tucked it into me. I kissed her gently on the mouth. I felt good with her there.

"Sweet dreams, Ada."

"You too, Graham."

Except mine weren't so sweet.

I dreamed I was on the job, working a shooting with my first partner, John Beverly. (He passed away a couple of years ago—bad heart.) John was tall and thin, with red hair and freckles, and I had never seen him without some kind of smile. He was not the kind of guy to go looking for trouble, but this dream version of John Beverly was definitely on the hunt for some. I knew someone would die by his hand. I stuck by him anyway. We were on the lookout for a suspect when I suddenly found the two of us in Charontown, standing before the pastor's house.

John kicked in the door, and we stormed in with our handguns drawn. Pastor Simon and Matthew were sitting on the sofa in the living room. They didn't say a word, just looked up at us as if expecting our presence. John opened up on them. I tried to shoot too, but my gun jammed.

Their bullet-ridden bodies sat there, heads slumped over as if in prayer. Vivid red blood oozed out like slime.

John turned to me and said, "*That's* how it should be."

I woke up.

My head was pounding.

It took me a second to remember that Ada was in bed with me. She was sleeping peacefully. I quietly rolled out of bed and went to the bathroom for a couple of ibuprofens, then returned and just as silently slipped back into bed.

I don't remember falling back asleep again. I woke up to the sound of my cell phone ringing.

Ada did too.

"I thought I had muted that," I mumbled. "Sorry."

"It's okay," she said.

I picked up the cell. It was Bill. The time was 6:30.

"I need to take this," I told her.

I answered.

Wished I hadn't.

"There's been another murder," said Bill on the other end.

41
The Apple Orchard

Henry Flood's body was under an apple tree at the Charontown Orchard. It was a family-owned farm. The eldest son found him. His upper body rested against the trunk of an apple tree, positioned in a way that made him look like he was napping. That is what the farmer's son thought he was doing when he approached the body from the side.

That was before he saw the blood-soaked T-shirt.

Gottert lifted up the T-shirt, revealing four small puncture wounds.

"Shit," I said, recognizing the body as my brother's ex-partner.

"Just like the others," he told me. "And he wasn't killed here. No other trace of blood around him."

"The kid has an accomplice," Bill said with certainty.

"But the entire town knows that an arrest was made in the case," I objected. "So why kill again now, unless Matthew Simon *does* have an accomplice, and they're trying to throw us off his trail? Or maybe Matthew is innocent, and the guilty party is just playing with us."

"In all my years in law enforcement," Bill observed, "I've never been involved in anything like this."

I knew Gottert would soon have to talk to Tommy, but all I could think about in that moment was how I was going to break the news of his ex-partner's death to my brother. In my head I prayed to the God I was angry with that Tommy had nothing to do with any of this.

It was something of a hollow prayer, of course: Tommy and Henry had broken up only recently, so that made him a prime suspect. No way around that.

Officer King was standing in the road, attaching crime-scene tape to three orange cones and blocking a portion of the lane. King had to remain on post to divert the occasional passing vehicle. A state trooper was helping him. She'd heard the call go out and came to assist.

The farmer's son was in his truck, parked along the road ahead of the yellow tape. The ambulance was in front of his truck. My car was on the other side of the two-lane road.

Bill notified Sergeant O'Born. He was on his way to the scene.

"Looks like he was dragged from a vehicle parked beside the road. You can see the path through the dirt and weeds," I advised. "Need to make sure no one walks over any possible evidence or tread marks."

"I'll tell them up there," Bill said. "I should go interview the son, too."

He exhaled, long and heavy. I felt like doing the same.

I had to tell Gottert. I could not keep something like this to myself. He was crouched down, looking at the body as if he expected it to speak to him.

"I need to have a word with you, Mike," I said.

He looked up at me. Snapped out of wherever he was.

"Yeah, of course."

He stood up and faced me.

"This man here was a friend of my brother's. They were close—very close."

"Damn."

"I don't know if Bill—if the chief ever told you, but Tommy has PTSD. He also happens to be agoraphobic."

"I knew about his agoraphobia. I didn't know about the other."

"This is going to hit him hard. I know you'll eventually have to talk to him, but let me tell him about Henry's death first, as soon as I get home. Plus I have to ask you if that conversation can wait until tomorrow."

"I don't think that'll be a problem."

Had I been more truthful with Gottert, I was sure it *would* have been a problem: I was sitting on the information that Henry Flood had been my brother's long-term boyfriend until their recent breakup. But I urgently needed to talk to Tommy first: I wanted to get his story and see how he reacted after I broke the news to him.

"Thanks. I'll tell the chief too."

"Did you know Henry?"

"No. I knew *of* him through my brother, but we had never met."

"Okay." He looked back at the body. "This is so fucked up."

"It is. This is also the first one that looks like the body was staged, propped against the tree like that. The others looked like they had simply been dropped callously where they were found."

"Like he wanted this one to be comfortable."

"I don't know what the hell it all means," I admitted. "Not yet, anyway."

"You really think Matthew could have an accomplice? It's either that or he's not even fucking involved, and we shouldn't have locked him up."

"Granted," I told Gottert. "But as bad as this sounds, locking him up revealed he had nothing to do with this murder."

"That's pretty fucked up. All the circumstantial evidence points to Matthew Simon: The two murders in Morsville, a few hours from where they used to live; his connections to the victims, through the NA meetings held at his father's church; the love affair and incriminating geolocations we found on his cell; and finally his car being in the area of the Birdhouse around the time when Jean Marie was murdered."

"Maybe the poor kid is just fucking unlucky. I honestly don't know what the hell to think. We sure as shit need to talk to his dad again, though."

"You're not thinking the pastor was involved?"

"Like I said, I don't know what to think."

Being hungover might have had something to do with it, too.

"Remember Matthew telling us the first time we interviewed him that he didn't have any friends here?" I asked.

"Yeah."

"Well, I think we should take another look at that too. See what the pastor has to say about it. I gotta tell ya, man—something about that surveillance photo still gets to me."

"You think it's someone else, don't you?"

"Yeah, I do. I'm gonna walk the scene."

"Fuck me."

There was no blood anywhere that I could see, except on Henry's shirt. I walked slowly along the path down which it appeared the body had been dragged; that one action had wiped away any footprints that might have been left. I could see where Henry's heels had dug into the ground. I confirmed it when I returned to the body.

"Lift his feet and look at the heels of his shoes," I asked Gottert.

He lifted the right foot.

"Dirt caked on from being dragged or something."

He lifted the left foot, and it was the same.

We both walked the edge of the area where he had been dragged and worked our way up to the road.

No tread marks or footprints along the dirt before the pavement.

"It doesn't look like he was dragged across this area," Gottert said.

"No—probably carried from a vehicle to the edge over there and set down. See this—"

I pointed to an area of the dirt that looked disturbed, as if something—footprints, maybe?—had been brushed away.

"Looks like he tried to cover his tracks here," Gottert said.

"Yeah. The suspect would have left footprints because of the weight of carrying Henry's body."

We scanned the area and then walked around some more. I could not find anything like a tree branch that might have been used as a broom, and the only trees in the vicinity were medium-sized apple trees; their branches were unlikely to fall this close to the road. Even had I found the branch, fingerprints could not be recovered from something so rough and porous.

"He may have used something from inside the vehicle," I suggested, "like a windshield brush for snow. This scene is clean.

"I'm going to have to roll out—talk to my brother before he hears about this on social media."

"I understand. I'll be here until we clear the scene."

"This shouldn't take long."

Time heals all wounds. What idiot said that? Time doesn't heal anything—it only allows the wounds to fester.

Tommy, for example—despite the passage of time, he never healed. Time had merely turned him into something else. Hopefully, that *something else* was not a monster.

42

Tommy Comes Clean

He cried after I told him. His tears seemed genuine.

When he had calmed down a bit, I said, "Tommy, the investigator is going to come over and talk to you tomorrow. I told him that you and Henry were friends, but I didn't say anything else about your relationship."

"Why? Are you ashamed of me?"

"Not at all. If I had told him you two were partners, he would have had to come here right away. The significant other is always a suspect."

"How the hell could I be a suspect? Tele-fucking-portation?!"

"You and I have to talk. That's why I broke away to come here."

"I don't have anything to hide."

I've heard that so many times. I can't count the number of times I've heard that.

"I also wanted to be the one to tell you first."

"How did he die?"

"Murdered. In the same manner as the other three victims."

"Oh, dear God. You don't think I possibly had anything to do with this? I mean how could I? And I thought someone was locked up for it. Did he get out?"

"No. I have questions, though. Some of the questions I have will also be asked by Investigator Gottert. One in particular won't, because I'm the only one who knows."

"What are you talking about?"

"A few days ago I saw you drive Dad's car off the property around two in the morning."

At first he looked confused. Then he wagged his head with an awkward grin, but not as though he'd been caught. His expression was more like *incredulous.*

"No you didn't."

"I did, Tommy. I'm not making this shit up."

"You could not have seen me drive off the property because I never did drive off the property. But you might have thought I did."

"I saw you open the garage door, Tommy. And I saw you drive the car out and leave the property."

"No you did not." He was adamant. "I'm not denying the first part. You just didn't see me drive off the property. I did drive to the road, but I never left. I tried hard to, but I couldn't make myself do it. I wanted to do it for Henry." His eyes teared up again. "But I fucking couldn't. I just parked there at the end of our driveway, like a sick, weak man. If you had kept watching, you'd know that's all I did. I don't even know for how long. I should've been able to leave—for him."

I didn't know what to say; because the trees *had* in fact obstructed my view. More than anything, I wanted to believe my brother.

"I've been doing that for a while. A couple of months at least. I can never bring myself to leave the driveway, though. I simply can't find the courage. I'm telling you the truth. I loved Henry, but I guess not enough to change who I am — who I've become."

"I'm sorry. I honestly thought you left and drove away. There's no reason for Gottert to know all this. I won't bring it up — and you don't either, all right?"

"I won't."

"Was it a bad breakup you two had?"

"Like how? If we fought?"

"Yeah — and was it in person or over the phone?"

"Sounds like you're interrogating me."

"These are questions that you will be asked. I'm trying to help you out here."

"I don't need your help, because I didn't do anything. For God's sake, I just lost the man I loved!"

"I know that, and I'm so sorry. But we still need to talk. Did you break up in person?"

"It was in person. When Dad was in the hospital. I didn't want to. I told Henry that the therapy was helping me, and I asked him to be patient. But he just couldn't anymore; he'd had enough. Plus I strongly believed he'd met someone else."

"Do you know who that might have been?"

"I have no idea. He had a lot of friends. He was social, unlike me."

"Are there any texts or anything on social media that might not look good? Between the two of you, I mean?"

"I texted him a few times after. Told him I loved him. Nothing bad, though. I can't believe this is happening."

"It'll be okay. Just be truthful and you'll have nothing to worry about. What friends do the two of you have in common?"

"Graham, I already told you: I don't have any other friends. Just Henry and Dad."

"He had to talk about his friends, right?"

"Yeah, but not in a long time. I friended a couple of them on Facebook, but we don't talk or message. I might like an occasional post, and so will they."

"Give me their names and whatever contact info you have for them."

"Okay."

My cell rang. I saw on the screen that it was Ada. Probably checking on how everything was going. I silenced the ring and let it go to message.

"You have to get that."

"It was Ada. I'll call her later. Did you know the pastor's son, Matthew?"

"No—but didn't you ask me that already?"

"I can't remember. Maybe. Did Henry ever mention that he was having problems of any kind?"

"No. Well, just with me; I guess I was the only problem in his life. This town has never had anything like this happen. Do you think I'm in danger too?"

"No," I said in a bid to comfort him. But I wasn't altogether sure.

What I *was* certain of, however, was that Tommy had nothing to do with Henry's murder. Still, I knew that he would be looked at—and looked at hard: Investigator Gottert might've been a rookie, but he wasn't stupid. Unfortunately, Tommy was the Boo Radley of this small town. He wasn't a murderer like they thought, but the image of the character was enough to stir the town up.

When I got in the car, I listened to the message that a concerned Ada had left for me. As I'd thought, she was simply just checking in with me. I texted her that everything was okay, and that I would talk to her later. She texted back with a heart emoji after I started the car.

I arrived at the police station parking lot to find the media out in full force. There was even a reporter there from *The New York Times*. Four murders in a small town was becoming a big story—not something we wanted to happen.

Family members were in attendance too. I recognized the mother of Jean Marie Evans; she was being interviewed by one of the reporters.

I gave Gottert the names of the Facebook friends that Tommy had confided to me. He scanned the list and said in a surprised voice, "Samuel Alvez?"

"You know him?" I asked.

"Yeah. He's the guy who reported the burglary the other night."

"That's pretty damn interesting. We need to talk to him."

43
The Knife

Henry Flood lived alone. We had recovered his wallet and cell phone from his person, as well as a laptop, some mail, and a couple of photos from his home that showed just him. His pay stub indicated he worked as an engineer for a company in Rochester. We also found several letters from his mother, who lived in San Pedro, California. Gottert would have to contact the jurisdiction there so they could make the unfortunate notification in person.

He appeared to have led a decent life. Nothing we found revealed his relationship with Tommy. Possibly got rid of all that after the breakup, but maybe the cell and the laptop would show more.

We made our way back to the station and through the menagerie that was the news media and their barrage of questions. After Gottert logged Henry's belongings into the system, we headed back out and drove around for a while to shake any reporters off our tail. We then made our way across town to the home of Samuel Alvez. He lived in an old but well-kept Victorian, with a large assortment of colorful flowers planted in front and in nice ceramic pots on the patio. A newer-model Toyota SUV sat in the driveway.

Alvez answered the door. He appeared to be in his late 30s, with wide eyes and a small nose that didn't seem to fit his very round face. His thick hair was black and shiny.

"Investigator Gottert," he said with no surprise.

"Mr. Alvez. How are you? May we come in and talk?"

"I'm working from home today, but of course."

We entered.

"This is Graham Sanderson. He's working with me."

"Nice to meet you, sir."

"Good to meet you."

"Do you have some news for me?"

"Unfortunately, we're here on another matter, but we'd like to talk about the burglary too."

"Sounds serious. Come into the living room."

We followed him.

"Have a seat on the sofa."

A fat, furry cat entered from the hallway, sat on the area carpet, and stared at us point-blank.

"That's George."

"Big boy," I said.

"He likes to stare. He's a little slow. What brings you here, then?"

"We got information that you were friends with Henry Flood."

"I am. Yes. Why would you ask that?"

"I'm sorry to say, Mr. Alvez, that he was murdered."

"He was what?"

"He was murdered sometime last night. I'm so sorry."

"That can't be. It can't be—I just saw him last night."

"What time did you see him?" Gottert asked.

"He was here for dinner and left at a little after nine. He went straight home."

"Did you talk to him when he got home?"

"No."

"And he didn't say that he was stopping somewhere on the way?"

"No. No. He said he was going home. He had to get up early. It can't be Henry. It just can't be."

Gottert produced a photograph taken from Henry's home that showed him on a beach somewhere. He handed it to Alvez.

"Oh no. No." He cradled his head and gushed tears.

His anguish and the staring cat made me uncomfortable.

Gottert gave him a minute, then said, "As difficult as this is, we have to ask you some questions."

"Oh my God." Alvez looked up at us. "How did this happen?"

"We're looking into that," Gottert said.

"You were close?" I asked.

"Yes," he stammered. "We were very close."

"Where was that photo taken?" I continued.

"California. His mom took it."

"How long have you known him?" Gottert asked.

"Only a couple of months. I moved here from New York City for work five months ago. Henry worked there too."

"Samuel," I asked, "what was your relationship with Henry?"

"We fell in love," he said through his tears.

Damn—he was the one Henry had left Tommy for.

"What did you do after he left your home?" Gottert questioned.

"I was tired. I went to bed. Do you know who did this?"

"Not yet," Gottert said.

"Did he suffer?"

"I don't think he did."

"Does it have anything to do with all these other murders?"

"We think they may be connected."

"Did the person who was arrested get out of jail or something?"

"He was held, but we won't have an exact time of death until there's an autopsy," Gottert lied.

We knew that Henry Flood had been murdered within a few hours of leaving Alvez's house—a time when Matthew Simon was still in jail. But Gottert was right not to reveal too much yet.

"So he could have done it before he was arrested?" Alvez speculated.

"We can't answer that yet," I said. I was afraid to ask, but I had to: "Did Henry have problems with anyone that you know of?"

It took Alvez a minute and some more tears, but then he said, "He had a hard breakup with someone he had been seeing for a while, but he didn't act worried or anything."

"Was there physical violence?" Gottert asked.

"No, nothing like that. I never met the guy in person, but we friended each other on Facebook after I met Henry. He had a lot of problems, but nothing Henry ever said he was worried about. He had agoraphobia and couldn't leave his home. Henry had a hard time with all that—it was the main reason they broke up. Well, actually because he met me, too. But if you're thinking it's him, am I in danger too? I mean, the man who broke in here had a knife. Was that who Henry broke up with?"

Gottert looked at me. I couldn't read him, but it didn't look good.

"We don't know yet. What was this person's name?" Gottert asked, but I knew he already knew.

"I just knew him as Tommy."

"And when was the last time he and Henry saw each other?" Gottert questioned.

"I'm not sure."

"Did Henry mention anyone else he might have had problems with?" I asked hopefully. "Or anyone new who came around?"

"No."

"Do you know anyone by the name of *Matthew*?"

"No. Who is that?"

"Henry never mentioned anyone by that name?"

"No, he didn't."

"I'd like to ask you a couple more questions about the burglary you reported, if you don't mind. Investigator Gottert may have asked these already, but it's just for me since I'm helping out here."

"Okay."

"Was there anything about the intruder that stood out? Anything at all, no matter how small it is?"

Samuel Alvez looked like he was thinking hard. My eyes shifted to that damned cat again, just sitting there. I wanted to kick him to the wall.

"He wore dark clothing, gloves, and a ski mask. I just don't know."

"You reported to Investigator Gottert that he had a knife."

"Yes."

"Can you describe the knife?"

"It was so quick. I only remember that it looked long and skinny and sharp."

"Skinny?" I asked. "You mean like the blade was skinny?"

"Yeah, but like circular and skinny."

Well, that just took a turn.

44

A Sit-Down with the Chief

On our way to meet with Bill at his office, Gottert asked:

"Did you know your brother was in a relationship with the decedent?"

"Yes, but I didn't know until recently that he had broken it off with him. I was going to tell you."

"Don't you think that's something I should have known right away?"

"My brother is not capable of murder. He can't even leave the house, so no—I did *not* think it was urgent."

"You know how this looks, right?"

"If this was DC or even Rochester, with a population of a few hundred thousand people, then it would not look good at all. But Charontown is a very small community, where everyone seems to be connected to almost everyone else in one way or another. I should have told you right away, but I had to be the one to tell Tommy myself about Henry's murder. I needed to see his reaction. I know it's hard to understand."

"You wanted to see his reaction because you thought your brother might have killed Henry Flood?"

"I didn't think or believe that at all. But I'm still a detective, even though I am retired. Our brains work differently than others, brother. And I was forthcoming with you right away about Tommy knowing Henry."

"But not that they were in a relationship! And that the decedent had broken up with him! Look—I understand that you want to protect your brother. But how do I know you didn't work with him on what to say when questioned? Or even help him dispose of evidence?"

"Don't be ridiculous. I planned on telling you today, but I never expected you'd find out like this. I told Tommy he would be questioned, and I urged him to tell you the truth—and believe me, he will. These murders were committed by a psychopathic serial killer or killers, and despite my brother's problems he is far from that. And think about it: If Henry Flood was the primary target all along, and the three before him were murdered to fool us into thinking that Henry was just another one of the serial killer's victims, why would Tommy be stupid enough to kill him when he knew you had already made an arrest?"

"Fucking reporters." Gottert had just turned onto the street that was home to the station, and we saw right away that the parking lot was still swarming with media.

They ran up and followed us to the front door, bombarding us with questions.

Inside, we found Bill Finn at his desk.

"Have a seat."

Gottert gave him a rundown. Bill looked truly surprised when he learned of Tommy and Henry's involvement. I believe Bill had no idea my brother was gay. I advised him in a nutshell what I had told

Gottert in the car. When I had finished, he slowly nodded his head without a word.

"We need to bring him in for questioning, Chief."

I jumped in right away: "You cannot drag him out of that house. He has not left home in years. He was diagnosed by a psychiatrist and is on medication for severe anxiety disorder and agoraphobia.

"Listen, if I believed he could do something like this, I'd be right there with you when you cuff him. All my brother is at this point is someone who was connected to a single victim, so please just conduct the interview at our home."

"I knew your father for several years," Bill replied, "and during that time I had many conversations with him about Tommy's agoraphobia and his PTSD." He turned to Gottert. "I see no problem with interviewing him at home."

"Copy, Chief."

"Thank you, Chief. If you want me to step out of this investigation, I'll totally understand."

"Right now, I think it'd be wise to just step out of the interview with your brother."

"Of course."

We left the office.

"It's a nice day for a drive," I said. "Can you call me when you're done?"

"Yeah, I'll call."

"Mike."

He stopped and turned to me.

"I should have told you right away. There was no ill intention."

"I believe ya, brother."

It was a short drive, because I decided to drop by Sweet Tooth to see Ada and grab a coffee.

There were no customers in the bakery when I entered. Ada was behind the counter.

"Hey there." She waved.

"Hi. Thought I'd drop by instead of calling."

"It's a good time. I'm not busy right now."

She came from behind the counter and planted me with a kiss.

"I need a strong cup of coffee, too."

"Have a seat. I'll join you."

She brought over two cups of coffee and set them down on the table.

"Be right back," she said and walked into the room behind the counter.

She returned with something that looked tasty on a plate.

"Just made these."

"Cinnamon buns. They look delicious."

"Apple cinnamon."

She sat.

I took a bite.

"Yes. Delicious."

"Can you talk about what's going on?" she asked.

"It's not good. Another murder."

"Oh no. I thought someone was arrested?"

"Someone was. I've never had anything like this my whole career. It's insane. Even worse, the man that was killed was very close to Tommy."

"That's terrible. Is Tommy okay?"

"He took it hard. The investigator is questioning him."

"Why aren't you there?"

"It's best that he do this without me. I'm too close."

"Are you okay?"

"I am now—I think."

45

Anonymous Tip

I left the bakery and drove around for about an hour. I was getting worried that I had not yet heard back from either Gottert or Tommy.

My cell rang as I was on my way back. It was Bill Finn. He asked that I respond to my house. He'd explain when I got there.

When I pulled in the driveway I noticed a marked unit and Bill's cruiser parked in front of the garage. Gottert's car was nowhere to be seen.

"What the fuck?" I mumbled.

I parked along the driveway and stepped out. Sergeant Jimmy O'Born got out of the driver's side of the marked unit and started walking toward me.

"I got a call from the chief," I told him. "But what are you doing here?"

"The chief is in the house with Officer King and your brother," was all he would say.

"Did something happen to my brother?" I was beginning to panic.

"No. They're sitting inside."

I knew something was wrong. As I hoofed it toward the house, O'Born called me back.

"Hold on there, Sanderson."

I stopped and faced him.

"Are you carrying?"

"*Carrying*? What the hell you talking about?"

"Gun. Are you armed?"

"Why would that matter? What's going on here?"

"You can talk to the chief, but before you enter I need to make sure you're not carrying a weapon."

"What the fuck, O'Born? This is my house, and you're on my property."

He approached me, but not in a threatening way.

"For our safety and yours. You should know that."

That's when I knew Tommy was in trouble.

"You need to pat me the fuck down on my own property, and you won't even tell me what's going on?!"

"I assumed the chief did when he called you."

"No, he didn't. So do whatever you have to do, and let me go see my brother."

He patted me down.

"Am I good to go?"

"Yes. Just doing my job. It's nothing personal."

I didn't respond to that. Instead I just walked to the front door and went in.

Bill and Dana King were seated on armchairs; Tommy was on the sofa. Tommy saw me first and said, "Graham, I don't understand this."

He was not in handcuffs. He looked like some kind of lost child.

King stood up.

"What's going on?" I demanded.

Bill looked concerned. He stood and approached me.

"Can we talk in another room?" he asked quietly.

"Tommy, you okay?"

"I, I . . ." he stuttered. "I don't . . . I don't understand anything about this, Graham," he muttered.

"We need to talk, Graham," the chief said sincerely. "*Please.*"

I looked at Tommy again. He did not look good. No injuries that I could see, but he did not appear to be in a good place mentally.

"I'll be right back, Tommy. Let me find out what's going on." I looked at the chief, hard. "The kitchen," I commanded.

We walked to the kitchen.

"Can we sit?" he asked.

I pulled out the two stools from under the center island. I sat. He scooted the other stool toward him and sat to my right.

"What the hell *is* all this, Bill? Did Tommy have some sort of breakdown?"

"No, no. But please understand: I have to go by the book on this one."

"Just talk."

"I'm going to be straight with you, so I'll expect the same consideration in return. As Gottert was interviewing your brother, we received an anonymous tip on the tip line. The caller said an older-model black Ford Explorer—much like the one your dad used to drive—was seen in front of Henry Flood's home on the night of the murder. The tipster also said Flood was observed entering the car's passenger side."

"A lot of cars would match that description around here."

"Let me finish. As the car drove off, the witness saw a bumper sticker on the rear: BACK OFF. I'M RETIRED."

I didn't respond, because I knew that was not good.

"I have personally seen that on the back of your dad's car before. I called Gottert immediately and told him. Tommy gave him permission to look at your father's car parked in the garage."

Chief Finn paused, but not for effect. He was truly troubled.

"When Gottert walked to the back of the car, he observed through the rear window what appeared to be blood smear on the floor mat."

"Fresh blood?"

"Dried blood. Caked."

"Okay, my dad used to hunt."

That was all I could say, because I had no explanation for the car being seen at Henry's home.

"Gottert's getting a search warrant for the car as we speak. I've already spoken to the state police; they'll put the swab along with a sample of the decedent's blood through their crime lab for analysis. Another big favor, and it won't take long at all. I'm afraid it's not looking good for Tommy, Graham."

"This can't be. It just can't be true. Tommy's not capable of murder. What did Tommy say about the car being parked in front of Henry's house?"

"He said it was impossible, and that he did not ever drive the car there. He doesn't know how it could've been seen there."

"What about the blood?"

"He told us he's never seen anything resembling blood in the vehicle."

That's when I started to worry. Bill must have read it in my expression: "Just tell me you didn't know anything about any of this," he implored. "Look me in the eyes and tell me, so I'll know."

I leaned forward and looked him straight in the face.

"I only knew he was in a relationship with Henry. I also know, without a doubt, that my brother is incapable of doing something like this." I said it as earnestly as I could, even though I had watched

Tommy drive Dad's black Explorer out of the garage at almost two in the morning, in the middle of the night just days before Henry's murder.

"I promise you we will look into everything. I'm getting assistance from the state police now."

"The blood will come back to an animal," I said, as though trying to convince myself.

"I hope it will, Graham. I truly do. But there's still the issue of the car."

And what the hell could I say to that?

46
A Bad Turn

I didn't see him in cuffs. Is Tommy under arrest?" I asked.

"He's just being detained right now," Bill reassured me. "I want this to be rock solid."

"Unlike that kid Matthew's arrest, you mean?"

"I understand your concern for your brother."

"I know there's PC to have Sergeant O'Born out there secure the car so Gottert can get a search warrant, but you don't have PC to be in here in our house, detaining my brother." I was bluffing because I knew that they did, in fact, have probable cause, but I continued anyway: "I could tell you to get out and not come back until you have a warrant."

"I think you know better," Bill said calmly, seeing right through my feint. "I have more than enough RAS to keep Officer King in here and detain your brother. In fact, I would say I have PC along with reasonable articulable suspicion to search the house, too—and even if the blood proves to be animal, that will probably still happen. Don't forget I'm the police chief of this town, trying to keep the people here safe. Four innocent people are dead."

"I want to cooperate, and I know Tommy will too. My concern is for his well-being right now. I need to talk to him in private. He won't open up otherwise."

"I'll give you that, Graham."

"Thank you."

Bill followed me back into the living room. Standing by the front door, he summoned Officer King.

I was left alone with Tommy on the sofa.

"You know what's happening here, right?" I asked.

"They think I killed Henry, don't they?"

"Listen, Gottert will return with a warrant for the car, then take a sample of the dried blood they found on the floor mat in the back. It'll be compared to Henry's. If that's not a match, they'll compare it to blood samples from all the other victims. Tommy, is there any chance that there will be a match?"

"How could there be?"

"A witness saw Dad's car at Henry's on the night of his murder. Even the BACK OFF bumper sticker! So tell me right now: Did you take the car to Henry's house? This is only between you and me. I want to protect you."

"I did not! It's just like I told you, Graham: I have not left this property! I've tried, but I could never leave. You have to believe me."

"I believe you. But that would mean either there's another car exactly like Dad's, with that same unique bumper sticker—which I doubt very much—or someone stole the car and returned it later. Which I also doubt."

"No. I hear everything. I would've heard the garage door opening and the car driving out. Even if I were sleeping it'd wake me up; you know what a light sleeper I am. But we never locked the side door to the garage."

"So anybody could've walked in?"

"Yeah, I guess."

"Then the only other possibility is that you're being set up."

Tommy looked like he was about to have a panic attack or something.

"Do you need any of your medication?"

"No, I don't. But who would want to frame me for Henry's murder."

"When Henry came to visit, did anyone ever come with him?"

"No, just him."

"Think very hard—who else knew that you and Henry were partners?"

"I don't know. Dad could have told anybody."

"What about your other friends with him, or on your social media?"

"We were very private. I mean, there are photos of us when he was visiting, and of Dad too. But I never posted any of those online. I don't like sharing my private life."

"But Henry could've shared *his* photos on social media, right?"

"Yes. I guess he could've, but I never saw any."

"The police have his laptop and his cell phone, but with all that has happened now, I won't have access to any of that. What about Henry's friends? You never met any of them?"

"Just messages and comments here and there on Facebook. They never came over. It's not like I get out, you know. I mean that was Henry's biggest problem with us." He cradled his head after. Sobbed.

"Tommy, I'm sorry, but the car alone and your breakup with Henry—it doesn't look good. Help me out here: What about your counseling sessions with Pastor Simon? Does he know?"

He looked up at me, eyes bleary.

"Only if Pastor Richard told him. Some of those Bible passages about homosexuality made me question my relationship with Henry, but that was a long time ago, and I only ever confided in Pastor Richard. Why would him knowing about that mean anything anyway?"

"You have to keep that to yourself, and if there comes a time when we have to get you a lawyer, then that lawyer is the only one you can talk to about this. Understood?"

"What?"

"Pastor Simon's son, Matthew, is the one we arrested, but the evidence against him is shoddy. I mean it, brother: You don't say anything when they question you. Are we clear?"

"So you think they're going to arrest me? Take me away?"

"I don't know. I don't know, but whether they do or not, you don't talk without a lawyer. I'll make sure you have one."

"I can't leave here. I'm not sure what I would do."

"Have you seen that blood in the back of the car?" I was trying to move Tommy away from where he was emotionally going.

"Only when I was out there with the investigator. Last time I opened the hatch was months ago. If I had seen it, I would've cleaned it up."

I was certain my brother was being set up, and that the blood on the mat would match Henry's, but the devil on my shoulder whispered, *What if he's a fucking lunatic and has us all fooled?* I had thought the same thing about Matthew, though. *Maybe* I'm *the one who's losing it?*

But then again, if Tommy was truly being set up, why wouldn't whoever it was simply have left the fucking knife? That'd be a slam dunk. And then there was the surveillance footage of a suspect whose physical description was nothing like Tommy's, and the description given by Samuel Alvez of the intruder with the knife, which didn't match either. My brain was a jumbled mess.

Gottert returned with a warrant to search Dad's car. He left with Bill for Albany right after collecting a blood sample from the mat. The Explorer was then towed away, and O'Born followed the tow truck. The GPS was older, and was out of date so unfortunately that would probably be useless because it could reveal that the car was never at or around any of the crime scenes. On the other hand, it could have been good for them because it could also have revealed that it was. I couldn't help the thought.

Officer King stayed in the living room with us.

I sat with Tommy and tried to pick his brain as much as possible, but he had nothing more to offer. He fell asleep on the sofa. All that worked-up adrenaline had shut him down.

I eased off the sofa and stood.

"I need a drink," I told King.

"Wish I could have one with you."

I walked to the kitchen and poured myself a double, then returned to the sofa. Ada called, but I let it go to message.

The hours passed and the day eventually slid into early evening. Tommy was now sitting up and quiet. King was still holding his same pose in the armchair, as though years of surveillance details had trained his body and mind to cooperate.

"A car's coming up the driveway." Tommy said it like he was talking to himself.

I stood up and went to the front door to meet them. King followed. I opened it and stepped out. I wanted to hear whatever news they had first, before they entered.

Bill and Gottert stepped up to the porch and faced me.

"The blood's a match to Henry Flood's," the chief informed me solemnly.

47

This One Was Not a Dream

Gottert was armed with both an arrest warrant and a search warrant for the entire home, including my bedroom and the unattached garage. Two state-police officers had been detailed to assist. The chief allowed me a moment with my brother to explain the situation. I knew it would not be good, but I never thought it would turn out this bad.

"They're going to have to take you, Tommy."

"I can't leave here. I can't leave."

"Remember what I told you before—I'll get you a lawyer. Don't say anything. Talk only to your lawyer, okay?"

He looked at me with wide, glassy eyes.

"They can't take me, Graham. You know that. I can't leave here. It's not safe."

"There's no other way, Tommy."

I had him stand up and tried to hug him, but he suddenly pushed me away and ran toward the stairs. Maybe, like a child, he thought he could lock himself in his bedroom and be safe? One of the state troopers tackled him before he got to the stairs. He could not subdue Tommy, so the other officers hurried to assist. Instinctively, I wanted to rush in and protect my brother. I felt a strong, restraining hand on my right shoulder. It was Bill. It was like he knew what I wanted to do. His hand there was all the reminder I needed to prevent me from doing that. The officers wrestled with Tommy, who was still trying to get away. He was not violent, so the officers showed restraint and blows were not thrown.

It probably took only seconds, but it seemed much longer until Tommy was placed in custody.

He collapsed on the floor, screaming, "I can't leave this house! I can't leave—it's not safe!"

All the words I had for him meant nothing. He was in a state of complete and utter panic. Nothing I could do or say would calm him down.

The chief decided to call for an ambulance.

I stood there in total disbelief. I tried hard to fight the tears, but they came like a stream.

By the time the ambulance arrived, Tommy's body was limp with exhaustion. He had to be dragged out, muttering unintelligibly. I had witnessed total strangers dissolve publicly like this on the beat in DC—more times than I cared to remember—but none of that compared to standing there helplessly and watching it happen to my little brother.

King got in the back of the ambulance with Tommy and the EMT. A state police officer followed behind as my brother was taken to the hospital for psychiatric evaluation.

"I need to go and get a drink," I told Bill.

"Can I join you?"

I nodded. He followed me into the kitchen once again. The officers began to search the house.

"I ordered them not to mess anything up."

I said nothing. Instead I poured myself a good measure of scotch, then did the same for Bill. After a sip or two, I managed to calm myself.

"He has to have his medication," I explained to Bill. "But I don't know where he keeps it. Probably on his nightstand or in his bathroom."

"I'll have that taken care of. Don't worry."

"This doesn't make any sense."

"It never does, my friend."

"No, I mean that Henry Flood's murder and the blood found in our car makes no sense. Then there's the surveillance footage of a suspect getting out of Del's pickup, and the description of the intruder that Samuel Alvez gave us. Neither of them matches Tommy."

I downed the rest of the scotch and poured myself another.

"And if my brother was really the killer, why would he make such a mistake? Whoever murdered Jean Marie Evans left no DNA evidence behind—nothing. Why would that person be so meticulous, but then so stupid as to leave clearly visible blood in the back of the car? It doesn't make sense."

"It would if it was something like a copycat killer."

"You can't honestly believe that Tommy would mimic the other murders just because he was angry about a breakup! How would he know about the weapon used?"

"I gave you the case jackets. Maybe he saw them."

"No, he is obviously being set up by the real serial killer. Convenient that Henry's murder happened while Matthew was in jail, and then on top of that you get an anonymous call with an incredible tip. C'mon, Bill."

"Are you suggesting the interim pastor?"

"Hell, yeah! I'm suggesting him or someone else associated with Matthew who we never got around to discovering."

"Graham, is there a chance your brother got into those case files I gave you?"

"Of course there's a chance. You know that. But if that's really what happened, then you also know the autopsy will reveal a dissimilarity in the knives used. I'm betting that won't happen, though. Tommy is not a murderer, and he's not a fucking serial killer."

"He could have gotten everything he needed to know about the murders from those files. And a stab wound is not like recovering a spent round with distinctive rifling from a body."

"Just do me a favor and check with the ME, okay?"

"I will, but that won't make all the other evidence we have go away. You know that."

"And take a harder look at Pastor Simon. Remember how certain you were that his son was guilty? Again, isn't this all too convenient?"

I know how I must have sounded to him, but I was desperate to save my brother.

"Tommy was set up," I told the chief. It felt like I was trying to convince myself at the same time. "You need to put him on a 24-hour suicide watch. Extreme agoraphobia is a serious disorder. Will you make sure to have that done?"

"I will."

Later that night, I woke from a dreamless sleep and remembered what had happened earlier that day. I had a hard time believing it was real. The authorities had not found any other evidence, either in the house or in the garage. They left my Glock 40 with me because it was properly registered. I was thankful for that, because I was starting to feel the need to carry it again.

I could not get the image out of my head of Tommy being dragged from the house. Overwhelmed with sadness, I cried until daylight crept in.

48
Vultures Gather

My morning routine did not follow. Instead, I sat in the den with my coffee and called Samantha Everett, a friend who lived in New York City. She was a recently retired Assistant U.S. Attorney from DC. She had heard about the murders. I gave her a brief synopsis of the events and asked if she could recommend a defense attorney in the Rochester or Syracuse area. Samantha knew a guy: His name was Dan Wolff, a classmate of hers from Syracuse University. After working as an ADA in Rochester, Dan had gone into private practice. She gave me both his office number and his private cell.

I called him as soon as I got off the phone with Samantha. He too had obviously heard about the murders. I advised him about everything I could think of regarding Tommy's mental health, and that I did not believe my brother capable of doing what he was accused of. Dan agreed to take the case, and I accepted his retainer fees. I told him to which hospital Tommy had been transported.

"I know the DA for that county," said Dan. "I'll contact her to let her know I'll be representing your brother."

And that was that. Dan said he would go to the hospital, then let me know what my brother's status was. I felt better after talking to him.

The doorbell rang shortly after I hung up with Dan Wolff. I looked out the peephole. It was a woman I had never seen before. She was attractive and in her early to mid-30s, with dark hair in a tight ponytail.

After I opened the door I immediately saw a stubby little man standing to her left and brandishing a video camera on his shoulder.

"Mr. Sanderson," she began.

"Get off my property or I'll call the police," I said calmly.

She turned to her cameraman and shot him a nod. He must have understood that to mean *No camera,* because he lowered it from his shoulder and pointed the lens down.

"Just a moment of your time, Mr. Sanderson. I'm a reporter with News Five out of Rochester—"

"Get off my property now," I demanded and shut the door.

I gave it a couple of seconds and saw them both walking back down the driveway toward the road, where their car must have been parked.

I knew that would hardly be the end of it. More would come. I had been through many a media circus before, but never one this personal. I knew what it was like for the victims and their families who had to go through it in DC. Not every crime reporter was a vulture, though. A couple I'd known were far from that, and we're still friends to this day.

About an hour later, the house phone rang. I never used Dad's old landline, so I knew this had to be the *more* I was referring to. I answered anyway. It was another vulture. I slammed the phone back on the receiver and disconnected it from the wall.

I called Bill on my cell, but it went to voicemail. I left a message that my brother now had representation and gave him Dan Wolff's name. I asked him to call back when he got a chance to let me know how Tommy was. I called Gottert after that, but it too went to voicemail. I left basically the same message.

I felt like I had been exiled. A pariah.

I had to do something. But what? I was hungover and my brain was numb. Still, I had to do something.

The doorbell rang again.

I hoofed it over there and threw open the door like I would rip it off the hinges.

"I said get off my fucking . . ."

It was Ada.

"Oh, damn," I said. "I'm sorry. I thought you were—"

"I figured that. There's a group of them parked along the road near your driveway."

"Damn them. Bunch of vultures."

"You didn't return my calls, so I closed up the bakery to come check on you. I was worried."

"I'm sorry. You shouldn't have done that. Come in. Please."

She walked in. I closed the door behind her. She wrapped her arms around me right away and we hugged.

"I'm so sorry about all that has happened," she said earnestly.

I didn't know how to respond to that.

"Do you want some coffee?"

"I'm all coffee'd out," she said.

We released our arms from one another.

"You shouldn't be here, Ada. It's a very small town, and you have a business to look out for. I mean, I'm probably bad for your business because of my brother's arrest."

"I came here to see *you*. But if you don't want to see me, I'll understand. I'm not worried about the bakery right now."

"I'm very happy to see you. I just didn't call because, you know . . ."

"No need to explain."

"Do you want to sit down?"

She nodded and we walked around the living room to the den. I could not sit in there because the traumatic scene with Tommy was still too fresh in my mind.

Ada sat beside me on the love seat.

I came right out with what was preying on my mind: "My brother is not a murderer," I said. "I'm sure of it."

"I confess I'm having a hard time believing it, too," she reassured me. "Especially after hearing so much about Tommy from your father, then meeting him in person. Plus didn't they already have someone in custody?"

"I know saying this does not help my brother, but I never wanted them to arrest Matthew Simon in the first place. There simply wasn't enough evidence. But still, something about him just doesn't sit right. His father the pastor too."

"Did they have good evidence on your brother?"

"Pretty damn good. In fact, too good."

"What do you mean? I hope you don't think the police fabricated evidence."

"No, not at all. There's just so much of it. I wouldn't know where to begin, but I do believe he was set up."

"Why Tommy?"

"Because he's convenient. I got him a great attorney, and I'm far from being done here. I will get to the bottom of this."

Whatever it takes.

"What are you planning to do?" Ada sounded worried.

"I'm gonna get through today and hopefully tonight, then start fresh tomorrow."

"Don't get yourself into trouble."

"I haven't so far in my life." I tried to comfort her with a smile. "And I don't intend to now."

"I'm a pretty good judge of character, Graham, and I know you're a good man. I'm also sure you were a damn fine detective. So be that detective again."

I leaned forward and kissed her lightly on the lips. No feelings of guilt after.

We sat and talked for about thirty minutes. Most of the conversation was one-sided, with me rehashing everything I had already discussed with the chief and going over what I planned to talk about with Dan Wolff. It was almost as if I were trying to convince a jury.

"I should get back to the store."

"I didn't scare you away with all this, did I?"

"No. Not at all."

"Just drive straight through them if you have to," I told her, referring to the reporters. "And by no means talk to any of them."

"That goes without saying, Graham," said Ada, sounding a bit wounded.

"I know I keep apologizing, but I'm sorry. Some crime reporters have no shame—so if you get followed, please call me. I'll leave it at that."

"I'm not worried about them. Why don't you let me bring you dinner when I close up at six? I'll get us a couple of cheeseburgers and fries from the pub."

"I'd like that."

I had a feeling it might be my last solid meal for a while.

49

A Courteous Conversation

It was just as I was reheating some mac and cheese for lunch that my cell rang. It was Gottert. He said he was a couple of minutes away and asked if he could stop by. He assured me that it was not about anything bad. I wanted to say *How much worse could it get?* but decided not to.

"How is my brother?" I asked after Gottert came inside.

"He's sedated."

"Have a seat." We both slumped forward over the tiling on the island.

"I'm not here to follow up on anything," he said, as if in apology.

"Okay," I replied. "So what *are* you here for?"

"I just can't wrap my head around a few things. I thought we might have a talk."

"*You* can't wrap your head around it?" I came back at him, mildly amazed.

"I didn't mean anything by that."

"But you have some questions?"

"Yes."

"Come out with them, then."

I sat there and waited for him to begin.

"Just so you know, the chief told me that the first murder happened before you even got here."

I let go of a quiet chuckle and said sarcastically, "Then you've ruled me out?"

"A lot of things came to mind when we got that anonymous tip about the car. You were a part of that too. No way out of it in my mind."

"Understood."

"I'm sitting here talking cop to cop, not like anything else. I gotta be honest with you—I did believe Matthew was the guy, but like you, I didn't feel good about the arrest because we didn't have enough yet."

"But now you feel differently, obviously?"

"That's what I have to wrap my head around."

He paused. I intentionally did not respond.

"And you alerting the chief to your reservations about Matthew's arrest also convinced me that you knew nothing about your brother, because you'd want that arrest to stick if you did."

"My brother is innocent."

Gottert didn't comment on that. Instead, he said, "The chief didn't tell me much about the conversation you two had in the kitchen. I asked him point-blank, but all he would say is that you wanted to make sure your brother would be treated well."

"Only partly true."

"That's why I'm here. Like you, I'm pretty damn good at reading people. I knew there was more, and I tried to pursue it."

"And Bill shut you down." I stated it as fact.

"Yep. Pretty much."

"Chief Finn is not a bad man, but he wants to—he has to put this to bed. He obtained that evidence—the dried blood from my dad's car—and then made an arrest that would never be questioned in order to put the mayor and this town at ease. It's politics, I get it. The last thing he wants to do is put anything in your head to make you question all that."

"I'm pretty sure you were telling the chief the same thing I wanted to: that there's something not right about the fact that Henry Flood was murdered while Matthew Simon was still conveniently in prison. There's that suspiciously timely anonymous tip, that led to that blood-smear evidence. And then the interview we had with Samuel Alvez, when he claimed that Henry had blamed Tommy's agoraphobia as the main reason for their breakup. It all feels just a little too pat."

"Amen, brother. Keep preaching. What are you going to do about it?"

He didn't answer, just shook his head. Gottert had said what he had to say, so in return I let him in on everything I had told the chief. He didn't respond after, probably because he didn't want to reinforce my impression that he was indeed on my side with everything. He pretty much had already suggested as much. I understood. Charontown PD was a tiny department, and Gottert's chain of command was directly to Chief Bill Finn when it came to something like this. Creating any waves was more than likely the last thing he wanted to do.

"Your brother . . . I have never seen anything like that. I've had a couple of domestic situations where the man or the woman had to be dragged out, but they were resisting arrest because they didn't want to go to jail. Your brother was terrified purely about being taken out of this house. It wasn't the same."

"He hasn't left the house in years. He has an extreme disorder. The chief put him on suicide watch, right?"

"Yes, I heard the chief instruct a nurse to that effect. We also have an officer posted outside his door at all times. And like I said, he's sedated—and restrained in bed."

"But if he goes to a cell, they'll have to make sure he's on watch. You'll take care of it for me?"

"I'll make sure to."

"And his medication? You recovered that?"

"I personally gave it to the chief. I saw him hand it to the doctor at the hospital."

"So aside from working with the prosecutor on the murder charges, you're just gonna leave it at that? You won't be digging deeper into Matthew and his father?"

"As far as the chief is concerned, the arrest of your brother has brought these four murder cases to a close."

"You didn't answer my question."

"Matthew was released. If I went off on him like that, it'd be harassment."

"No it wouldn't. It'd be doing your job."

Gottert scrunched his face awkwardly and shrugged.

"I get it," I tried placating him. "No worries. I should warn you that I'm no longer bound by your kinda rules."

"Promise me you won't go doing anything stupid, Graham."

"I've never been known for that—but I was well-known for being a determined hound dog."

50
Sleep Paralysis

The news van had left by the time Ada arrived. As difficult as it was for me to resume a ritual I had shared with Tommy, we sat on the deck to eat. It was unseasonably cool for late spring. Ada said it was not normal, but weather here could be unpredictable.

It was nice to have her company. I tried hard not to reveal the heartache I felt, but I sensed she could see it in my heavy, puffy eyes.

I told her about Dan Wolff, the lawyer I had hired to defend Tommy.

"He sounds good."

"Let's hope he is."

We retired to the den for an after-dinner drink. I made her a Manhattan, and I had a pour of the whiskey I used to mix hers. My dad's good bottle of single malt was long gone.

Ada stayed late but could not spend the night because of her daughter.

"I'd like to meet your daughter one day."

"I'd like that too. How about Saturday for dinner? I'll cook."

I liked how she was always quick to initiate. I was not. Never had been, so it was a good balance.

"I don't know if that's a good idea. The news reporters out there are trying to dig up more information. Last thing you want is them going through your life."

"I told you I'm really not concerned with all that. Besides, knowing all that you know, wouldn't it be simple for you to lose a tail if you were being followed to my house?"

A tail. It gave me a bit of a chuckle hearing that phrase come out of her mouth.

"Yes, I could manage that. Did they bother you when you left?"

"I shielded my face and drove. I didn't notice anyone following me."

I didn't say anything about her license plate, or about the fact that almost every crime reporter has a source at some department that could run it.

"Saturday would be nice."

"How about five o'clock?"

"I'll be there with pleasure."

I walked her to her car. We kissed. She hugged me after. A nice long hug.

I went back in, hoping for a long nap and to wake up fresh. To face the day with a new set of eyes. I was going to dive into this shit. I didn't know where to begin yet, but it would come to me.

I dreamed that I was in bed, but it was my old bed from DC. It was not my old bedroom in DC, though; it appeared to be this one. I could make out certain things like the blanket, and the walls. Suddenly a great heaviness came over me. It was like a presence sitting on me, holding me down. Unseen. My whole body was weighted against the mattress. I could not move. My worry turned to panic when I tried to speak and found I couldn't move my lips. I tried to say *Wake up,* but it came out as only incoherent mumbling. I could move my head but not lift it. I turned my head to my left. Elena was sleeping there. I tried hard to lift my arm so I could touch her, let her know she had to wake up so she could wake *me* up.

"Wake me up," I mumbled several more times. Each time it felt louder, trying to break through my closed lips. I managed to tap my left hand against the mattress. With each tap I inched closer to Elena until finally I could feel her.

I was awake but still could not move. I knew where I was.

"Wake me up," I called out and finally broke through sleep.

I breathed heavily. The back of my neck and the pillow were soaked in sweat.

I sat up. Despite knowing that she was gone, I felt certain I would find Elena asleep beside me. I turned and she was not.

"Fuck me."

I sat up on the edge of the bed. The inside of my head felt like it was being crushed by life. Reality was a motherfucker, but sleep was just as bad.

51
Dan Wolff

Dan Wolff called me after he finished at the hospital with my brother. We agreed to meet at the diner outside town, the same place where Gottert and I had lunched. Not much chance of my being recognized there.

Dan had informed me he'd be wearing a tan seersucker suit and a light blue shirt without a tie. I didn't tell him I had already googled him and found several photos, along with details about some of the cases he had worked as a defense attorney. Mostly corporate stuff, and only a couple of murder trials—including one that resulted in a not-so-good plea for his client.

He was tucked in a corner booth away from the large window. A weathered brown leather satchel rested beside him on the seat. He was a short, round-faced man with black-framed glasses that seemed too big for his face. He had thick black graying hair and appeared to be in his 50s.

As I approached the booth, he slipped off the bench and stood.

"Graham Sanderson. I'm Dan Wolff. Good to meet you."

We shook hands. He had a firm grip.

I took the bench across from him.

"So . . . Samantha said you're a retired DC homicide detective?" he asked after we sat.

"I am. You were checking up on me with her?"

"Getting a little background is all. She also said you're good people."

The waitress walked up before I could reply, gave us menus, and offered coffee. We both accepted.

"I'll give you some time with the menus." She smiled.

"Thank you, sweetheart." Dan winked, but not in a way that appeared flirtatious.

After she left, Dan sipped his coffee for a moment, then fixed me with a level gaze. It was a calm look that probably worked well with jurors.

"I'm afraid I couldn't get much out of your brother."

I straightened up. That worried me.

"He seemed well cared for," he continued. "But he was heavily sedated, and that made things difficult. I assume he's under the care of a psychiatrist?"

"To be honest, I'm not sure how often he sees his psychiatrist anymore. He was going through therapy and other counseling. I can try to get all their names to you. I know one of them is the pastor of his church, Simon Guerre. Pastor Simon also happens to be the father of Matthew, the kid suspected in the murder of Jean Marie Evans."

"No kidding? That's interesting."

"Yeah. Very—"

"Get me all the names. And based on what you told me about your brother over the phone, and what little I've seen of him at the hospital, I'd like to get an outside psychiatrist to evaluate him."

"You mean to assess whether he's competent to stand trial?"

"Yes."

I hated the thought of that, but realized it was probably how things would play out. I was a realist.

"I spoke with the Assistant DA who will be prosecuting, and the evidence against your brother appears to be overwhelming."

"He's innocent. Again, not capable of leaving the house at all. I know he was set up."

"That's another reason why it would be good to get an independent psychiatrist who specializes in Tommy's kind of disorders. I also have a very good investigator who works exclusively for me and will look into everything."

"I'd like to meet him."

"*Her,*" he corrected me. "Hilda Burkett. I'll have her give you a call."

He picked up his menu.

"You hungry?" Dan asked.

I wasn't, but I scanned the menu anyway. The waitress returned. Dan ordered a tuna melt with fries. I ordered a BLT. She topped our mugs off with more coffee and bustled with the menus.

"Don't be offended, Dan, but have you ever handled a case like this before?"

"Before I crossed over to the dark side," he began with a slightly devilish half-smile, "I was an ADA in Rochester. During my time there I prosecuted more than a few murders. Mostly your standard drug-thug shootings, but I had a couple of more high-profile cases too."

"I'm sure that gives you an edge as a defense attorney."

"Certainly does."

"I confess to having checked up on you too, but I couldn't find much online. I did find that one case where your client pled out to something like thirty years. That's a hard plea."

"Oh yeah—that one. But better than a life sentence, right? A woman went missing from her home in Palmyra. State police handled it. They believed the husband, my client, had killed her. The investigator was persistent. The husband retained me as his attorney, claiming his innocence. There wasn't enough to arrest him. Months later, after part of the canal was drained, her remains were found. She'd been wrapped in heavy construction bags, with cinder blocks weighing her down."

"They drained the canal?"

"Parts of the canal are drained every winter by dropping the sluice gates. They do it for maintenance. To make a long story short, they recovered DNA that linked my client to the murder, but by then he had disappeared. In the wind. He was caught, of course."

"I guess he was lucky to get that plea deal, then."

"Luck had nothing to do with it. It was all me."

"Okay, but that doesn't exactly inspire confidence in your plea-negotiating skills—especially when the case concerns something that's happened to an innocent man."

"Last thing I want is for an innocent man to go to jail. I'm at the beginning of this case. I need to go through everything carefully, and that includes hiring a psychiatrist. The one I have in mind is not cheap."

"I've managed to put away a more-than-comfortable life savings. Plus our father left some inheritance."

"Okay. I do have to talk to your brother, but unfortunately I can't do that until he's stable. This might take a little time."

"I understand."

No reporters were on the road in front of the house. I was sure a few of them were lurking around town, trying to uncover more for their story. I sure as hell hoped that didn't mean finding Ada. She was the last person I wanted to see dragged into this.

I got a call about an hour later. Hilda Burkett. She wanted to come over in the early afternoon. We agreed on one o'clock.

Dan moved quickly. I liked that.

52

A Troubled Man

I started working on a running résumé for Hilda that night and finished it in the morning, then printed it out on the machine in Tommy's bedroom, which doubled as his remote office.

This was the first time I had been in his bedroom since moving back to the house. Normally I admired Tommy's neatly organized desk, but now it was a mess. Gottert and his team had gone through all its drawers and everything on its surface. At least it was not torn apart, with everything scattered on the floor. His clothing was in a pile, but that was to be expected: They had to go through every item of clothing in their search for trace evidence such as hair, fibers, or blood.

I felt my mind reverting to previous bothersome thoughts: *What might the Charontown police find on the few items of clothing they had confiscated, let alone on Tommy's laptop and cell phone?* Deep down, I knew my brother was innocent. But how many more times would I have to convince myself of that?

The doorbell rang and I automatically clenched my teeth, debating whether to answer it. *But who knows what they'll do to our property if I let it go?*

My eye went up against the peephole once again.

Pastor Simon.

Shit. What the hell does *he* want?

I stepped to the window and looked out. He appeared to have come alone.

I thought about it for a couple more seconds before answering, then opened the door and stood there without saying a word.

"Graham," said Simon, feigning deep concern.

"What can I do for you, Pastor?"

"I'm so sorry to barge in on you at a time like this, but when I tried to call the number I had for your father it just kept ringing. I don't have your cell-phone number, so I thought I'd come by."

I didn't bother telling him I had unplugged the land line.

"Okay. What can I do for you?"

"As you know, I took over the previous pastor's membership counseling, and I did have virtual meetings once a week with your brother."

"Yes—I knew that."

"As his pastor, I wanted to assure you, despite what Tommy has been accused of, that I am still here for him—and for you too, Graham."

In a moment of clarity, I realized that chances like this don't come often. I had to take advantage of it, so I said, "Would you like to come in?"

"That would be nice."

We stepped into the living room. He sat on the side of the sofa where Tommy normally sat. I wondered if that was intentional. I took the armchair to his right.

"I want you to know I was shocked when I heard the news."

"But I imagine you're happy to have your son back."

"That's behind us now—I'm here for the two of you. I also want you to know that the church's prayer group is praying for you both."

"Well, I appreciate that—and I'm sure my brother would, too. Did Tommy share with you everything that was going on in his life?"

"He did."

"I'd like to know all that he talked about with you. It's important to me."

"My counseling sessions with Tommy are confidential, of course, but I can share with you that he is a very troubled man. A very angry man."

I restrained myself.

"My brother is a loving soul, yet very frustrated with himself. He may be scared of life, but that does not make him an angry man."

"I'm sorry, Graham, but he does have a lot of anger."

"What gave you that impression? Did he say what he was angry about?"

"I don't feel comfortable talking about that without Tommy being here with us."

Total bullshit, but I played along: "Well, did he talk to you about his relationships? That much you can tell me."

"He did."

"So then you know he'd just broken up with someone."

"I know he was having problems."

I needed to squeeze more water from this stone, but I would have to be careful how I broached it.

"Pastor, having gone through this yourself with Matthew, I know you understand how difficult this is for me. It's actually unfathomable."

"I do. That's why I'm here."

"I mean, I was helping to investigate the murders, only to find . . ." I deliberately left the sentence hanging.

"God is merciful and the source of all comfort, but you need to come to Him."

"Sorry, but I'm having a hard time with that. I'm more than a bit angry with that God right now."

"It's okay to be angry with God. Some great men of faith wrestled with the Lord. Moses took his complaining right to him."

"And were you angry?"

"When Matthew got arrested? Of course I was—and also when my wife died. I turned to the Lord and cried out like David did in the Psalms. I cried on my knees and asked Him *why* continuously. It's not biblical, but I truly believe God will never put you through more than you can handle. God can heal and restore. Go to Him with your heavy heart and burdens, Graham."

He was convincing, but there was something deeper—an uneasy sensation gnawing at my insides. There was something fundamentally off with the guy. His face when he spoke seemed sincere enough, but when I looked in his eyes they reminded me of a dead man's stare.

53

“We are all sinners here”

Is what you and I talk about confidential, too?” I asked Pastor Simon.

“Yes.”

“The man who was murdered—Henry Flood—was my brother’s boyfriend.”

“I did not know that. How terrible.”

“But you knew my brother was gay?”

“Not from your brother. When he approached me about continuing his counseling after Pastor Richard McKearn left, I called Richard to get a better understanding of Tommy’s background. About ten years ago, Richard told me, when your brother first came to the Lord, he was struggling with the Bible’s stance on homosexuality. He was looking for spiritual guidance. Tommy didn’t talk much about that with me, however; he seemed mainly troubled by coming to grips with his childhood trauma.”

“And his agoraphobia,” I stated.

“He never mentioned that to me. That’s about all I can tell you—I’m sorry.”

"You're telling me he never discussed his fear of leaving this property?"

"He did not."

"Well, did Pastor Richard have anything to say about it? You were looking for background on Tommy, and that's a pretty big deal."

"Pastor Richard did tell me that Tommy suffered from agoraphobia, but my counseling with your brother had more to do with his childhood trauma."

I left it at that. In the course of searching Tommy's laptop, I knew Gottert would find out about Pastor Simon's Zoom sessions with my brother. The police would then subpoena his ass for everything concerning Tommy, and I found it hard to believe that Tommy had not discussed his agoraphobia with him. I didn't want to tip off Pastor Simon to the wisdom of "disappearing" any notes from those sessions.

"I'd like to continue our talks," I deflected. "They are helpful, and I appreciate your time. I'd like to know how you and your church feel about Tommy being gay."

Pastor Simon paused thoughtfully for a couple of seconds.

"The Word of God has quite a bit to say about that. In Leviticus, God says that 'You shall not lie with a male as with a woman; it is an abomination.' And in Corinthians, God correlates homosexuality with other sins like idolatry, drunkenness, and theft, and goes on to say that its practitioners shall not inherit the Kingdom of God. To answer your question, our Presbyterian church, myself included, stand by the Word of God."

"So you think Tommy is going to hell?"

"There is only one Judge, Graham. I have committed my life to helping those who are seeking the Lord, no matter what their lifestyle. Our church doors are also open to everyone. We are all sinners here."

"Tommy told me that you had stopped by to give him a book."

"Yes. A book by C. S. Lewis."

"I have it upstairs if you'd like it back."

"That's not necessary. In fact, I think you should read it. Lewis had a lot to say about grief. 'I sat with my anger long enough until she told me her real name was grief.' I love that line of his. It's not from the book I gave Tommy, but it says a lot, don't you think?"

"Yes, it does."

In fact, it opened my eyes.

Pastor Simon and I talked a while longer until finally I told him I was expecting company.

"By the way, Graham, we found a new pastor for the church. He'll be here within the month."

"That's good."

"Yes, it is. Matthew and I will be leaving so that his family can move into the house we've been living in. The church owns it."

"Where will you be going?"

"We're going back to Virginia for a short visit, then wherever the church sends me. We'll see where I land."

"Does Investigator Gottert know about this?"

"Not yet. But I assume, based on the recent unfortunate events, that it won't be a problem. I'm sorry to say that."

I didn't respond.

I ushered him outside just as a car pulled into the driveway. A young woman was at the wheel, and she parked next to the pastor's car.

"Must be your company," he said.

"Have a good day, Pastor."

"You too, Graham. I hope we can talk again soon."

I opted not to respond to that either.

He walked to his car as a petite and very attractive young woman—I assumed it must be Dan Wolff's PI, Hilda Burkett—stepped out of her small car. She spotted me at the front door, then smiled at Pastor Simon as they passed one another. I couldn't tell if he smiled back.

The pastor opened his car door but did not get in right away. Instead he turned toward me and nodded his head a couple of times. His eyes were as flat as stones.

54

"Humor me, Mr. Sanderson"

Private Investigator Hilda Burkett wore an olive-green skirt and matching blazer, a white blouse, and fashionable black sneakers. On her shoulder was a medium-sized black leather satchel. She looked to be in her late twenties but carried herself as if she were older.

We sat in the den.

She slipped the manila envelope I gave her inside her satchel.

"I'd like to look around Tommy's room, if I may. The garage, too."

"What purpose would that serve? The police took everything they thought might be useful, including the car."

"It's how I like to work. Humor me, Mr. Sanderson."

"It's *Graham*. My dad was *Mr. Sanderson*."

"Graham," she said with a quirky smile.

"I have no problem with you looking around, Hilda, but I'd like to pick your brain a little bit first."

"I'm thirty-two, single by choice, majored in political science at the University of Rochester and I don't like cats. I was an officer with

RPD for four years, worked plain clothes and narcotics, but quit three years ago after realizing it was not the life for me. I've been working for Dan Wolff for two years—"

"Alright, I get it. But did Dan talk to you about how I feel about everything concerning my brother's arrest?"

"He said you believe he was set up."

"I do. And that man you passed on the way in—be sure to remember his face and name. Pastor Simon Guerre."

"I take it he's not a family friend."

"Far from it. But he was Tommy's pastor."

"Your brother went to church? I thought you said he couldn't leave the house."

"Attended virtually. Simon Guerre also counseled my brother for a bit. His son, Matthew, is the one who was originally arrested."

"I did read that. About the son of a pastor, I mean."

"He's an interim pastor at the Presbyterian church here. Took over after the previous one retired. Pastor Richard something—I don't know his last name. You need to find him too."

"May I ask why?"

I broke down the conversation with Pastor Simon that had taken place just before Burkett's arrival, including my suspicion that he had indeed known Henry Flood was Tommy's partner. I also relayed Pastor Simon's dubious claim of never having counseled Tommy about his agoraphobia, the condition that was tearing up my brother's life.

"But why would the pastor lie about those things?"

"I have no idea. Let's just say it wouldn't look good for my brother if the police heard all that bullshit coming from Simon, especially any mention of Tommy's alleged 'anger issues.' I'd also be interested to know more about the conversation Pastor Simon said he had with Pastor Richard about my brother."

"I'll see what I can find out."

"Hilda, there's something off about that man—his son, too. The police aren't going to look into them anymore. As far as they're concerned, the investigation is closed. I know what you might be thinking—that I'm fishing for anything I can because I can't face the fact that my brother is a serial killer. That's partly true. But when you've been doing this for as long as I have, sometimes no matter how it looks, you have to go with your gut."

"I understand that perfectly."

I showed her Tommy's room and left her alone to do what she had to do.

"I'll be in the living room."

"Thank you."

Hilda Burkett came back downstairs about twenty minutes later.

"I'd like to see the garage."

I walked with her.

"The automatic doors are always kept closed, but Tommy said he never locks the side door. I'll be in the house. Just come right in."

"I won't be long."

Hilda returned after a few minutes.

"Find anything useful?" I asked.

"I didn't really expect to."

"Then why waste your time?"

"Because it's always that one time when you don't . . ."

"You are right about that."

I walked her to the door. We exchanged cell numbers.

"I expect to be kept informed," I told her. "About everything."

"You will be."

"And if there's anything I can do to help—"

"I'll let you know."

I watched Hilda Burkett walk to her little hybrid and get in. I liked her and felt confident she'd turn up something new. Sometimes all it took was a fresh set of eyes. Hers were green, though.

I got a call from her the next day around four.

"I found Pastor Richard."

"That was fast."

"He's in an assisted-living facility in Ithaca. Suffering from dementia."

"That's not good."

"No, it certainly isn't. But it does get better. Are you home?"

"I'm here."

"On my way."

Hilda arrived at my place about forty-five minutes later. It was a nice day, so I decided to move our conversation out onto the deck.

"Nice property."

"Felt nicer with my brother sitting in the rocker over there."

"I'm sorry."

"I miss that damn creaking sound it made, so let's bring him back."

What could she say to that? Nothing, if she was smart.

"Pastor Richard's son lives in Ithaca. In fact he's the one Pastor Simon Guerre spoke to—*not* his father Richard, as he told you."

According to Hilda, the retired pastor, Richard McKearn, had been in assisted living for more than two months. His son reported that Pastor Simon had contacted him six days ago. That would have been when Matthew was still in jail. The son advised Hilda that Pastor Simon claimed to have the pastoral counseling sessions for several church members his father had been counseling. The son went on to say that Pastor Simon told him he needed more background information on some of them *and asked if his father had notes* or files. The son let Pastor Simon go through his father's boxes for those sessions. *He told him he could make his own notes but he could not remove anything.* The pastor then spent more than an hour going over the session files.

"In fact, the son allowed me to do the same thing," Hilda recounted. "One of the boxes had Tommy's file in it. I photographed everything and made copies."

She pulled a folder from her satchel and handed it to me.

"This file is for you. I highlighted the passages I think are important. You'll find them on the pages with the sticky strips."

It was a fairly thick file. All handwritten notes. I scanned the highlighted sections, which contained a trove of details about Tommy's agoraphobia and his relationship with Henry. Some of the notes even mentioned Henry's first name and the date of their breakup—which, according to a date at the top corner of one of the pages, would have happened months ago. Multiple mentions of pain, fear, shame, and loneliness. But nothing that I could find having to do with anger or revenge.

"I find it very intriguing that he lied to you about not knowing any of this," Hilda told me. "And I think Dan will find these notes quite useful for his defense."

"This is excellent work, Hilda—thank you."

After she left I spent the rest of the day and well into the night combing through all of Pastor Richard's voluminous session notes. Around two in the morning, I realized what it was I had to do.

My dinner with Ada and her daughter was scheduled for Saturday, and I wanted to stick to that. So I would begin on Sunday.

55

Crystal Clear

Early Saturday afternoon I was pleasantly surprised to get a call from Dan Wolff. He advised me that late yesterday afternoon a judge had ordered Tommy to a state-run psychiatric facility for evaluation. Dan apologized for not calling me sooner, but he got caught up in other things.

"It's a forensic psychiatric center," he said. "But I'm still going to bring in another psychiatrist; I don't really trust anyone from a state-run facility."

I asked Dan if he'd had a chance to review my running résumé and what he thought about everything Hilda had uncovered? He agreed that it was intriguing—and definitely worth investigating. I did not tell him what I intended to do, however. I kept that to myself, just in case it went bad. I *was* a bit out of practice.

I made my way to Ada's for dinner. Lasagna. Sweet comfort food. Her daughter, Olivia, was a lovely, polite young girl. I felt awkward, though, knowing she was privy to my brother's situation. How could she not be? She never mentioned Tommy's name or asked me anything about him. Maybe her mother cautioned her not to bring it up.

Despite my slight discomfort, it was a pleasant evening. Olivia left for her bedroom shortly after dinner, granting us some nice alone time.

I filled Ada in on what had been going on and where they took Tommy. Left it at that. We spent the rest of the evening listening to Leonard Cohen, snuggling and occasionally kissing.

I left Ada's around ten o'clock, went home, changed my clothes, and secured my holstered gun on the right side of my waist with a belt. The button-down short-sleeved shirt concealed it well. I found one of Tommy's ball caps in the hall closet and slipped it on.

I headed for the thorn in Bill Finn's side: the Birdhouse. Tomorrow evening I would begin my surveillance of Pastor Simon's house.

It was a Saturday night in Charontown, when even the pub closed early, but not the Birdhouse. It attracted people from all the surrounding towns. No stools at the bar, but damn if one of them wasn't occupied by my boy Matthew Simon. (I guess it takes a small town like this to get that lucky.) I noticed it was Matthew when he turned casually to talk to Crystal—wearing even less than she had been the last time I saw her.

Matthew's back was facing me, but there was a chance he could make me in the large mirror behind the bar. Crystal I wasn't worried about—probably didn't even remember me. I scanned the area and noticed an empty table with two chairs. It was against a wall and far enough back that I wouldn't be easily made.

It took some time before the waitress showed up—the same surly one from my previous encounter here with Crystal. I ordered a Jameson on ice. Surly returned with it long minutes later. I wished I was a fly on the wall for their conversation at the bar. Crystal's hand was on Matthew's thigh near his crotch. He turned to her several times all smiles, working hard to charm her.

I was almost done with my second drink, and they were still

chatting. *How much more time would Crystal spend with him before moving on to someone more profitable? Or had they already taken care of that part?*

My attention was diverted by a young couple at the next table. They looked like they were moving on to the next level. He was a large, tattoo-riddled man with a thick beard. She was a large woman too, but with less ink and questionable fashion sense: Her red sleeveless dress, at least two sizes too small, revealed certain areas of her body that shouldn't be revealed in public.

I turned back to what interested me most. Nothing had changed.

Everything changed a few minutes later, though, when I saw Pastor Simon stepping in from the front door. He was looking around. I had to turn and conceal myself as best as I could, but not for long. It looked as though he had found what he was looking for.

He threaded his way through the crowd and placed his right hand on Matthew's shoulder. Matthew turned. He did not look happy, and neither did his father. Crystal's plastered-on smile dissolved in confusion as Matthew stood up to address his father. A couple of seconds later, Crystal turned her attention back to her drink. Matthew shook his head, then reached into his pocket and removed some money. He hurriedly counted out a few bills and slapped them down on the bar, then set his drink down hard on the money to hold it in place. It looked like Crystal said something to him, but he didn't acknowledge her.

Matthew walked toward the front door with his dad.

I waited for them to exit, then hoofed it to the front door and opened it in time to see Matthew walking a bicycle to their car. The pastor opened the trunk and helped Matthew stuff it inside as best they could. Then they both got in the car and pulled away.

I walked back inside the Birdhouse. Matthew's stool beside Crystal had not been reclaimed, so I grabbed what remained of my drink and made my way over there. It should be interesting to hear what she had to say about their interaction.

56

One Hundred Dollars

Someone sitting here?" I asked Crystal.

"All you," she said.

"It's *Crystal*, right?"

She looked at me. Studied me for a second.

"I remember you," she beamed. "Jean Marie's friend."

"Yeah—Joe."

"What brings you back to town?"

"Some things I have to take care of. I was sitting in back and saw you talking to that young man, so I didn't want to bother you."

"Wish you would have."

"Oh, really? Why's that?"

"Just wasting my time."

"Sort of looked that way. I've met him before. At that party I told you about where I first met Jean Marie."

"Oh yeah. Okay."

"He's *Matthew*, right?"

"Yeah."

She downed the rest of her drink. I did the same.

"Rum and coke, right?"

"Ooh, good memory!"

I summoned the bartender and ordered us both another round.

"Who was that man Matthew left with?"

"Looked like he coulda been his dad or something. He's been in here before."

"With Matthew, you mean?"

"Naw. Just sitting at the bar by himself."

"About how long ago was that?"

"Still Mister Question Man, aren't you?"

"Just trying to have a conversation."

"I saw him in here last week. He was drinking at the bar."

The bartender returned with our drinks.

"I was at the table back there," I told the bartender. "The waitress started my tab."

"Got ya, babe."

I turned to Crystal with a smile and said, "Well, I certainly don't want to waste your time."

"Hmm, that sounds promising."

She placed her hand on my thigh. I didn't like it, but I went with it anyway. Had to play the game. For a while, anyway.

"You ever get with that boy, Matthew?" I asked with a playful grin.

"Oh, you into that sort of thing?"

"Not really. I just don't like him because of how we met. I just want to know is all."

"No, I haven't—but it was heading that way until that man showed up."

"Really?"

"Yeah, Question Man. *Really.* So how about you?"

"What about me?"

"What are you looking for here?"

"Only your company, for the time being. I can take care of you just to hang with me."

"*Take care of me* how?"

I removed my wallet from my back pocket, pulled out a few 20s, and handed her three.

"Thank you, sweetie."

"Will that buy me a few minutes of conversation here with you?"

"If that's what you're into. Sure."

Crystal softly stroked my thigh. I tried not to think about it.

"I gotta be honest with you. I'm looking for some information, too."

"*Information*? What's that mean?"

"I've taken it on myself to look into Jean Marie's murder 'cause the cops aren't doing shit."

"She must've had some impact on you."

"That she did."

"The police arrested someone for those murders, you know. So what're you thinking?"

"No, that arrest was for a different man's murder, not Jean Marie's."

"That's not what I heard."

"Then you heard wrong. Like I said, I never liked the way that Matthew kid was all over Jean Marie at that party."

"I wouldn't know about that."

"Was he gonna take you somewhere tonight?"

"Listen, Mister—"

"Joe."

"Okay, *Joe*. I don't want to get involved in anything having to do with what you might be thinking."

"I didn't mean to make you nervous, Crystal. Truth is, I cared for Jean Marie a great deal. That's all."

I took a nice swig of Jameson. She rubbed my thigh some more, creeping her fingers a little too close to parts I'd rather not share with her.

"Were you gonna take her away from all this, Joe?" she asked in a teasing tone. "Was that what you were gonna do?"

"I guess that's what I thought, yeah."

"Truth is, I was surprised when that man came up to Matthew like that. At first I thought he must be jealous."

"Jealous? Of Matthew being with you?"

"Yeah. I couldn't make out what they were talking about, but then I heard the dude call Matthew *son,* so I figured it must be his dad."

"Okay, fine. But why *jealous*?"

Crystal hesitated. Not like she was afraid, though. It was something else. I grabbed two more 20s from my wallet and handed them over.

"What made you think the guy who barged in here was jealous?"

"I don't talk about my clients, Joe. That's why I didn't go on further about that man. I want you to know that. You get me in the car with you, or we go to a motel outside of town, that's our business. I don't tell no one about our business."

Well, she had just given up Pastor Simon without *technically* giving him up. I had to give her credit for how she handled that, but I still wasn't satisfied.

"The car or the motel with him?"

"Both."

57

Stakeouts

Crystal was getting a little too hands-on for my comfort and clearly wasn't good for any more information. What she had given me, however, was worth the hundred bucks I dished out: The good pastor and that piece-of-shit son of his weren't looking good at all.

Regrettably, that assessment wasn't substantial enough to pass on to Dan Wolff for Tommy's defense. I would need a lot more than that.

I rested most of the next day, ate a good dinner, then prepared for a night of surveillance. I filled a thermos with hot coffee, then emptied a wide-mouthed bottle of juice from the refrigerator into the sink. That would be my piss container. There were several homes on Pastor Simon's block, and it wasn't like I had a sketchy car that would draw attention, but stepping out to piss in the gutter most certainly could. Countless hours of past surveillance had taught me the importance of being prepared.

I left the house at dusk, found a good spot along the curb under two large-trunked maple trees. Their house stood on the other side of the street, about a quarter of a block away. I had a good view of the front door, one side of the house, and their car in the driveway.

It was a quiet neighborhood. Occasional residents walked by on my side or the other side of the street. A couple of older folks left their home opposite the Simons, got in their car, and drove past me. I scrunched down to make myself less conspicuous.

Dusk rolled into night. The front porch light at the Guerre residence was illuminated, along with a couple of lights on the first and second floors. The curtains were drawn. The ghostly silhouette of a figure passed a first-floor window on the visible side of the house. That was all the movement I would see that night.

The break of day came early. That was when I left for home.

I slept for most of the day.

Gottert called me later that afternoon with news from the medical examiner: The puncture wounds in Henry Flood's chest were as close to a match with those on the other victims as you could get. Gottert also told me that the search of Tommy's cell phone had revealed several calls made to Henry's phone, including two calls just a couple of days before his murder. There were none after.

Was it Henry that I heard Tommy arguing with on the phone through his closed bedroom door that evening?

Their breakup had occurred months ago, according to Pastor Richard McKearn's counseling-session notes, but I guess Tommy couldn't let go. Gottert wouldn't tell me anything more.

The call from Gottert was disheartening at best. When I phoned Dan Wolff it went straight to voicemail, so I left a message. It did not look good for Tommy.

That evening I went through the same routine, leaving earlier but parking in the same spot. Spent the whole night there with no luck. The same lights were on, but this time an upstairs light went off around one in the morning. That was it.

* * *

I was getting discouraged and starting to worry that my surveillance scheme might never pan out, but I was not one to give up. *What the hell else did I have to do?* Well, there was Ada. I called her from the car as early as I dared Tuesday morning and told her I'd be busy working with the attorney on Tommy's defense.

"I'd like to see you soon, though," I added.

"You do what you have to do. I'm not going anywhere."

How the hell did I get lucky enough to meet someone like Ada? Damn, I hoped I wouldn't fuck it up.

Dan Wolff called not long after my chat with Ada. He had just picked up the information I left him in my phone message the day before.

"I want to wait until Tommy gets a full evaluation from our psychiatrist too before I sit down with the ADA. The last thing we want is for this to go to trial."

"Don't tell me you're considering a plea?"

"Graham, the evidence against your brother is just too overwhelming. If he is found competent and we go to trial, Tommy won't stand a chance."

"How long will it take for the evaluation process?"

"This is a complex case, so it could take as long as a week. But then again, depending on the psychiatrist, it could go a lot faster."

"Then he'd go back to jail?"

"Yes."

"Let me know right away if he's going back. Don't discuss a plea deal with anyone until you talk to me first."

"Okay."

* * *

After a dreamless sleep, I woke up rested Tuesday afternoon and returned to my observation post. The unpredictable weather revealed itself and it was uncomfortably humid. This wasn't exactly a stakeout in some drug-infested corner of a large city, so I turned on my car's AC but of course kept the lights off. I wasn't about to sit there all night sweating through my clothes.

Just before midnight, a curtain on the front window to the left of the porch opened slightly. I couldn't tell if it was Matthew or Simon, but they appeared to be peeking out. Awaiting someone's arrival, perhaps? By the time I got my binos out to take a look, the curtain had closed.

Night No. 3 and the Guerres had yet to leave the house. Maybe there was a deck in back where they hung out like Tommy and I did? The car remained exactly where it was on the first day of surveillance. During his surprise visit to my house, Pastor Simon did say they'd be moving out soon. Could be busy packing everything up?

Objective reason would call this a big waste of time, but I went with my gut feeling instead. Desperation? Possibly. But just maybe it wasn't.

58

Blindsided

3:33 a.m. Still the third night, and my back was starting to feel it. I drank my last cup of coffee over an hour ago, and the caffeine wasn't working anymore.

Then the front door opened. I noticed it because light spilled out from inside. Matthew stepped out onto the porch. I didn't need my binos to know it was him. He stood there, looked left and right a few times, then closed the door behind him.

I trained my binos on him to get a closer look. He appeared not to be carrying anything. Matthew headed for his dad's car but did not get in. Instead he walked up the driveway toward the back of the house on the side I could not see. I lost sight of him.

I thought hard about leaving my stakeout and sneaking up there. The trees across the street from his house might conceal me, but I didn't want to take the chance.

Moments later, Matthew returned carrying a shovel.

A fucking shovel.

He entered the house with it.

I've had a few of those *You gotta be kidding me* moments in my career, but none like this.

I debated what to do next. It was unusual enough that I should have called Bill or Gottert. I sure as hell should have done that, but I didn't. Instead I got out of the car, quietly closed the door, and made my way toward the house. I wanted to get a look through a window.

I got up to the front door and listened for anything that might be considered *exigent circumstances*. That'd be when I'd call 911. I didn't hear a sound. I walked to the driveway and toward the rear of the house. All the curtains were drawn. There were three small rectangular windows at the bottom of the house about four feet apart and inches above the driveway. Their ice-textured design made them opaque, but it was obvious the lights were on in the basement.

I made my way to the rear of the house. Sure enough, there was a deck. The backyard was not fenced in. I walked up the five steps to the deck. Through a sliding-glass door I could see a small, sparsely furnished family room, with a flat-screen TV affixed to the wall opposite a sofa.

Light bled in from another room.

Only blinding concern for my brother led me to contemplate what I was about to do; as a detective, I never would have considered it. I was hoping to discover something so incriminating that the authorities would not arrest me for burglary while armed. Such a charge would definitely fuck my brother. Me too.

I was able to slide open the glass door about a quarter of an inch before it caught on the cheap latch. I took out my pocketknife and jimmied it until it unlatched itself. I slipped the knife back in my pocket and unholstered my weapon, then slid the door all the way open and entered.

I walked as lightly as I could, but the old wooden floor creaked a bit. Not enough to worry me. The door to the next room that was lit was open. The kitchen. I stopped before entering and listened for a moment. A muffled scraping issued from another room. It didn't stop so I entered the kitchen with my gun in the tuck position. At the far end of a short walkway was an open door emitting a dim light.

Creeping around, I saw that the door opened onto a dining room, with steps leading down on the far side. Had to be the basement. I moved slowly along the wall toward those stairs, then stopped to listen again. Same sound, but steadier—every couple of seconds. It was definitely coming from down there. I moved closer, stepped back a bit, and bent down to peek in.

A bare bulb dangling from the ceiling lit the basement stairs. I could hear huffing, like someone was working out, but then I realized it was more likely the sound of Matthew or his father digging.

Thoughts of another dead body raced through my mind.

My right foot hit the first wooden step, and the damn thing creaked as loud as Tommy's rocker. I moved closer to the wall, where I knew the treads would be firmer, then continued making my way down.

It was a dirt floor. To the left was the HVAC system. The ceiling was a maze of PVC pipes, with all kinds of wires hooked to two-by-fours.

The sound was coming from the other side of the HVAC. Gaps and holes pocked the basement's old stone walls where the mortar had crumbled over time. I followed the darkest part of the wall to the rear of the HVAC.

The digging noises had stopped. I stopped too, listening intently. My adrenaline kicked in, making me ready for anything. I stepped back to a more tactical position and moved slowly around so I could see.

Pastor Simon Guerre lay inert on his back on the damp dirt floor, his chest caked with dried blood.

I quickly moved back, gun at the ready.

Matthew jumped out from the other side of the HVAC and swung the shovel like a baseball bat. I lost my footing trying to dodge the blow, managing to get a single round off, but the shovel blade hit me square on the side of the head and I fell to the ground.

I felt myself going out. My gun was no longer in my hand. Matthew was a blurred figure standing over me, shovel held high and ready to come down for what I knew would be the end of me. My head felt like it had been split open. I was losing myself.

"I couldn't take it anymore!" I realized Matthew was screaming at me. "I couldn't take it anymore."

My right hand scrabbled around in the dirt, hoping to find my gun, while my mind fought to say something.

Then, a familiar voice. It sounded like a woman shouting commands: "Down! Down on the ground!"

And I went out again.

59

Hard Head

I tasted blood.

I was in and out of consciousness. I thought I might still be in the basement.

The voices I heard around me were indistinct. The last thing I could recall was two hazy forms lifting me from the ground.

I opened my eyes to bright fluorescent light. My head felt like it was compressing with intense pressure and throbbing at the same time. I saw through the corner of my left eye something that confused me at first, but then I realized it was thick gauze.

An IV was in my left arm. The bag was hanging on a hook near my gurney.

I was in a hospital room.

I remembered what happened.

The clock on the wall read *12:20.*

There were no windows in the room except the large window in front, with a view to the hallway. I didn't know if it was afternoon or after midnight.

A nurse came in.

"You're awake," she smiled.

When I tried to scoot myself up in bed, she ordered, "Please don't try to move, Mr. Sanderson. Just lie down."

"How long have I been here?" I asked. My mouth so dry the words barely came out.

"You've been here for almost eight hours. Let me take your blood pressure."

"Who brought me in?"

"The ambulance."

"Someone was with them, though."

"It wasn't my shift, so I wouldn't know."

"Little water, please?"

"Of course, dear. I'll be right back."

She walked out and returned shortly with a small bottle of water, opened it, and leaned toward me.

"Let me help."

She tipped it slightly against my lips.

I sipped.

"Thank you."

The nurse set the bottle on a rolling tray beside my gurney.

"It's there if you need more, but try to remain still for a bit. Use the call system if you need anything at all."

She took my blood pressure.

"Looks good."

"How bad is my head?"

"The doctor will be in shortly. Just try to rest for now. And remember, if you need anything, use this button to call me."

She set the call system on the edge of the thin mattress and walked out.

The doctor came in a few minutes later. He told me I had sustained a head injury with concussion and mild cerebral edema, but

I was lucky to have escaped a skull fracture. From the upper left of my forehead down to my eyebrow on that side did get split open, however.

"Probably from the curved edge of the shovel blade," the doctor said.

Eighteen stitches and a decent scar, he told me.

"You might feel dizzy and nauseous for a while, and I want you to stay overnight to monitor you and bring the swelling down."

"So I'll survive?" I asked.

"You'll survive this. But try not to stand in the way of any more flying shovels, okay?"

"I'll try my best, Doc."

After he left I found my cell phone on a wooden stand beside the gurney. Only one missed call: Ada. I listened to her voice message. *I'm just calling to check in and say hi.*

She didn't know.

Though I didn't feel like talking, I wanted to let her know before the news got out. Pretty sure she'd be at the hospital if it already got out.

Bill and Gottert entered the room. So much for not talking. Gottert's clothes were rumpled, and he looked as tired as I felt.

"How you holding up?" Bill asked.

"Doc says I'll live," I joked.

"That's good. We had to sneak out the back of the station because of all the damn reporters. A couple of them have staked out the front of the hospital too."

"Don't worry. I have nothing to say to them."

"Happy to see you're okay," Gottert said.

"Thanks. I just want to get the hell outta here."

"I doubt that's happening anytime soon," Bill said.

"Well, I'm not in handcuffs, and there's no uniform posted outside my door, so I plan to be out tomorrow."

"If I could arrest you for stupidity, I would," said Bill. "You should have called me."

"For a man with a shovel on his own property? I'm not familiar with that crime."

"A guy we suspected of several murders getting a shovel out of his garage at three-something in the morning and taking it inside is pretty damn suspicious. Especially with the dirt basements these old homes have."

"Maybe in some awful TV crime show," I conceded, attempting a weak smile.

Bill's tone turned serious. "What you did is straight out of one of those stupid shows, my friend. But you're you, and what's done is done."

"You got one hard-as-hell head there, Graham," said Gottert.

"I'm not real clear on how I got here, but I'm pretty sure a PI named Hilda might have had something to do with it."

"You got that right," Bill said. "Hilda Burkett. She was sitting on that house too, and you didn't even know it. She was surveilling it off and on every day and night since Saturday, when she followed Matthew to the Birdhouse, then followed him and his father back home."

Bill knew I'd been at the bar. Didn't even have to say it.

"Is the kid still alive?" I prayed that Matthew had survived so we could get the full story.

"He did, but you might need to get yourself back on the range. You shot a hole right through the HVAC."

"I don't even remember firing my weapon."

"You did get one off. You must have slipped on the dirt floor."

"Yeah—that's gotta be what happened."

Bill chuckled and said, "Gottert and a state police investigator interviewed the kid. His lawyer was there too. It was not a long interview."

Bill paused to collect his thoughts. "You know you'd be dead right now if it wasn't for your young private-investigator friend. You know that?"

"I do know that. And I'll make sure to thank her for it as soon as I see her."

"She heard the gunshot and called 911, then went in on her own," Bill continued. "I visited the scene, and we recovered that tri-edged dagger. Damn thing even had *Matthew* etched on its hilt, along with a skull and crossbones. We also retrieved his bloodied clothing and shoes from a construction bag I'm sure he was about to dispose of after he buried his dad. The living room was the crime scene. Messy as hell even after he tried to clean it up."

"Where did you find the knife?"

"On the dirt floor of the basement. Probably left it there after he stabbed his father. In fact we probably never would have found it if you hadn't showed up."

"What about Tommy?"

"We've got Guerre only for the murder of his father, and for your attempted murder. But based on everything else we have, I'm hoping your brother will be okay." Bill looked away from me after saying that. I couldn't tell if it was guilt or shame.

I looked at Gottert.

"You didn't get enough on him for all the murders?"

"At this point we don't know if it was him or his dad," Gottert began. "He said he'll talk, but only with you. His lawyer ended it immediately after that."

"Me? Why the hell me?"

"He didn't say. Just totally shut down."

"You going to be up for that?" Bill asked. "Guerre's not going anywhere, so I'm not suggesting it should be today. We can bring him back up from jail when you're ready. You're all we have, brother."

I didn't know what to say. As much as I loved getting in the box, getting in with him was not something I looked forward to. Matthew Guerre had gotten the best of me, but I had Tommy to think about.

"I want Tommy out and home," I said.

"Get a confession from that kid and I'll make that happen right away."

Despite everything they had on Matthew, I knew they had damning evidence on Tommy too. For all they knew, my brother had been in on it somehow. Tommy had to be conclusively ruled out.

"You make sure Tommy is on watch and safe, and I'll be there tomorrow."

"I'll do that," Bill assured me.

"I should be good by the afternoon."

"I'll arrange for the deputies to bring him back. Now listen, I know you probably have more questions, and we'll get to them. But I have to do my job. Gottert's going to get a statement from you now. Okay?"

"I understand."

I felt like my head was about to fall off my shoulders, but I gave him everything I had. It didn't take long at all.

60

My Savior

Private Investigator Hilda Burkett—my savior—appeared at the window of my hospital room in the late afternoon. She stood there looking in, and looking a bit silly. I guess checking to see if I was up. After she realized I was, she waved, raised her brows, and pointed to herself, then to me: *Okay to come in?*

I smiled and mouthed *Yes* with a nod.

Hilda walked in and said, "At least your head isn't fully wrapped. That's a good sign."

"Yeah, it is good. Pull up a chair."

She slid a chair closer to the gurney and sat. Stared at me with that quirky smile, as if waiting for me to open the conversation.

I obliged.

"Thank you, Hilda," I said sincerely.

"No need to thank me."

"Hell yeah, there is. But why didn't you tell me you were following them too? That you were sitting on the house?"

"I don't work for you," she said in a firm but nice way.

In a way she did work for me—I was the one paying her salary—but I let it slide.

"You *can* tell me what you've learned, though," I said.

"I know about as much as you do at this point. The police are being very tight-lipped about everything."

"What led you to start following the Guerres?"

"It wasn't both of them—just Matthew. Wolff asked me to. He had managed to get his hands on the police reports pertaining to Matthew's arrest. Then, based on a lot of what you said, he directed me to stay on him for a while, see what I could dig up."

"I'm damn grateful to him too, then. Were you armed when you came in?"

"I carry, yes. But I could have handled him without a gun."

"I'll bet you could've."

But what did that say about me?

Hilda continued: "I got him face down. I guess he didn't want to get shot."

"It's important for me to know as much as you can remember. For some reason Matthew told the investigators that he would talk only to me."

"That's . . . interesting."

"Yeah. Did he say anything to you before the police arrived?"

"Only that he *couldn't take it anymore*. Kept repeating that over and over like a child."

"That was all he said to me, too. Did he give up anything about the murders?"

"Not at all. He wouldn't even acknowledge his father lying dead on the ground a foot away. I helped him sit up and tried talking to him, but I got nothing."

"I remember seeing the body. The blood looked dry."

"It was. I've been on a few homicide scenes as a cop, so I've seen my share of dead bodies. This one was starting to get a little ripe. I think it's safe to assume that Matthew killed his dad a couple of days ago—maybe even Saturday night, when I was right on the block in my car."

"The chief said he was stabbed, so you wouldn't have heard any gunshots."

"I have no guilt."

"I wouldn't either."

"Is there anything else he said or did?"

She lowered her head, thinking hard, then looked back up at me.

"He did say something incoherent, but the only words I could make out were *for Mom*. Other than that, nothing."

"*For Mom?*"

"Yeah—it was weird."

"His mom died."

"Maybe he was praying to her."

"*For Mom?*" I mumbled to myself.

"Did you talk to Matthew or his dad in the bar?" she asked.

"No. Chief said you followed him there, so you know when I arrived and walked in."

She nodded.

"When I saw him sitting at the bar with Crystal, who I knew was a prostitute, I found a good spot to sit and hoped he wouldn't make me. He didn't. I got the feeling they were about to walk out together. But then Pastor Simon showed up and interrupted their conversation. Matthew looked upset and embarrassed. Once they left, I went over and sat with Crystal."

"She a talky working girl?"

"Talky enough. Matthew would've been a first time with her, but not Daddy."

"Well, well."

"I felt like I needed much more than that, so I decided to sit on the house myself. But I didn't start surveilling it until the next night, which was Sunday. You know the rest."

"You're damn good at what you do, though, Hilda: I never saw ya, and I'm pretty damn good at what *I* do. At least I thought I was until all this happened."

"I don't use my personal car when doing surveillance. Otherwise you probably would've made me."

I chuckled at her obvious effort to make me feel better.

"What's next for my brother?" I asked.

"We wait for Dan to get everything from the ADA. Hopefully that'll be exculpatory evidence—or, even better, you'll get a confession."

"I don't like that *hopefully*. You one of those glass-half-empty types?"

There came that quirky smile again. "I can be an optimist sometimes."

"Be an optimist now, because I'm going to interview Matthew Guerre tomorrow afternoon."

"You had some sort of effect on him. You up for that?"

"I will be. I like you, Hilda. And I owe you big time."

"I like fine red wine. Preferably Italian."

"Well, I'll more than likely have to go to Rochester for that bottle or two."

"No rush," said Hilda, standing. "I have to go."

I reached my hand out and she did the same. We shook. Her grip was firm.

"You can have my back anytime," I volunteered.

She shot me a knowing look, turned, and walked out.

As if on cue, Dan Wolff called shortly after Hilda left. He apologized for not coming to the hospital, but he and Hilda had both been running around trying to get the full story from the police. I told Dan that Matthew wanted to talk, but only to me. He advised me to be careful and to call him right away, especially if he confessed, so that he could huddle with the DA about Tommy.

"Do you know who Matthew's defense attorney is?" I asked.

"Tonya Stein. She's overworked, but decent."

"I can't count how many debriefings I've sat through with a suspect's defense lawyer present. I'll be fine."

I called Ada next. She sounded upset that I hadn't informed her earlier, and insisted on coming to the hospital to see me. I begged her not to. I didn't want her to see me laid up this way but that's not what I told her.

"I'm just so out of it. I had to give a statement to the police and all that."

She understood.

I told her I would be released tomorrow, but didn't know the exact time: *Could she come pick me up and take me to my car?* Ada said she'd be happy to do that—so long as I filled her in on every last detail.

The doctor checked up on me again. Then there was a steady stream of nurses throughout the night—changing the IV, taking my blood pressure, having me swallow anti-inflammatory meds, and doing whatever else they needed to do. All that TLC didn't allow me much sleep.

In the early morning I got another MRI and was told I would have to wait for the doctor to read the results before I could be released. When the doctor finally came by, I refused his offer of pain meds but took him up on the prescription ibuprofen. That would help my throbbing head.

After a predictably awful hospital lunch, I got the thumbs-up and was discharged.

Ada picked me up and drove me to my car. "I have to be at the station in a couple of hours," I told her.

"Are you sure you should be doing that?"

"The doctor said I was good to go so long as I don't attempt anything strenuous. And all I'll be doing at the station is sitting on my ass."

I didn't tell her about having to interview Matthew Guerre.

"Is your brother going to be released?"

"We still have to follow up on a couple of things." I was being vague in order not to tempt fate, but his release is precisely what I was praying for.

"And that guy is not going to get out?"

"No, he's not."

I got home in time to shower and relax a bit before I had to leave.

I reached the police station about an hour before Matthew was scheduled to be transported there. I wanted to watch as much of the video of his initial interrogation as I could.

Gottert leaned toward me, resting his elbows on the cubicle divider like he was tired.

"This was all we got out of him yesterday. There were a lot of holes in his story, and we thought we were about to break him and get him to talk about the murders, but he shut down and said he'd talk only to you."

"I don't know what he's up to. Maybe he wants to apologize for trying to kill me?"

"We could use that," Gottert said with a smile.

He started the tape of the interview. We watched it on the computer monitor. His lawyer, Tonya Stein, sat to his right. She looked to be in her 50s. Her yellow legal notepad was on the desk and her pen was at the ready. Gottert and the state troopers' homicide investigator sat across from them. The bulging case jacket lay on the table before Gottert.

Matthew was advised about everything they had on him—the murder weapon, the bloodied clothing, all the evidence they needed for the murder of his father and the attempted murder of me. The state investigator mentioned that the inscribed dagger recovered from the Guerre residence would more than likely match the wounds on the other murder victims too.

They had a lot. But what they did not have was any concrete evidence that Matthew had murdered those other people. The killer could have been his dad. Or it could have been father and son acting in concert.

It took Matthew a few moments to respond, and what he had to say was not what they wanted to hear. He played the abused kid terrified of his father. Tried to make it look like his father was the serial killer. *But how could you know that?* the investigators pressed him. *Why did you stay? And most importantly, why not just go to the police?* That was when he shut down.

The look on Matthew's face moments after he said *I'll only talk to that retired detective Sanderson* changed to the same kind of look I'd seen on Tommy's face in the mirror when I was shaving the back of his head.

Dead.

But Tommy's eyes held the life his face had temporarily lost. I remembered that well. In Matthew's eyes there was only darkness.

So what did he want from me?

61

Back in the Box

My head was killing me. I should have taken the doctor up on those painkillers. Ibuprofen 800s were worthless. I didn't like the idea of walking into the interview room—with raccoon eyes and a bandaged head. Made me look weak. But hell, I was there and still standing, so maybe not so weak.

Tonya Stein introduced herself. She looked tired. Her eyes drifted to the side of my head covered in gauze. It was subtle but obvious.

"Graham Sanderson," I said, then sat into a chair across from them.

Matthew did not acknowledge me. His handcuffed hands rested on his lap, fingers interlaced, his head bowed slightly toward the table. Matthew's eyes were open, so it did not suggest an attitude of prayer—more like a thousand-mile stare.

"I want you to know, Mr. Sanderson, that your presence here is just as much a surprise to me as I'm sure it is to you. I advised my client against it, but it's what he wants."

"Well, I'm here," I replied, looking directly at Matthew. He did not return my gaze. "What is it you'd like to say to me, Matthew?"

After a moment with no response I said, "You got me here, so there must be something you wanted to talk about."

Suddenly I longed to get up and walk out of the box, but I managed to restrain the urge. Allowed him a little time.

He looked up with those lifeless eyes and that same disturbing expression. I knew then that this was the real Matthew Guerre, and that he'd been putting on an act the two previous times I'd been in here with him. In that stone-cold face was no fear.

"So after your father died," he asked almost sincerely, "you left your life in DC to come all the way up here to live with your brother?"

"Who told you that?"

"My dad."

"Yes, I did," I said without hesitation.

"Why?"

"What did your dad say?" I returned instead.

"That your brother had a lot of mental issues, and you had to take care of him."

He said it like Tommy was dead, but I played along.

"Tommy doesn't need me to take care of him. But he does have severe agoraphobia and suffers from a lot of trauma, mostly from his childhood. Why were you talking to your dad about my brother?"

"Just came up in conversation."

I left it at that. For now. I wanted him to think he was in control, and I wasn't all that interested in whatever he was after. I got the sense that I was talking to a different kid from before. Not that I believed Matthew suffered from dissociative identity disorder, just that Gottert and I had been duped by his naïve, apple-pie act. He had played us well before, and he might be trying to do the same thing again. But this time I was on to him.

"What kind of childhood trauma?"

Matthew knew more than he was letting on. Maybe he had even

read the notes that his father had wheedled out of Pastor Richard's son. He was trying to set something up, probably for his own legal defense, and he thought I would inadvertently help him do that. I seriously doubted that his interest in my brother's past amounted to anything more than a quest for personal advantage. I had to get past all that shit with him, though.

I had read the same notes, so I decided to play along. Truth became my tactic, because I didn't know how much Matthew knew, and if I wanted this to go anywhere I could not let him catch me in a lie. That might shut him down again.

"An abusive mother."

Obviously pleased by my answer, he allowed himself a throaty grunt and a slight half-smile.

"And your dad did nothing about it?"

"Why all this interest in my family? That can't be why you wanted me here."

Tonya Stein regarded her client with concern. I am sure she was worried about what he might say.

"Fair question. When you and that investigator interviewed me before, you said it was all about getting to know me. Gaining trust. Was that a lie?"

Matthew needed to believe he was in control.

"No, it wasn't. My parents were divorced. I lived with my dad. We didn't learn about the extent of the abuse until Tommy was older. But what about your own mother? Was she abusive?"

"I don't want to talk about my mom."

"I got the sense when we talked before that you loved her and missed her. Was I wrong?"

"No."

"What about your dad, then?"

"I already talked about all that with the other two cops."

"Yeah, but not with me."

"I'm sure they told you all about it before you came in here."

"Not really."

"I'm sure they did. My dad buried your dad, huh?"

He wants me to play his game.

"He did—and you think that connects us somehow?"

"If you had known what kind of man he was, you never would have allowed him to bury your father."

Here we go.

"Wasn't my choice, but you're probably right."

"I know I'm right."

"What's your point, Matthew?"

"Just having a conversation is all."

"Then it shouldn't be so one-sided. Tell me more about your relationship with your father."

Matthew lowered his eyes, intent on what to say.

Or how most convincingly to lie.

62

Control

I did watch the recorded interview with you, and how you claimed your father was abusive."

"*Claimed*? He *was* abusive."

"Okay. The obvious question then would be why you chose to come here with him? I mean, you seem smart. You worked construction in Pottstown, and you do masonry here. You're old enough to make your own decisions, so why not get out on your own?"

"Do you know anything about emotional abuse?"

"A bit. I know it can be just as bad as physical abuse."

"It can be, but I think it's your brother who really knows. Not you."

"You're right. I only know about it from Tommy, and the work I did as a detective."

"But you've never lived it, so you can never really understand."

"True—but I can see the harm it's caused my brother, and that's more than enough understanding for me."

"That man was very controlling. My whole life was controlled since childhood. My mom drank herself to death because of him. I ended up becoming an addict because of him. I . . ."

He stopped himself. Gathering his thoughts or was about to say something he shouldn't have.

"I lost my job. My credit's still shot. I can't even buy a used car. It was either him or life on the street—where I probably would've fallen back to drugs."

"So after you got clean, you still chose to live with an abusive father?"

Matthew took a moment. Slowly shook his head at my incomprehension.

"He had me so turned around I didn't know right from wrong. It was like I couldn't make any kind of decision on my own. He controlled everything."

"Maybe we should talk, Matthew," his lawyer jumped in.

"I *am* talking," he said, angrily continuing to eyeball me.

"I mean in private," amended Tonya.

"I don't need to talk in private."

Tonya Stein took in a telling breath. Her fatigue was evident.

"Give me an example of how you didn't *know right from wrong*," I prompted him.

"Matthew, we should talk," Tonya tried again.

"Those were his words, Counselor. I'm just asking for clarification."

Before Tonya could stop him, Matthew blurted out, "I knew what he was doing, and I knew that it was wrong."

She placed her hand on his shoulder in a bid for his attention.

"Matthew—" she pleaded.

"He was a hypocrite," he stated, ignoring his attorney.

"Because he liked to pay for sex with prostitutes, then guiltlessly preach about redemption and salvation through Christ Jesus on Sundays after?"

I had taken a chance. The look on his face instantly changed from lifeless to surprised, then dismayed. I gave him a couple of seconds to take it in. He resumed his dead eyes as if aware he'd gone too far, but I glimpsed something powerless there, if only for a moment.

But that was all I needed to see. My gamble had paid off.

"Yeah, I know all about that," I added. "That had to upset you, didn't it? Especially since he pulled you away from one of his girls at the Birdhouse. *Crystal*, right?"

He continued to stare at me blankly.

"I was there, Matthew. Close enough to see and hear everything. In fact, I'm gonna be honest with you: I talked to Crystal afterward. She told me your dad had paid for sex with her on several occasions, both in motels and in his car."

He seemed confused.

"Is that one of the hypocritical things you were speaking of? Or didn't you know?"

He shook his head again, but quicker this time.

"I knew what he got up to, but not about *her*. But yes, that's one example. You were there?"

"Yeah. I was embarrassed for you. It must have been hard on you having a dad like that. A man of God, even. I can't imagine."

Matthew simply nodded.

"Was that night at the Birdhouse—how he humiliated you in front of Crystal—something like a trigger? Was that why you killed him?"

"I've already confessed to what I did, but I'll tell you too: Yes, that was part of it."

"What else led up to what you did?"

"Years and years of shit. I don't know where to begin."

"Then start with my innocent brother. Tell me that's why you really wanted me here."

Matthew smiled. After what I'd just said, it was the last thing I expected him to do. He seemed to believe he'd regained control of the exchange.

But was it too soon?

Had I fucked up?

63

Cob

Tell me what you really want to say. What your dad did when you were in jail."

Matthew stared at me with his lips tight against one another.

"Tommy is innocent. There is no other reason I can think of that you would want me here. Despite everything you've had to go through and all that you have done, I know you have decency. Don't allow another man to suffer just because of your father."

Tonya Stein broke in: "If you know something, Matthew, you should tell him. It could help you."

"My dad was a murderer. He followed me in Pottstown a couple of years ago when I was going to meet my dealer. He killed him in front of me."

"With your knife?"

"No, I didn't have that yet. He stabbed him, though, with a steak knife."

"What was your dealer's name?" I asked.

"I only knew him as *Cob*."

"Was anyone else there at the time?"

"It was in a parking lot. I didn't see anybody else."

"Why didn't you go to the police?"

"I was scared to. My dad convinced me I was responsible, then made me pray with him for forgiveness. I told you he was a master manipulator."

"When did you get your knife?"

"I ordered it online about a week after that, for protection in case my father turned on me."

"Tell me about Tommy."

"When I was arrested the first time, Ms. Stein here told me I would probably be released, because they had just caught the *real* serial killer."

He had to take a moment before continuing. I could not read him. He had no expression.

"Matthew thought it was his dad who'd been arrested," Tonya clarified.

"I was honestly surprised it was not him," Matthew went on. "When I got home from jail I confronted him about it, because I knew. He told me he did what he had to do to protect me—just like he had to with Cob."

"So he set Tommy up by killing his boyfriend, Henry Flood, at a time when you could not possibly have done it?"

"Yeah, he told me he had done 'what was necessary. Just keep your mouth shut and everything will be okay.' "

"Did he tell you what else he did to set Tommy up?"

"He planted some kind of evidence. I don't know what it was or how he did it, and I didn't ask."

"But how did he know about Tommy's relationship with Henry?"

"I didn't ask that either. I assume it came out of the counseling he was giving your brother. Oh—he had the former pastor's notes, too."

I could tell he knew more than he was letting on.

"Thank you for telling me that, Matthew."

"It's the right thing to do, isn't it?"

Strange how he said that—almost as if he didn't know.

"But I still can't understand why you stabbed your father to death. Why didn't you go to the police instead? Would have saved you a whole mess of trouble."

He had to think about that.

"After he came up to me like that in front of Crystal at the bar, I lost it. We got in a bad argument when we got home, and it was like I went blank. I don't know . . ."

"Was the knife on you at the time?"

"Don't answer that, Matthew," cautioned Tonya Stein.

Then, to me: "I need to speak with my client in private now."

Matthew ignored her. "I don't remember where the knife was, or how I got it. I only knew my father had to be stopped."

"You know that your knife is a match for the murders of Pauly Savell, Del Thomas, and Jean Marie Evans too, right?"

"Obviously, his father committed those murders," Tonya cut in.

"Why Jean Marie, though?"

"What are you suggesting, Mr. Sanderson?"

"Why would your dad use *your* knife for those other murders? You said he thought he was protecting you, correct? So why your knife? Why those people? Jean Marie especially: Was he paying for sex with her too?"

"No!" he burst out.

"Why not Alice Winters? Why wasn't *she* killed?"

I had surprised him again. His lawyer, too.

"You've admitted that you were having an affair with her, a married woman with two young children, and your NA sponsor."

"Again, I don't know where you're going with all this," Tonya

Stein protested, "but I am going to have to insist that you permit me to speak with Matthew in private."

"Of course. Just knock on the door when you're ready for me to return. Keep in mind, however, that I know exactly where I'm going with 'all this,' and that it would be in Matthew's best interest to answer truthfully. Because he won't get another opportunity. And based on my experience, you might lose your chance to make a deal with the prosecutor."

It wasn't my place to say that, but I did.

"My client just cleared your brother," Tonya retorted in a wounded voice.

"And I thanked him for that."

I closed the door behind me.

64
Privileged Information

Bill was sitting with Gottert when I got out. They switched off the volume on the monitor.

"I'm not going to question what you just said," Bill advised. "Let's just hope Ms. Stein doesn't end this."

"If she's smart, she won't."

"She's smart alright."

"I want my brother out of jail today."

"I'll make a call to the DA. It'll be taken care of by end of day."

"I talked to a detective in Pottstown," said Gottert. "He's looking into Cob's murder and promised to get back to me."

"If I'm in the box, text me whatever you discover. I'm convinced that Matthew is good for murders, including the two in Morsville."

"I agree," Bill said. "He's working on a temporary-insanity defense for murdering his father and nearly killing you, and he intends to pin all the other murders on his dead dad. Bad thing is, if it goes to trial, it just might work."

"Let's see where it goes," I said.

After a few minutes came a knock on the door from inside. Gottert reactivated the monitor sound.

I entered and sat down.

"Matthew has something to say," Tonya Stein declared.

"Okay."

"My father did not know about Alice, and I'd like to keep her out of this. My affair with her was wrong. I don't want her life ruined because of me. She's married and has kids. It was a mistake."

"So what you're saying is she's probably alive today because your dad didn't know about her?"

"I have no idea, but he definitely did not know about her."

"Okay, let's start with Pauly Savell and Del Thomas. Why would your dad kill them? Before your arrest, you were a suspect in their murders. What did your father have to say about that?"

"He told me not to worry—that he'd figure something out."

"And you knew he murdered them."

"Not back then, but now I do for sure. Like you said, my knife was a match on those murders."

"So Pastor Simon never confessed to you?"

"No, but after he told me he'd killed your brother's friend, I realized he'd killed Del and Pauly too."

"But why kill those two?"

"They were both dealers, and both going to the same NA meeting I was going to. That's probably why."

"How would your father have found out they were dealing drugs?"

Matthew pondered that one for a moment, then said, "I talked to him about it once or twice. It was happening in his church, after all."

"And when their bodies were discovered, you chose to remain silent?"

"Asked and answered, Mr. Sanderson. Let's leave my client's trauma and child abuse to the professionals."

"I just find it hard to believe, despite the emotional abuse you say you've suffered, that you would not go to the police."

"He's already explained that," objected Tonya.

"All right, let's move on. Why Jean Marie Evans? Remember, the knife was a match."

"I don't know. He knew I liked her, so maybe he thought she would ruin me. Or maybe he offered to pay for sex with her but she refused, so he went off on her and stabbed her all those times."

I shot a quick glance at Tonya to see if she'd picked up on the fact that her client had just incriminated himself. She betrayed no sign that she had.

"You never told me why you think your father would use your knife."

"Because he's crazy. How the hell should I know?"

"You witnessed the murder of Cob, and your testimony will help the Pottstown Police Department close that case. It could help you, too. Did he go off on Cob like he did on Jean Marie—stab him multiple times?"

"No."

"How many times, then?"

"I remember it clearly. It was four times, to make sure they were dead."

"*They*?" I repeated.

"I meant *him*. Cob."

"By the way, Matthew, no one in this department ever said Jean Marie was stabbed multiple times."

Tonya perked right up at that.

"I must have heard it on the news."

"Her manner of death was never released to the media. Now . . . do you need time with your client again, Ms. Stein, or can we get to the truth?"

65

Return to Morsville

I stepped out again—something I've had to do several times in my career. Rarely was it a big deal, though—especially if we'd made a strong case. Most public defenders, swamped by heavy caseloads, would prefer to see their clients plead out than go to trial. I was hoping Tonya Stein would realize that with Matthew Guerre.

"He slipped up," Gottert said.

"He did."

Bill smiled.

Gottert took a call on his cell. A couple of minutes later, Tonya knocked on the door.

I stepped back into the box. Before I could retake my seat, however, I got a text: Gottert.

"Give me a second," I said.

I tapped the message open, then tried hard to maintain a strict poker face.

Cell phone in hand, I sat down and asked, "So, can we get to the truth here?"

"My dad was a murderer, not me."

"Are you sure you want to stick with that?"

He nodded.

"Investigator Gottert just got off the phone with a detective in Pottstown. He was able to locate a case jacket."

I turned my phone around so Matthew could see the screen.

"Is this the guy you knew as Cob?"

"Yes, it is," he said immediately.

"Wonderful." I slipped the cell back into my pocket. "Now I'm going to be straight up with you, Matthew: That case file I just mentioned revealed the presence of two witnesses in a parked car." I paused, hoping to elicit a reaction. Nothing—not even tight lips pressed together. "The Pottstown detective described them as *credible witnesses*. They reported seeing a young man—someone who fits your description damn well—jump Cob and stab him in the chest four times, just like you said. Ms. Stein knows what will happen next: Once they're done with you here, they'll transport you to Pottstown, where they'll collect your DNA, contact the witnesses, and do a lineup. The way the witnesses described the attack, you more than likely left some DNA at the scene, and possibly on Cob's body as well. Do you have anything to say?"

Silence.

"I highly doubt those witness recollections will be accurate after two years have elapsed." Tonya was scrambling.

"You never know, Matthew is a pretty memorable guy. I wouldn't want to take the chance. In fact I'm sure the police now have more than enough to make a solid case for all the murders. Best thing your client can do is tell the truth. They don't have a death penalty in this state—but they do in Pennsylvania."

Matthew tried to grasp one final straw: "It was self-defense."

This time it was his lawyer's turn to shake her head.

"Pennsylvania wouldn't give him the death penalty for a single murder," Tonya said.

"There was more than one, though. Two other homicides took place in Morsville, and investigators there recovered DNA from one of the crime scenes. I'm terrible when it comes to wagering, but I'd sure as hell bet that the knife the police recovered here in Charontown will match the wounds of those two victims in Morsville."

"Morsville?" asked Tonya.

"ViCAP revealed the two murders there after Investigator Gottert submitted the information about the ones here. They were identical to the murders here. Will the knife match, Matthew?"

He didn't answer.

"Did Cob emotionally abuse you too?"

He glared hard at me and then suddenly lunged forward, but the table and the handcuffs thwarted him. I didn't flinch, but Tonya jumped up and almost out of her chair.

Matthew slammed his cuffed hands down on the table with a loud thud.

"I told you that was self-defense!"

Gottert was in the room fast.

"It's okay," I assured him.

Matthew sat back and straightened his posture.

Gottert retreated and closed the door.

"The two witnesses in the car said you jumped Cob," I said calmly.

"Yeah—because I feared for my life."

"Have you been searching street-lawyer forums online?" I asked. "Are you going to tell me your father used your knife to murder those two victims in Morsville too? This is getting ridiculous already, Ms. Stein."

"Matthew, I'm not licensed in Pennsylvania, so I can't represent you there."

"Your father tried to cover up for you, didn't he? Helped dispose of a few bodies? Even killed Henry Flood, then planted his blood in my brother's Explorer? He drove Del Thomas's pickup truck back to Del's place after getting rid of his body, didn't he? We got that from a surveillance camera."

"*He's* the monster—he's rotting in hell. They all deserved what they got!"

"Even Jean? You said you really liked her. Your father didn't help you clean up that mess too, did he?"

"She's a whore. It's all about money in the end. She was no different."

Before Tonya could intervene I asked, "Just tell me why you stabbed them each four times, Matthew?"

"Matthew—" his attorney tried again.

"I don't know," he said flatly, cutting her off. "OCD, I guess? It just felt right—made sense."

66

Ashes to Ashes

I stepped out. Sergeant O'Born and Officer King had joined Gottert and the chief in viewing the monitor that showed proceedings in the box. They were all smiling. Tonya Stein stayed in the room to talk things over with her client.

"That'll do it, Graham," Bill told me. "Great job."

He stretched his hand out to shake mine.

"Thank you for that, Chief. It got the results you needed, but unfortunately, sometimes you never really learn the *why*."

"I don't care why he did it, just so long as we got him—and you did. Leave the *why* to the criminal profilers who will probably visit him in prison. Tonya Stein is known for pleading out her clients if she thinks she can't win in court. I'm sure that's what'll happen here. But if this does end up going to trial . . ."

"You know where to find me. I don't plan on going anywhere."

I walked toward Gottert. We shook hands.

"Great working with you, Sanderson."

"Likewise. I'll see you around, Mike."

"It's all about exhausting the leads, right?"

"Yeah—and if that fails, hope for a bit of luck."

I phoned Tommy's defense attorney, Dan Wolff, as soon as I got in my car. Told him about the interrogation and that Chief Finn had called the DA to get my brother released.

"I want to make sure you'll follow up on that today, Dan. I want Tommy out."

"I will. I was happy to hear you got out of the hospital okay."

"Thanks—I was lucky he didn't brain me for good."

"You saved me a lot of work."

"Then let your bill reflect that," I returned.

He laughed, but it was the kind of laugh that suggested *That'll be the day.*

After walking in the front door of our house, my first call was to Ada. I told her about everything, and we made plans to see each other again once I had confirmed that Tommy was okay.

"My daughter's with her dad this weekend. Maybe dinner?"

"That'd be nice."

I picked Tommy up from the facility he was in. He had dark puffy bags under his eyes and didn't smile. We hugged and cried a bit. Happy tears, though.

When we got home, we sat out on the deck. Our comfort zone. I watched his hulking body move the rocking chair. As expected, it creaked. I would simply wait for him to broach everything he had gone through in the last few days.

We sat there companionably, our nightmare now over—his so much worse than mine.

I gazed out over the pasture. There was this spot farther back that I liked. It gave me an idea.

I turned in early.

Upon waking, I did not remember any dreams.

Later that day, I drove to a big nursery outside Charontown that carried every variety of fruit tree. My car wasn't huge, so I was limited to a certain size; it would have to be tied to the roof rack or shoved in the hatchback.

I found a Turkish fig. The perfect size for me to plant myself. The gal helping me said Turkish figs do well in this climate: "They grow tall, with thick limbs that twist and turn like a wonderful living sculpture."

Elena had loved figs, so I bought it.

The young tree was secured to the roof rack, its tightly wrapped root ball facing forward.

I drove home.

Perfect *size*, sure, but that fig tree was one heavy mother, so once I got it home I had to enlist Tommy's help to lift it down from the car and set it on a wheelbarrow. Most of it hung over the front, making the wheelbarrow tippy.

I had Elena's urn with me. I set it securely in the bottom of the barrow, beneath the burlap.

"Want me to go with you?" Tommy asked.

"No thanks—I'm good."

He smiled for the first time in a while.

* * *

I got the shovel, set it atop the fig tree, and wheeled it out to the spot in the pasture that I had admired from the deck. It would always be visible to us.

I dug a deep hole, wrestled the fig tree into it, and shoveled in some dirt. I stepped back to make sure the trunk was plumb, then shoveled in a bit more.

I picked up Elena's urn, kissed it, and carefully poured the ashes all around the root ball. I covered them with the rest of the dirt, then tamped everything down. I set the urn near the tree's trunk, put the shovel back in the barrow, and retreated a few steps to consider the effect.

Just like my dad's own green burial site, Elena would help to enrich the soil here. The fig tree would grow. Its fruit would ripen.

I turned back toward the deck, about half an acre away.

Tommy was sitting out there. Watching. Rocking.

I waved at him. He waved back.

I turned to face the fig tree as if it had something to say.

It did.

Our past was all that remained.

There was a certain comfort in that.

ACKNOWLEDGMENTS

I want to thank my wife, Jennifer, for her patience and love and for being my first reader and critic. I'd like to thank my incredible agent, Deborah Schneider of Gelfman Schneider, for her invaluable advice, support, and patience in guiding me through this process. A huge thank you to Josh Kendall, my brilliant editor at Mulholland Books. As morbid as this might sound, I know that if I died in the middle of a book, Josh could pick it up and finish it in my name. He knows me that well. Thanks to the entire team at Mulholland and Little, Brown and Company for their unending support—specifically, Liv Ryan and Michael Noon. Michael always manages to connect me with the right copyeditor, like Allan "Conan the Grammarian" Fallow, who worked on this book.

I'm grateful for all my brothers and sisters in the writing community and law enforcement. All of you are always there when I need you, and for that I thank you. And a really big thank you to all the bookstores, libraries and booksellers everywhere who carry my books. I am forever grateful.

ABOUT THE AUTHOR

David Swinson is a retired police detective from the Metropolitan Police Department in Washington, DC, having been assigned to Major Crimes. He is the author of the critically acclaimed Frank Marr Trilogy, including *The Second Girl, Crime Song,* and *Trigger*, as well as the stand-alone novels *City on the Edge* and *Sweet Thing*. He lives in New York with his wife, Jennifer, their two boys, and their neurotic cat and dog.